2 nd INSERT by   John Varga
HARRY

rsg

1   Smiling the Boy Fell Dead   B95-2143

MURDER AT HERNE HOUSE

The first of three Michael Delving mysteries
featuring Dave Cannon.

"one of the most satisfying books in many a
month"

—*Washington Star*

"the book has a great deal of easy charm . . ."
—*New York Times*

"a cracking good mystery."
—*St. Louis Post-Dispatch*

"delightful!"

—*Saturday Review*

for Gerald—and high time, too

SMILING
THE BOY
FELL DEAD

by MICHAEL DELVING

Belmont Books   ●   New York City

SMILING THE BOY FELL DEAD
A BELMONT BOOK—July1971

Published by

Belmont Productions, Inc.
185 Madison Avenue
New York, New York 10016

Published by special arrangement with Charles Scribner's Sons.

1

It was like being in a dream. I suppose everyone who goes abroad for the first time has this feeling, although when they get home, being by then experienced old hands, they can't admit it. I knew all about England from novels and travel books and movies, and of course my business kept me in touch with the history of the land and, more directly, with English dealers. Actually being there was quite another matter. So different that nothing seemed real, and the unfamiliar speech of people around me was like the speech of actors in a play. I had to keep telling myself they weren't just putting it on.

The color of the sky was different, the sunlight had another sort of gold, and the great massed clouds seemed to shape themselves according to patterns established long ago by the painters of the Royal Academy. Even the smell of the air was different: coal fires and foreign earth.

And nothing could be more different than the spot

where I stood, between two stone gateposts topped by carved herons blackened with age, flanking a wide drive lined with ancient beeches. You never see beech trees like these in Connecticut, let alone a gate two hundred years old that is a mere modern afterthought to the house behind it.

Oddly enough, it all made me feel more American than I ever had before. I wanted to drawl through my nose, hitch up my galluses, and spit. Instead, I lit a cigarette and started the walk up through the park to Herne House. It was a real park, too, although it showed signs of neglect. Cows kept the grass shorter than any mower would have done, and there were trees four feet thick which managed to look domesticated. They had none of the unruly quality of forest trees, and after a while I realized that it was because their lower limbs and foliage had been trimmed off to a consistent six feet from the ground. I wondered whether the cows had been trained to gnaw the stuff off, because I knew Mrs. Herne was broke and I figured she couldn't keep a staff of gardeners.

Well, no. Maybe I didn't actually know that she was broke. But I suspected it from everything Dr. Crouch had told me when he first tipped me off to the *Raimond* manuscript.

Crouch was an old friend of Dad's. They had met during the war, when Dad was stationed in London doing decoding or translating or something that used his fantastic knowledge of languages. Later, when Dad went back to the business, Crouch acted as a liaison for him in England, more out of friendship and amusement than because he needed the money. He was well-to-do, and the "Doctor" was of Phil., not Med. Because he knew so many top-drawer people, he often learned of the sale of manuscripts or private libraries before they went on the market, and was able to put Dad in the way of some wonderful buys.

When Dad died, it was only natural that Crouch should go on doing the same thing for me.

He had written to me about the *Raimond* in July, when he first heard that Mrs. Herne was thinking of selling some of her uncle's stuff. By the end of August the thing had firmed up, and he sent me the extract he had taken from Sir Francis's own handwritten catalogue, made back in 1890, which he said he thought would draw me, knowing my interests: *Holograph mss. by one, Raimond de Poitiers, fifteen vellum pages appearing to be part of an account in verse of the crusade of Richard Coeur de Lion. Similar to that of Ambroise. Purchased through Killie from Comte Jean deVérac, whose family has owned it since medieval times, May 31, 1890.*

Dr. Crouch was right, it drew me. It got me so excited that I decided not to use an agent but to go and see for myself. I had always wanted to visit England, and this was a bona fide tax exemption. Bob, my partner, had no objection—or, at any rate, none that couldn't be argued down, and on the seventh of September I was on the plane. I had had a couple of marvelous days in London, had met Dr. Crouch who had already written to Mrs. Herne and made the necessary arrangements. And I had then rented a car and driven to Heronwick early this morning, all in one wild whirl, but in time for my eleven o'clock appointment.

I could see the house, now, through the shrubbery and it gave me a shock. I had expected one of those stately mansions you read about, with a Palladian front designed by Inigo Jones. I saw two battlemented walls in which window openings gaped, showing the trees beyond. Inside this shell of crumbling stone, a warped house of brick and timber, narrow and tall, with steep roofs of various pitches, and dozens of chimneys, was built. The timbers ran at different angles and it looked as though only the outer cloak of stone, the remains of a castle, was keeping the whole thing up.

A young fellow stood by the side of the drive, with a wheelbarrow full of firewood. As I came abreast, he gave me a quick look up and down, just his eyes moving, and then he said, "Got a cigarette?"

I didn't like the way he said it, something between a whine and a sneer. I didn't like anything about him, not his long, curling, dirty hair, nor his tight blue pants, nor his pointed high-heeled shoes, nor the smell that came from him. But what the hell, I wasn't going to make an issue of anything for a cigarette, particularly since I was smoking myself, so I offered him one.

He put it in his pocket, saying, "Ta. Going up to the 'ouse?"

I nodded.

"If you've got anything to sell you're wasting your time. *She* won't buy nothing." He kept eyeing me in a way that was probably intended to be disconcerting, and was. I was taller and broader than he was, and in pretty good condition, but I didn't like the look of him. There was something animal-like about him, so that you couldn't guess what he was going to do next, run off, or suddenly pull a knife on you.

"I'm not selling a thing," I said, and started to walk on.

"You a Yank? Or a Canadian?" he asked. "I like Yanks. They're rich and they know what to do with their money."

"Yeah, well I'll see you later," I said.

"Hey, what about another cigarette?" he called after me.

"Turn blue," I said.

He gaped, unsure of what I meant.

When I came to the front door I could see that the

house was even more dilapidated than I had thought. Quite apart from the wear of centuries, it showed a lack of upkeep that argued carelessness or poverty. Some panes were missing in the latticed windows and had been patched with cardboard, holes opened here and there in the brickwork, and one of the rain gutters was hanging loose from its bracket. The shrubbery and flower beds were overgrown, and I figured that the man I'd met was good at keeping trees clipped but not much of a hand with gardens.

There was a heavy iron ring on the front door, but no sign of a bell. I knocked, waited a while, knocked again. After a time, the door opened and a woman looked out suspiciously. She was as drab as the house, with a dirty apron and her grey hair coming loose from a bun.

"Yas?" she said.

"I'm Dave Cannon," I said. "I have an eleven o'clock appointment with Mrs. Herne."

"Eh?" she said.

I repeated the whole thing.

"Come you in," she said. "I'll tell madam."

The hall was large and dim and darkly paneled, and I suppose had once, long ago, been the main room of the house. A steep stair midway along led to a railed gallery above, and around the walls hung dusty trophies of arms and a few pictures so dark that they were like cellar windows: you could just make out imprisoned faces peering hopelessly out of them. It was cold, too, as cold and dank as if it were midwinter instead of a mild, sunny, September day. I was shown into a room off this hall, conventionally furnished with overstuffed chairs and a sofa, a good deal brighter and obviously more lived in than the hall if not much warmer. But here again, the upholstery was worn and unpatched, and the springs of one of the chairs were sagging to the floor. I wasn't kept waiting long. A woman came in with a vigorous, quick step.

"Mr. Cannon?" she said. She had a penetrating voice, not loud but authoritative. By contrast with everything else, she was neat, even dapper, in a plain black dress with a silver chain and locket that set off the silvery grey of her hair.

"Mrs. Herne? How do you do?" I said, in my best professional manner, holding out my hand. She ignored it.

"I expected someone a little more mature," she snapped. "You are very young."

I had run into this kind of thing before, although not quite so abruptly. "Age isn't everything in my business, Mrs. Herne," I said, with a wooing smile. "I assure you I have a great deal of experience."

"Yes, I know that you Americans make a cult of youth."

There was a sharpness in her tone which took me aback.

"I'm sorry if you don't like Americans," I began.

"My liking them has nothing to do with it. When Dr. Crouch put forward your name, I agreed simply because everyone knows how wealthy America has become at the expense of other nations. I was under the impression, however, that you would be about Dr. Crouch's age."

I was beginning to lose my temper. The English upperclass accent and tone can convey a biting contempt much stronger than anything we can manage. This is sometimes quite unintentional, I've found, but in this case it seemed pointed.

"I have been buying and selling books and manuscripts for fifteen years, Mrs. Herne," I said, stiffly.

This was stretching it a little. I did a lot of work with Dad all through college and summer vacations, but then I had had a couple of years with the Coast

Guard. After that, Dad had taken me in as a partner and we'd had eight years together, a wonderful, rich, exciting time. After his death, Bob had bought in with me and we'd had another couple of years as partners.

I went on, "I'm not rich, whatever you may think. But I do know the market and I'm prepared to pay well for good items. Any dealer in my position would say the same. I didn't come all the way to England to argue with you, but if you'd rather not show me the manuscript you want to sell—"

"Not at all," she broke in. "You're very touchy, aren't you? It is, after all, a very valuable article. One must be careful that one is dealing with the right people."

She gave me a quick, rather acid smile. "I'm sure you can see the justice of that. Have you had a pleasant journey?"

"Um—very nice," I mumbled. She knew how to throw you off balance.

"Splendid. Then would you like to look at the manuscript now?"

Without waiting for an answer, she led the way into the hall and up the staircase. It wasn't well lighted, and it was as steep as a ladder. I almost lost my balance near the top and had to grab the carved bannister. She opened a massive door at the head of the stairs and I blinked at the unexpected flood of light. This room was long and low-ceilinged. The outer wall had three bay windows with leaded panes and snug seats, looking out over an untended enclosed garden. Between the windows were bookshelves, and the whole inner wall was glass-fronted bookcases and cabinets. There was a fireplace at the end furthest from the door, but inside its generous cavern made for big logs, there stood a little iron box of a grate with a few short chunks of what we'd call stove-wood in it. A long writing-table and a couple of chairs faced

11

it, and in one corner stood a brown globe of the earth on a mahogany pedestal. It was a pleasant, comfortable place, just right for reading, and I said as much.

"My uncle was confined to a wheelchair for the last fifteen years of his life, and he spent much of his time here," said Mrs. Herne. "My father rarely used it. I myself have no interest in books, but I find it a very liveable room."

She selected a key from the bunch she carried, and unlocked one of the cabinets. She drew out a flat leather case which she put on the desk.

"You have, of course, seen the description taken from my uncle's catalogue," she said. "Just before the war, I had the library appraised for insurance purposes. A man came down from Saxby's, in London, and went over the entire collection. Here is his valuation. Number Three is this manuscript."

She handed me a sheaf of papers clipped together, each one with Saxby's letterhead: I knew it well, having done a good deal of business with them by mail. I was interested to see that Number One on the list was an illuminated thirteenth-century book of hours, and Number Two a fifteenth-century missal. Number Three was: "Manuscript on parchment, a rhymed Chronicle in Old French, probably 12th century, by Raimond de Poitiers. Twenty-two pages, 16th century binding, no illuminations or initials. £500."

"What about One and Two?" I asked.

"They are no longer in my possession," she replied, curtly. "I hope, however, that you are satisfied that the manuscript is authentic. Saxby's is an old and reputable firm."

"Yes, ma'am," I said.

"Furthermore, I feel that £500 no longer represents the true value of the manuscript. Prices have risen in the most scandalous way, and that appraisal was made in 1937. In any case, the pound was worth considerably more then than it is under the present Socialist-dominated regime."

"Well, Mrs. Herne," I said, "I'd like to look at it and study it. If I'm satisfied with it, and it's what I want, I assure you I'll offer you a fair price. I suppose Dr. Crouch has told you that I'm particularly interested in medieval manuscripts. I don't mind going high for something like this, but you can see that neither your uncle's idea of it nor Saxby's is enough to make me shell out a lot of money. They're not buying it; I am."

"What do you propose to do?" she said, tightening her lips.

"I'd like to examine the manuscript at my leisure. I'll do it right here at this desk. I'd just like to be left alone to study it."

"I beg your pardon? Left alone?" She drew herself up.

"Look, Mrs. Herne," I said, patiently—I had been through this before with customers. "I'm a dealer, not a burglar. I'm not going to steal your manuscript, and I'm not going to cut little bits out of it. I know how to handle these things. It won't be damaged, I promise you. But it's going to take me half an hour or more to look it over, and I can't stand somebody sitting and staring at me while I'm doing it. It makes me jumpy. You want me to do this thing justice and make you the best possible offer, don't you?"

"Very well," she said, after the slightest of hesitations. "Half an hour? If you wish to speak to me before that time, ring the bell." She indicated a button set in the wall.

"Thank you," I said. "I'll be as quick as I can."

She stood for a moment, and then very deliberately she locked the cabinet from which she'd taken the manuscript. She went out, leaving the big door ajar.

I pulled up one of the leather chairs and sat down before the desk. What I had told her was true, of course: sellers hovering over my head while I was inspecting something drove me nuts, and I had once offered a man more than his books were worth just to get rid of him. But it wasn't only that: I wanted to savor this moment alone, to have the delight of finding out for myself if this was what I thought it was.

I'm not a medieval scholar by any means, but I've always been interested in that provocative period known as the Dark Ages. It's full of contradictions, not least of which is the fact that it's called the *Dark Ages* in spite of its architecture, its poetry, and its learning. You get such wild extremes: deep religious feeling and widespread heresy, a Universal Church which was anything but universal, holding the awful power of excommunication which was largely ignored by those who should have feared it; men who could be pious and chivalrous and at the same time unbelievably savage and hysterical; a positive adoration of women and of the Virgin in particular, along with the most barbarous treatment of women in general. . . . I could go on for hours. One of the most contradictory characters, for me, in this whole contradictory time, was Richard the Lion-Heart, and one of the most intriguing puzzles is wrapped in the accounts of his crusade to the Holy Land.

There are two contemporary chronicles, both of which purport to be by eye-witnesses. One is the *Itinerarium Regis Ricardi,* the Itinerary of King Richard, by someone who may be named Richard of Holy Trinity. The other is the Chronicle of a French poet named Ambroise. The first is in Latin prose, the second in French verse. Nobody is very clear who either of these people were, and there are so many exact parallels in the two accounts, sometimes almost word for word, that it seems clear one must have been copied from the other. Or, according to some authorities, there was a third chronicle, a true eye-witness account, from which both the others were copied.

It had been the phrase, "similar to that of Ambroise," in Sir Francis's catalogue which had hooked me. Suppose that this manuscript, an account in verse of the Third Crusade by a twelfth-century French poet, were that lost original?

I pulled the leather case towards me. It was made in two parts, and I drew off the outer sleeve, and opened the flaps of the inner one. The binding of the manuscript itself, much worn but still a lovely job of tooling with traces of gilding, had been put on at a much later date to protect the pages. As I opened the book, something flipped out and sailed to the floor. It was a piece of paper folded in three, old but well preserved from being inside the binding. On the outside was written in brown ink what I finally decided was "Chas. Nowlle Esq." I opened it carefully because the creases were knife-sharp. It was dated 5 May 1895. I skimmed through it hastily to see whether it had anything to do with the manuscript. I've hacked my way through medieval script in three languages, but modern English handwriting is often beyond me: there have been times when Bob and I have puzzled for hours over a handwritten communication from an English dealer. This was no exception, being cramped, small and terrible, so that the first words seemed to say, "I am coviting to you my dist lhurts," which couldn't be right. However, I could make out that it was a personal letter of some sort, and I couldn't find any words that looked like "manuscript" or "Raimond," so I folded it up and laid it aside. I could struggle through it later, if it seemed necessary.

I turned to the manuscript. The parchment looked right; so did the ink, and the lovely, shaded strokes of the quill. I settled down to read.

Ieu sui Raimond del vil Poictier
E longue estoire ja traicter . . .

That second line was almost identical with the first line of Ambroise. But this first line, "I am Raimond of the town of Poitiers," seemed to fit better with the slightly changed: "And a long history I have to tell." I was quickly absorbed. The first twenty lines were all like that, close to Ambroise but different, at first in some small points, then in what appeared to me a growing richness of detail. There were places, too, where words had been crossed out and others substituted, so that I began to feel, with mounting excitement, that this was just the kind of draft a poet might have made. When he began to describe the knights in their painted mail, a forest of banners fluttering over their heads, "with squires and serjents, a worthy company," meeting at Vezelay with the two kings to renew their oaths, there was a compelling quality of observation which made me feel this man had actually seen Richard and his ally and rival, the king of France. This thing needed far more scholarship than I could bring to it, obviously. I had no proof: it could be only a preliminary re-copying of Ambroise. But to me, it looked good.

I was yanked out of the twelfth century by a clatter like that of a knight falling off his horse. I looked up. There was my cigarette-mooching friend with the long hair and the pointy shoes. He had brought in a bucket of firewood and had just finished emptying it into a metal container next to the grate. He straightened, and grinned at me, showing large dazzling teeth as if he were unveiling an international display of cheap crockery.

"Whatcher doing?" he said. "Reading?"

"That's right."

He came over and leaned on the table, squinting

down at the manuscript. "What would it be—a letter, like? One of them old-time books before they had printing? Worth a fortune I shouldn't wonder. This room's full of 'em. A temptation, ain't it?"

His feral smell made me shove my chair back.

"Look, I'm trying to work," I began.

"Wouldn't be like as if it was stealing. Nobody so much as goes near the stuff now. You can see the dust on 'em. Wouldn't do no harm to turn some of these pretty books into a few hundred quid. Now, would it? But she keeps 'em all locked up tight."

I had a hard time understanding some of what he said, his accent being like nothing I'd ever heard before: "tight," for instance, became "toight."

He leaned closer. "You wouldn't have the key, I suppose?"

"You must be out of your head." I almost laughed, looking up at him. "Do you seriously think I'd help you steal books from Mrs. Herne?"

"Take it easy," he replied. "Who said anything about stealing? You did, not me. I never used the word. I only asked you if you had the key."

"No, I haven't." I stood up. "Now, would you mind leaving me alone? I'm busy."

"Ooh, we are dainty! *Would you maind?*" he repeated. He lowered his head and began staring at me as he had when we first met. It was not a challenging look; there was nothing active in it. His eyes simply went dead and cold.

He got my back up. "Okay," I said. "I'm in somebody else's house, and I'm not going to start a fight with you. But I've got no time to fool around. Are you going?"

"One of them tough Yanks, ain't yer?"

I considered, for a minute, whether it might not be worth it to poke him one in the jaw. But I was there as a dealer, not an upholder of American honor. I started for the door, to call Mrs. Herne. Then I remembered the button and went and rang that, instead, deciding it would be better not to leave him alone with the manuscript. It was just as well, too, because as I turned back again I saw him straighten up from the table. I strode over, picked up the manuscript, and closed it with a snap.

He watched me. "None of it missing, is there?" he jeered.

He picked up his bucket. "Bye bye, big shot. I only take what's mine, look."

He met Mrs. Herne at the door and stood aside for her. Her glance swept him up and threw him away. As he went, he shot a sudden murderous look at her over his shoulder.

"I take it you've come to a decision, Mr. Cannon," Mrs. Herne said.

"Well, I was interrupted, ma'am," I answered. "I believe it may be what I'm interested in. If you have no objection I'd like to study it a little longer, and then I think I'll be in a position to make you an offer for it."

"Now? I'm afraid that's impossible. I have to go out very shortly."

"It doesn't have to be now. To save time, I want to cable my partner about it. Tomorrow'd be all right."

"I have two committee meetings tomorrow," she replied. "I had not anticipated this would take so long. After all, you have Saxby's report on it. I find your caution a trifle unreasonable."

"Mrs. Herne, I don't know about you, but I've got to think carefully before I start handing out large sums of money," I said. "I'm perfectly serious. I didn't come all this way to play games. I can tell you this much: my offer will be in four figures."

That got to her; I could see her blink. But all she said was, "I prefer not to do business on Sunday.

However, if you will come on Monday morning, at about eleven, you may have as much time as you require."

I couldn't resist a parting jab. "I guess you'd like to check the manuscript before I go, and make sure it's okay," I said.

Well, of course, I should have known.

"Quite so," she said, coldly. She riffled through the pages and inspected them, and then put the thing back in its case. "Thank you. It seems to be in order."

What could you do with a dame like this, I thought, as she showed me out with the kind of distant courtesy she might have displayed to a doctor she didn't really trust.

I had just about made up my mind about the *Raimond*. I had also made up my mind that I didn't like Mrs. Herne. While I wanted to be fair about the price, a streak of horsetrading in me, along with my annoyance at the way she sniped at me, made me decide to try for the lowest figure I could. My great-great grandfather, after all, had sold wooden nutmegs over in New York State to the Dutch farmers and had built our house in New Canaan on the proceeds. I thought I'd start off with £1,000. That was $2800, and twice what it had been appraised at some thirty years before. But I knew that if she took the manuscript to Saxby's or some other auction house, it would probably bring a little more than that: not too long before, a poem by Alain de Lille had brought £1,000, while a thirteenth-century manuscript of King Arthur had made five. If I was right, and this turned out to be a genuine link between the two chronicles of the Third Crusade, and somebody caught wise, the bidding would be brisk indeed. I had to make my offer high enough so that she'd consider she was playing me for a sucker, but not so high that she'd catch on and send it to the sale room.

In the end, after considerable thought, I decided to start at £1,500. Then, reluctantly, I'd let her dicker until I blurted out that it was worth about seventeen hundred, and that I'd give her two thousand. I'd be helped by the fact that there were no pretty pictures, no golden initial letters to make it seem more tasty. Even so, that was going to come to nearly six thousand bucks, so I had to explain it to Bob and get confirmation.

I went back to the pub where I had taken a room—the Goat & Compasses, it was called—and asked Mrs. Davies, the owner, where I could send a cablegram direct, without phoning it and risking a mistake. I had to go all the way to a big town called Ross-on-Wye, clear in the next county, but it gave me a chance to practice driving and to look at the scenery. It wasn't so much staying on the left that bothered me, as shifting left-handed. Furthermore, I confirmed what I had suspected when driving up, that English drivers were pretty crazy people. I had thought maybe it was just my unfamiliarity with the wrong side of the road. But no, on roads that looked like our Connecticut back lanes they shot along at sixty, they passed you on hills and blind curves, and if you tried to be cautious at bad spots they sat on your tail as if they wanted to look over your shoulder at your speedometer. I guess it could be called the spirit of Drake and Hawkins, that adventurous lust that once sent them out across the Atlantic in little sailing ships and made them carry their empire all over the globe. Since empires stopped being the In thing, they let it loose in driving.

But the countryside made up for it. That part of England, the northwestern corner of Gloucestershire and its neighboring Hereford, is not so much hilly as sharply crumpled. The land slopes up and drops steeply back down, so that from any high point you see tilted pastures criss-crossed by stone walls, clumps of beech and oak often growing in circles in the midst of fields, tiny cows and sheep scampering like bits of blown paper, villages with roofs of stone slabs instead of shingles, and houses built of stone that changes its color to match the weather, and winding among it all the glint of water. All this careful, neat, minute detail makes you feel like a giant—something like that poem by Stevenson, "The Land of Counterpane." By contrast, the sky is enormous so that you remember you're on an island, and across the shadows of splendidly heaped-up clouds the gulls, never far from the sea, caw and wheel above the ploughland.

And coming leisurely away from Ross after sending my cable, stopping in a village named Goodrich to look at the ruins of a medieval castle, I realized why I had bristled so at that long-haired slob, Mrs. Herne's gardener. It was not because he was rude and disagreeable, nor because he had seemed to propose something crooked to me, but because he struck a jarring note in what I thought England ought to be. This great castle, Goodrich, its wreckage still full of beauty and power, showing the successive hands of builders from Norman times to the fifteenth century, gave the same sense of a long continuity, of human work and habitation, that I had felt at Herne House. An ancient and honorable past, much labor, centuries of villainy and splendor, and a deep, strong sense of poetry: these were England for me, summed up by all that I had read and heard. And here were the heirs—the gardener and young men like him whom I'd already seen in London and now in Ross, with their pointed shoes and sideburns and fake American clothes, their sleazy Way Out look, their bogus beatnik-knackery, neither real rebels nor dashing bohemians, neither part of the American world nor the English but cheap imitations of a modern style like the sort of abstract art made to hang in the windows of furniture stores. They had nothing to do with the continuity.

Well, you know, I was romanticizing. I was wrong. But I wasn't to know it for a while.

2

The weather changed. Suddenly it was autumn:
grey heavy skies, a steady cold drizzle, the smell of
wet clothes and mould. I was taken aback when I
came down to breakfast and Mrs. Davies, sliding an
enormous plateful of fried eggs, bacon, sausages,
grilled tomatoes and fried bread in front of me, said,
"Fine day, isn't it?"

"It is?" I said.

"Ah, well, it's not actually pouring with rain, you
see," she said, comfortingly. "Might be worse, now,
mightn't it?"

"I suppose so."

"We had a saying in Malvern, when I was a girl,
that if you could see the hills it was going to rain, and
if you couldn't see them it was raining." She gave a
rich chuckle.

She was a comforting sort of woman all around,
and all round was what she was, too: round body,
round arms, a round little nose, round blue eyes, and

a round solid head with grey tight curls all over it. Her husband, on the other hand, was a craggy man, large and slow-moving, with a deliberate way of speaking that turned the most casual observation into an address to Parliament.

He was cleaning up behind the bar when I went in to get a pack of cigarettes, and I said, "I guess there's not much to do in a village like this on a Saturday?"

"No, there is not," he replied, polishing a glass thoughtfully. "Nor on a Monday, nor Friday either. But they are highly festive occasions indeed compared to Sunday. On the other hand, there are some who prefer it that way. Ah, sir, when you have had the glitter and bustle of a great city, you find that the tranquil uneventfulness of the country is more to your taste. Or do you not think so, Mr. Cannon?"

His voice had a soothing sing-song quality, which made his oratory even more persuasive, and I found myself agreeing with him.

"But I live in the country myself, in America," I said.

"Is that so?" he replied. "I suppose it is all great distances there, with the wide open spaces, the mesas (he pronounced it *mee-sa* so that at first I couldn't think what he meant) and the prairies. Our island must seem as constricting as a wardrobe for midgets to you after that."

"Well, not all of America is quite the way you describe it," I said. "Connecticut looks a lot like England."

"Oh?" he said, politely, obviously not believing a word of it.

"You see, you British get your ideas about us from movies, just as we do about you. We could both be wrong."

He straightened, holding up his towel as if it were a bill he was about to propose. "I am not English, Mr.

Cannon. I am Welsh, and my home is Bridgend, a lovely place but wet. Nevertheless, it is a sound point you have made there, and I can see the justice of it."

He bowed mournfully, to the applause of the back benches.

His son, Ted, a boy of about eleven, came in and announced that he was going down to the Scout Hut, and with no change in his tone Mr. Davies continued, "Wipe your nose, and put on your Wellingtons, boy, do you think you are journeying through the Sahara, or what?"

"All right, Dad," said the boy. "Good morning, Mr. Cannon, sir."

"Hi, Ted, how's it going?" I said.

"Okay," he grinned. "I like the way you Yanks talk. I'm going to America someday." He was struggling into a pair of high rubber boots, and he stopped to puff. "I'd like to go to Disneyland. You been there a lot?"

"No, I'm afraid I've never been there."

He stared up at me. "Never? You live in America and you've never been to Disneyland?"

"It's a long way from where I live, Ted. About three thousand miles."

He snorted in disgust. "Cor! If it was me, I'd walk there if my feet fell off. So long, Dad. Be seeing you, Mr. Cannon."

Mr. Davies shook his head. "Begging your pardon, and no offense to you, sir, but they all try to talk like Americans these days. It is from the telly and all. I cannot say that it delights me. It is not becoming."

"I agree with you. It doesn't sound natural, somehow. I felt the same way meeting a young fellow who works for Mrs. Herne, a guy with pointy shoes and long hair—"

"Ah, that would be Charlie. One of the local yobs. He comes here nearly every night with his friends.

But he is not so young as you might suppose. Might be thirty now, I should think, or a bit more."

"What'd you call him—a yob?"

"It is the word they use nowadays. *Boy* spelled backward, because they are backward types, you see. He is not an angel, our Charlie. He has been before the magistrate several times. When the scent of him comes down wind in the High Street you cannot hear yourself think for the slamming of doors and windows."

He lifted a flap in the bar and went to unlock the front door. "I am open now, Mr. Cannon," he said. "Would you like to have a drop of something?"

"You mean, people are going to start drinking now? At ten in the morning?"

"Oh, yes. Why not? A pint of beer helps to lubricate the wheels of a trying day, and what with the way the world is now there are few days a man can face without some internal support."

"Well," I said, "I was asking what to do on a Saturday and I got an answer."

I had a half-pint, and another, and people drifted in, drank their beer and exchanged a few desultory words with Mr. Davies, chewed over the news, and drifted out again. Nobody seemed to be in a great hurry, and it struck me that there was a timeless quality about this place, that the villagers had been dropping in for beer for a long long time, in just this way. It wasn't anything like a bar at home. It was more like a clubhouse, or, no, like the old-time general store with a cracker-barrel and a stove: everybody's living room.

In the afternoon, I strolled up to visit the church. It stood among dark yew trees, surrounded by blackened stones and tombs, a small but attractive building with a fine square tower. I read the notices in the porch: "Pray more for the clergy; pray for more clergy," times of services, and, rather severely, "This is God's house. Conduct yourself as a guest." It was colder inside than out in the drizzle, but a husky man stood in his shirt sleeves before the altar giving directions in a loud voice to a girl who was arranging some flowers. At the clank of the door, he glanced round at me and smiled.

I smiled back, but I was looking at the girl. I'd always heard about the pink and white complexions of English girls, and here was one for real, like living porcelain. She had short smooth red hair and the kind of smile which peaks down in the center and quirks up on the ends and is full of devilry.

"Do you mind my looking around?" I asked.

The man said, "Not at all, not at all."

"Nice church you've got here," I said, inanely, still staring at her.

"You've hardly seen any of it yet, have you?" the girl said.

"I'm seeing all I want to," I replied.

That brought a blush. Like a ripe peach. It went beautifully with the coppery hair.

"I'm the vicar," the man was saying. I could see, now, that he wore a backward collar. "Would you like me to show you round?"

The girl put in, "If these are satisfactory, Jack, I'll push off. Father's coming home to tea and you know what he is."

"Right-ho, Lucy. Let's foregather with the ladies next week, to settle the Harvest Festival details, shall we?"

"Okay." She shot me a look which started out to be sharp and was ruined by an explosion of laughter. "Sorry," she choked, and ran past me.

"Spendwell's my name," the Vicar said, pulling on

his jacket. "Not my nature, I'm afraid. Can't afford to. But then, who can?" His laugh was large and hearty, not at all affected.

"You don't look like a vicar to me," I said. "I always thought of vicars as mild, gentle, white-haired men pottering around in gardens or collecting flint arrowheads."

He grinned. "I hope you're not too frightfully disappointed."

"Nope. It makes a change."

"You're an American, aren't you? On holiday?"

"No, I'm in Heronwick on business."

I could see he was burning to know what business I could possibly have in a village like this, but of course he wasn't going to ask.

I put him out of his misery. "I'm a dealer in rare books and manuscripts. I've come to see Mrs. Herne."

"Oh, yes, the library. I was allowed a quick peep at it once, after a dinner party. Some quite good things, I believe."

"Not bad."

"Well, would you like to see the church? I mean, really the church this time," he added, slyly.

"She is a knockout, isn't she?" I said.

"A knockout? Oh, yes, of course. Rather!"

"A local girl?"

"Are you going to be here long?" he said.

"I hope so."

We both laughed.

He took me around, pointing out the brasses of medieval wool merchants shown wrapped up like their own bales in their winding sheets, or proudly dressed in their Sunday clothes for posterity with the tiny figures of their sons and daughters kneeling on either side of them. There was a carved rood screen, a Norman font, and on one wall a stone plaque which said:

Beneath this spot there lies John Higgs,
A famous man for killing pigs.
Killing pigs was his delight
Both morning, afternoon, and night.
His knife is laid, his work is done,
I hope to heaven his soul is gone.

In the south transept stood the carved tomb of a portly gent in a splendid peasecod doublet and padded trunks, who lay, palms joined together, frowning sternly up at the ceiling.

"Sir Nicholas Herne," said the Vicar. "Founder of the house. Had literary pretensions. Perhaps, as it's in your line, you may have heard of his book, something about the evils of tobacco."

"Wait a minute," I said. "Of course—*The Indian Weed Expos'd,* wasn't that it? He was a buddy of James I."

"Yes, I suppose you could put it that way. Some jolly pointed things were said about their friendship, I believe, though my history's a bit shaky. James, you know, raised money for his Irish wars by creating a new dignity—baronets—and Sir Nicholas paid up his thousand pounds and received his title. Over and above that, he contributed quite heavily to James's purse, and when he was given Heronwick it was with the unusual stipulation that the property can descend to any heir, either male or female. Keeps it in the hands of the family, you see, although the baronetcy has lapsed, owing to Mrs. Herne not being a man. Not," he went on, "that she doesn't sometimes act like one."

"She struck me as being a forceful personality."

"I'd have used a stronger word myself. She has dominated this village ever since she was a child— tried to, anyway, although these days a good many people resist that sort of thing. Times have changed, you know. Not so much of the tugging at the old fore-lock, and the 'Iss, my lady, 'ee be raare good to Oi' sort of thing. For one thing, she hasn't the money her father and uncle had. She still has her pride, however."

"In the family, I suppose you mean?"

"Yes. I'm afraid I rather sympathize with her, although as a parson I ought to oppose the sin of pride. But there, the old girl hasn't much else left. The Hernes have been here since 1614, after all."

I was struck by a thought. "How come she's Mrs. Herne? If she married into the family—"

"Oh, no, she didn't. She's a Herne, all right. Her father was half-brother to Sir Francis and inherited the estate at the end of the last century. She married a distant cousin, Reginald Herne, of Sussex. Rumor had it, I'm told, that she looked for a husband with the same name so that she wouldn't have to change it. There's family pride, if you like. It may not be true, but it's in the tradition. Margaret Herne, who was lady of the manor in 1770, married a chap named Ott-right and made him change it to Herne. He got a baronetcy of his own—profiteering during your American Revolution."

He had been leaning back against a pew, and now he straightened and gestured towards the wall. "And there they all are, the Hernes, or a good many of 'em, some of them under the floor and some in the churchyard. There's Margaret's stone, and her husband's, and Sir Francis, and Sir Alastair, and Reggie. You Americans are very keen on this historical business, aren't you?"

He grinned. There was no malice in it, just amusement.

"I guess so," I said. "Aren't you?"

"Well, we're living in history, you know. That's what people forget. I do glance backward from time to time, but it's the present I'm mainly interested in. Thatched cottages are pretty, but some of them are simply pretty uncomfortable. I think it's a mistake to think of England as a quaint old-fashioned sort of place where we drive on the wrong side of the road and take cold baths every morning, and vote Tory. A great many of us really prefer central heating, and vote Labor with surprising regularity."

He broke off short. "I'm terribly sorry. I'm being very rude."

"I don't know how," I said. "There's nothing rude about speaking your mind. And I'm not disagreeing with you."

"Good. Well . . . seen enough?"

"Yes. I'm afraid I've kept you from your work."

"Nothing I like better. Besides, showing off my church is my work, isn't it? Where are you stopping?"

"At the Goat & Compasses."

"Ah, there's an interesting piece of history for you," he said, as we strolled toward the door. "There are several inns about the country with that name. And one theory has it that the original name was God Encompasseth Me."

"That's quite a change, from God to Goat."

"Yes," he said, with unexpected gravity. "Some might find it sinister."

The drizzle had ended, although heavy clouds still raced overhead.

"Not very promising," said the Vicar, looking up. "And we've got the last match of the season laid on for tomorrow. Have you ever seen a cricket match? No? Why not come and watch, then?"

"Sure. Where and when?"

"Just outside the village. I'll fetch you at the Goat, at about one-thirty, shall I? We're playing the Nottswood Exiles. I'll explain something about the game to you as we go, and then perhaps afterward you'd like to come along to the pub—not the one where you're staying, the other one, the Falcon. We generally have a few pints, and it gets very musical there later on."

"Great," I said. "I'm looking forward to it."

We shook hands, and I set out for the God Encompasseth Me, feeling, somehow, suddenly at home.

There were three bars in the Goat & Compasses, as in most English pubs: a lounge for people who wanted to lounge, a public bar for the public, and a smoke room for everybody else. Most people crowded into the saloon bar, which was the largest of the three, had a darts board, and was somehow the cosiest with its leather-covered benches, its otter heads (M.O.H., Wyre Piddle, 1937), its glass cases of stuffed fish (Taken by Eustache Throgg, Esq., Bagman's Brook, 6 lbs 4 oz), and its gallant trophies of Mr. Davies's Indian service during the war. The bar counter was in the public room, with openings into the other two rooms on each side, so that Mr. Davies himself, moving with gravity from one end of the bar to the other, could handle all requests.

I sat in a corner that evening with a pint in front of me. I was still trying to make up my mind whether I liked English beer, which seemed watery and faintly sour to me. People were standing in clusters with drinks in their hands; there wasn't room at the corner of the bar for more than one or two to queue up for refills so a lot of people just never did bother to sit down. I listened to the babble of speech and was amused at the fact that I couldn't understand most of what was being said through the strange, rustic accents, although we were all supposed to be talking the same language.

My friend the Yob, with a couple of yobbish chums, was over near the darts board, and he grinned and nodded to me. One of his pals had blond hair down to his shoulders, framing a long bony face with a flattened nose. The other was undersized and his thick hair was carefully waved and as glossy as that of a girl in a TV commercial, but the rest of him was grubby, draped in a leather jacket and indecently tight blue jeans. Before I could stop, I found myself answering the greeting with a nod of my own. Such is social intercourse; like sexual intercourse, it has automatic responses.

I finished my beer, and sat for a while staring into the dimpled glass mug while the hum of voices rose and fell around me. I was feeling dream-like again. The bench I sat on, the table ringed with the marks of glasses, the room and its characters in a play being English and typical as hard as they could, all became insubstantial, thinned out and faded as if at any moment I'd wake up. So it was with no particular surprise that I looked up and saw the red-headed girl standing at my table and smiling at me. I accepted it. Anything could happen in a dream.

"Hi, Lucy," I said.

"How did you know my name?"

"Mr. Dogood—Welldone—what's his name?—Spendwell the Vicar, told me."

She giggled. "Do you mind if we join you? It's rather crowded in here."

"Love to have you."

A young man I hadn't noticed before stepped from behind her. He was handsome, but on the thin and pallid side. Behind thick glasses, blue eyes, the same color as hers but without her animation, peered with a certain apprehensiveness.

"My brother, Alan. And I'm Lucy Nicholson. And you're—?"

"Dave Cannon. So now we're all nicely introduced and everything, and what'll you have to drink?"

33

"Oh, no, let me," said Alan. "Another pint, Mr. Cannon? And you'll have a gin and lime, as usual, Luce?"

He went off. She sat down opposite me.

"I'm sorry I laughed at you in the church," she said. "I couldn't help it. American accents always give me the giggles. They sound like the films."

"I know what you mean. I've been sitting here thinking the same thing about the English accents."

We were silent for a moment.

"How do you—" she began.

"—like English beer?" I finished.

That pointed mouth quirked up. "I suppose everybody asks you the same questions. Actually, I was going to ask how you find being in an English village on a Saturday night. For an American, it must be very dull."

"Not any more it isn't," I said, just to see her blush again. "Anyway, honestly, I don't know what you think Americans are like. Do you think we spend our evenings in night clubs and theaters? On a Saturday evening, at home, I'd probably be going over to a friend's house for dinner, and then we'd sit around and gas for a while. Or maybe I'd go to a movie. The big thrill comes when once in a while the local amateur theater does *East Lynne*. This is really more gaiety than I'm used to."

"I'm sure you're exaggerating."

"I never exaggerate. Do you know what it's like where I come from?"

"I can't imagine. I only know America from the films, or watching *Peyton Place* on the television. I'm sure it's really quite different."

Her brother returned with the drinks, and squeezed onto the bench next to me.

"Cheers," he said.

"Thanks," I replied. "Well, New Canaan's a village, but it's spread out considerably more than this one is.

34

There's more of a shopping center, almost like a small town here, I guess, and there are a lot more houses and people. But it's in the country, and it's quiet and rural, and I think we probably live pretty much the way you do."

"Except that you're a lot richer, aren't you? You all have deep freezes and two cars and color television sets and all those marvelous gadgets I see advertised in magazines like *The New Yorker*. Delicious, but far too expensive for any of us."

"Really, Luce!" her brother put in.

"Oh, Mr. Cannon's used to being teased. He's good at it himself."

"Yeah. I deserved that," I grinned.

She mimicked me. "Ye-ah. What on earth brought you to Heronwick? There aren't any sights worth seeing and no stately ruins except our lady of the manor, Mrs. Herne."

I explained about the manuscript.

"Gosh! I wonder if we have a rare book around the house that we can flog to you," she said. "Some fine old paperbacks of the pre-Penguin era? I do hope you won't pay Mrs. Herne too much money, though. It might give her even bigger delusions of grandeur than she already has."

"I gather she's not greatly loved."

Lucy made a face. "She imagines we're still living in the Middle Ages. She thinks of Heronwick as *her* village. It's true, a number of families were once her tenants, but they've long since lost that servility tenants are supposed to have had before the war—you know, 'I am an 'umble man, Mr. Copperfield.' And lots of new people have moved in, people who work in factories as far away as Gloucester. They've bought or rented houses that are newish and they haven't any feeling for her at all. But still, she loves to boss things. The Harvest Festival, for instance—poor John Spendwell's having a hard time trying to keep her satisfied and still allow the committee to get any work done."

"And from what I heard in the church, you're on that committee?"

"I've had my difficulties with her. She particularly doesn't like me because she and Father have had a few brushes. Father's ex-army, and he doesn't have much tact. He has told her in public—in parish meetings, for instance—what he thinks of her." She dropped her voice an octave, and barked, "Nothin' but damned interference, madam! Your mind's stuffed with outdated rubbish."

Her brother laughed nervously. "Jolly good. Sounds just like Dad."

Lucy finished her drink. I said, "Let me get you another. And what are you drinking, Mr. Nicholson?"

"Oh, brown ale, please."

I forced my way to the counter and ordered.

Mr. Davies said, "Enjoying yourself are you, sir? We are rather crowded tonight. I hope you do not feel lonely."

"No, I've found some friends."

"That is good. It is a sad thing to be alone in a strange place among strangers. I have felt it myself, from time to time, living here with the Saxons. They are warm-hearted enough, but there isn't a really good baritone among them."

When I got back to the table, I found I had more friends than I had bargained for. The Yob was there.

Lucy wasn't looking at him. She was sitting very straight, her lips compressed, staring at the wall. Her brother sat motionless and silent in his corner, behind his thick glasses. The Yob was leaning affectionately over her, and I heard him say, "You didn't give me half a chance, you know. What you want's to come and visit me in my little chapel again, one day."

"I've got nothing more to say to you, Charlie, so push off," she snapped.

"Make it a pilgrimage, like," he went on, chuckling at some private joke. "Why, I hadn't even started—"

I jostled him aside. "Sorry," I said, putting the drinks on the table. "I'm sitting here, if you don't mind."

He goggled at me. He must have had a few because his eyes were swimming. He gave a neighing laugh, and said, "'Ere, Yank, whatcher think of this bird, won't even talk to an old friend what went to so much trouble for her like what I done. Showed her my etchings, I did. My itchings is more like it."

Lucy moved as if to rise. I said, sharply, "You heard the lady tell you to buzz off. What are you waiting for?"

"Oh?" he said, teetering slightly. "Oh-ho. We're gallant, ain't we? The Americans to the bloody rescue."

I stood close to him. "Listen," I said, "we're not in Mrs. Herne's library now, and I don't have to be polite. I'd enjoy knocking your teeth down your throat, if you'd like to step outside with me."

He backed away, making his eyes blank in the way he had, flat and expressionless like those of a wild animal.

"No? Then beat it," I said.

He disappeared into the crowd without another word.

I sat down, and Lucy murmured, "Thanks" without looking at me.

"What was that all about, with charm boy?" I asked.

"Nothing," she answered. "Nothing important. When you live in a village like this one you know people . . . and they change. What were we talking about? Oh, Mrs. Herne."

But she said nothing further, and we all three sat

for a bit like people at some ghastly formal function, waiting for the silence to do something with itself.

I felt the evening collapsing. I said, "Are you going to that cricket game tomorrow? The Vicar invited me. I've never seen one."

"I'd love to go," said Alan, "but I don't think we can. We shall have to go to Somerset with Father. Too bad. I try never to miss a local match. Cricket's a wonderful game, even village cricket. Awfully good fun."

"One of the dreariest ways I can think of to spend an afternoon," Lucy said, with some of her former liveliness. "Even a Sunday afternoon in England in the country, and that's about as dreary as you can get, for a start. We English have always believed there was some virtue in tormenting ourselves. That's why we've resisted central heating so long. And we play games for the same reason, not because they're really fun but because they're supposed to be good for our souls. Take fox-hunting—somebody called that the unspeakable in pursuit of the uneatable—"

"Oscar Wilde," said Alan. "And you know what *he* was."

"Sort of a Third Programme shocker in his day, yes, but he had the right idea. All those blokes galloping over the fields to prove what solid sportsmen they are. Or rugger, you watch some of those poor little kids from St. Edmund's School scampering around in the frozen mud with their knees all blue, on a winter day, well, that's intended to toughen them up. All it really does is give them colds."

"Oh, Luce! Cricket's nothing like that," giggled Alan.

"No? Not half! It's the only sport in the world played in slow motion. No other country'd stand for it. They expect a game to have some action."

"I suppose you mean the way the West Indians

play it," Alan said. "Those who aren't on the pitch are hurling bottles."

"That's better than noble immobility, broken only by an occasional 'How's that?' The last time you took me to a match, you remember, I fell fast asleep after an hour, and when I woke up nothing had changed except the position of the sun."

I listened to this spirited exchange between them with delight, and didn't want it ever to end.

"I expect I'll enjoy the game," I said. "It's all new and interesting to me."

"Good luck to you." She drained her glass and stood up, as Mr. Davies, from the bar, called, "Last orders, gentlemen, please."

"Won't you have another?" I asked.

"No, thanks very much."

I got up, too. "Will I see you again?"

"It depends how long you stop on here." She grinned, the corners of her mouth tucking in, the upper lip peaking wickedly. "Perhaps I'll sneak away from Dad and come to the match after all. If I know John, he'll somehow entice you into playing."

"Not me," I said, walking her to the door with Alan following. "I don't believe it's proper for a foreigner to mix himself up in the internal affairs of another country."

The night was moist and mild, and some pungently sweet flower smell filled the air so that it was more like late spring than September. I walked them to the road, for the Goat was set back a little way in its own garden. I said good night, and turned back, stopping for a moment to light a cigarette.

As I threw the match away, three men stepped out of the shadows of the shrubbery. Enough light came from the window of the pub to let me see that it was the Yob and his two buddies.

I wasn't thinking: I figured they were on their way

to the gate. But they moved in on me and stood in a row, their eyes fixed on me. They all cultivated the same stare. It was unnerving.

I didn't say anything, just stood smoking. I never imagined they'd try to do anything, so close to the pub, so near closing time. So it took me by surprise when one of them, without warning, kicked out at me. The pointed toe of his shoe caught me on the shin.

Luckily, it wasn't a direct blow. It hurt, but it didn't knock me over as he had probably hoped.

I was mad, but more than anything else I was shocked. I never suspected they were the kind that did any fighting.

I made a grab for the nearest one, who happened to be the short one with the marceled hair. I got hold of that pretty hair and yanked him over to one side, like pulling up a weed. I slammed him into the blond fellow and I could hear their heads rap together.

The Yob—Charlie—jumped me. He was snarling like a dog, going "Gr-gr-gr" between his teeth. The seams of my jacket popped as I swung around, staggering under his weight, trying to shake him off. He kept trying to punch me in the ribs, but he was too close. At that point, the others piled in and we all went down.

We were too mixed up for anybody to do much damage to anybody else, but I got hold of a throat and started squeezing. A bright light burst on us as the pub door opened, and a minute later men ran out and pulled us apart.

"Who is it?" said somebody.

"What is going on?" That was Mr. Davies.

"Just—" I had to swallow. "Just a little boyish fun. It's all right." I began dusting off my jacket, mechanically.

"Charlie," said Mr. Davies. "And Alfred Fewes, and young Henry. We don't want any trouble here. We don't want your sort doing this kind of thing." His voice shook, and under its ministerial boom was real anger. "I won't have it, not in my house I won't."

"I'll call the policeman, shall I, Mr. Davies?" a man said.

"No," I said, "that's not necessary. It's over."

I looked at Charlie and he looked back at me, his eyes glittering.

"Well, let them go, then," said Mr. Davies. "But don't set your foot in the Goat again, *bach,* nor your friends either. I don't want your custom."

Charlie spat on the ground. The short one was already running a comb through his waves. I was glad to see that the blond one had a bloody nose which he kept mopping with his handkerchief. They walked away, still without a word.

"Are you all right, Mr. Cannon?" Mr. Davies said.

"I'm great. Is your bar all closed up?"

"Not to residents," he replied, softly.

"Good. I could do with a drink."

We went in, and I looked at myself in the bar mirror. I had a dark lump on the jaw which was beginning to ache a little, and my jacket was torn under one arm, and my shin hurt now that I thought about it. I downed a whisky, and asked for another.

"It was a good day on the whole," I said. "I can't complain if it ended with a bang."

"Cheers," said Mr. Davies, solemnly.

3

My room was cold, and I didn't want to get out of bed. I felt stiff, and my face and my leg were painful. One tiny electric heater with a single bar, fed by shillings, was supposed to keep the place warm and I lay under the blankets wishing somebody would come in and turn it on. But the sun was fingering the crack in the curtains and eventually I jumped up and opened them and after a little study found out how to open the window, which had a complicated arrangement of bars with holes in them and pegs and hooks which looked as if they had been invented in the Middle Ages. As I had suspected, it was much warmer outside than in.

I'm not much of a church-goer, but this morning I felt I had to go, first to see what it would be like in that little, ancient church, and second to see how the Vicar looked in uniform. Everyone I met on the way said good morning as if I were an old friend, and I was shown to a pew by a rosy-cheeked man who looked provokingly familiar until I remembered that he had been in the pub the night before and had helped break up the fight. I looked around for Lucy but neither she nor her brother were there. I saw Mrs. Herne, however, in a carved pew up near the pulpit, straight-backed and severe. The service was higher than I was used to, but it seemed to go with the records of the past that surrounded me. Spendwell wore his vestments with dignity and I never would have recognized him for the same man until he got into the pulpit, and then he preached a sermon on the text, "The race is not to the swift nor the battle to the strong . . . but time and chance happeneth to them all," in which he pointed out that it was with life as with cricket, which is in a way the mirror of life (said he) and in which even the Eleven which plays well may sometimes find itself facing reverses owing to some chance—such as the absence of players from the team—and that to stand up manfully to a deadly bowler was sometimes more important than to score centuries, and that in short good sportsmanship in the British tradition was more to be prized than winning. It puzzled me a little, that sermon, but it was punchy. However, it was all made clear when, coming out of church, I shook hands with Spendwell and told him I'd enjoyed the service.

"Ah, and did you like my sermon?" he asked. "I'm afraid I got carried away. I hadn't intended to give so much play to cricket, but I was preparing the village for what may turn out to be rather a sticky game this afternoon. Two of our men can't make it, you see. Well, at any rate, we couldn't ask for finer weather. Er . . . I don't suppose you'd like to try your hand?" he added, glancing sidelong at me.

"What? Me play? Don't be crazy, Vicar. I don't know the first thing about it."

"Mm, yes. Well, I'll see you at one-thirty, as we agreed."

I strolled down the High Street feeling like an old inhabitant. As I came to the lane that led between stone walls to the Goat, a policeman wheeling a bike came up to me and touched his helmet.

"Good morning, sir," he said. "Mr. Cannon, isn't it?"

"That's right." I tried to sound casual, wondering what law I'd broken.

He was a young policeman, and very serious. "You had a bit of trouble at the Goat & Compasses last night, sir, so I'm told."

"I guess you could call it that."

"I'm very sorry, sir. Would you mind telling me what happened?"

"Look, is it necessary? I had a run-in with a guy. It won't go any further."

"I hope you're right, sir. I know the men in question, and two of them have been up before the bench in the past. Quite frankly, sir, I do not wish to have any trouble in Heronwick, and besides that, seeing as what you're a visitor from the Other Side—"

"I understand, officer. I'll try to keep my nose clean, and I'm pretty sure the others will drop the whole thing. I don't want to bring any charges, if that's what you're getting at."

"Very well, sir. I just thought I'd mention the matter."

"Thanks." I took out my cigarettes and offered him one.

He accepted it, and put it in his breast pocket, saying, "Thank you very much, but I hope you won't mind if I smoke it later, after my dinner, sir."

"Do you live in Heronwick?" I asked.

He grinned widely, looking about sixteen years old. "Oh, yes, sir. I've been transferred from London. My wife likes it, and we've got a nipper two years old, and when we was offered the move we thought the country'd be good for him. London's no place for a kid."

"I see. But it must be kind of strange being a London cop and living in a village like this."

"Well, I've got to watch my step," he admitted. "Friendly, but not too friendly, like balancing on a high wire, if you take my meaning. Some people think they can get away with anything if they're chummy with a policeman, and there's others won't say good morning on principle. But the wife's got her friends and her Women's Institute meetings, and I collect Oriental weapons—"

"Oriental weapons? You mean swords and daggers?"

"All sorts. Mostly, I'm interested in Jap stuff but it's very pricey these days. Still, I've got one short-sword signed by Sukesada of Osafune that I found in the back of a junk shop in Newent. I took it in to Mr. Robinson at the V. & A. on my day off, once, and he said it was first rate."

He beamed, and I regarded him with astonishment. "Don't tell me you read Japanese?" I said.

"Oh, no, sir. Just a few of them squiggles I got out of books, so I could read the signatures of the sword-smiths."

"I'd like to see your collection sometime."

"Whenever you like, sir." He was shyly pleased. "Just drop in. My house is the other end of the village, next to what's called Kingsmill. You can't miss it: it's got a sign on it saying *Police*. He hesitated. "How long do you intend to stay in Heronwick, Mr. Cannon?"

"I'm not certain. A few more days, I guess."

"Come and call on me if there's anything I can do for you. Um ... *anything*," he added, emphatically.

"I understand. But I don't think there'll be any more trouble."

"That's good, sir. I hope not, I'm sure."

He saluted and went off, and I chuckled as I walked on, thinking that this was the damndest policeman I'd ever met, with his quiet way, and his Japanese swords.

The Vicar drove me in a tiny noisy old Morris, the back seat of which contained two large canvas bags and a very tall man who was hunched up with his knees almost to his chin. "Jeffrey Parr," the Vicar said, and the man nodded glumly as if answering a sad roll call. On the way, the Vicar tried to explain the game to me.

"It's quite simple, really," he said. I had not been in England long enough, at that time, to know that when an Englishman began a sentence that way something horribly complex was coming. "You see, there are eleven men a side. One side bats first. They put their batsman in and if he hits the ball, he and his partner try to make a run, or more. They change wickets, so to speak—er—they run back and forth, you see, as often as they can. That is, of course, unless he hits a boundary. Well, but that's not really the object of the exercise. The object is for the batsman to defend his wicket, and for the bowler to take it. You follow me?"

"Uh-uh," I said. "What's a wicket?"

"Look here," the Vicar said, briskly, "the best thing would be for you to watch the game for a bit and you'll get the hang of it. Of course, if you'd consent to play—"

"Lay off, Vicar," I said. "I was never even any good at baseball."

"Ah, but this is nothing like baseball."

"No dice."

"No—? Yes, I see what you mean."

He drove up a dirt track and into a wide, level field. Men in dazzling white trousers and shirts were moving about on it, and others were gathered near a long wooden shack with a large window facing the field, above which was a clock. Cars were parked along one side of the field under a row of trees, and the Vicar slid into a narrow space between two of them and leaped out. Parr climbed out of the back seat, and they went off together, leaving me alone.

After a few minutes, the Vicar returned bearing a cricket bat, a kind of wide, flat paddle with a long handle. He fiddled with this for a moment, looking sheepish, and at length said, "Look here, Mr. Cannon, I—er—I do wish you'd change your mind. Two of our chaps can't come, and it's not going to be much of a match. The Nottswood bunch are jolly good . . . and as it's the last match of the season . . . I know you'd enjoy it if you gave it a try, it's really rather an interesting game. . . ."

I burst out laughing. "Miss Nicholson warned me against this," I said. "Okay. If you're really in a spot and you don't mind my ignorance, I'll play. What the hell, I'm going to be here watching anyway and if you keep looking at me like that I'll start crying."

"Splendid!" he said, warmly. "I've already put your name in."

"One thing, though, let me just try hitting a few balls with that bat, will you?" I said. "I'd like to get the feel of it."

"Absolutely. Oh, Willie, half a tick, please." This was to a thickset man with wide shoulders who was walking past. "Would you mind bowling a few to Mr. Cannon? Mr. Cannon's an American visitor who has kindly consented to play for us. Mr. Cannon, this is Will Brock."

Brock reached out an enormous hand. He had a heavy, slab-like face and no neck to speak of. Two small blue eyes were set like buttons above cheeks ruddled with purple veins, and they had about as much expression as a pair of buttons. He got a ball, while I tried with the Vicar's help to get the knack of holding the bat. It was awkward and heavy, and unlike a baseball bat had to be swung with a kind of sideways, or underhand, stroke. The Vicar left me, and Brock tossed me a few balls in an odd, stiff, overarm way, not using his wrist. I missed every one.

By the time the Vicar came back, I was wondering why I had let myself be talked into this. Brock had said nothing, and to add to my embarrassment two or three other men had gathered around and were watching me with broad grins. Among all their shining white clothes my slacks and blue shirt made me as conspicuous as if I were walking around naked.

"They won the toss," the Vicar said to Brock. "They'll go in first. Jeffrey'll lead off. . . . Ah, Mr. Cannon."

"Dave," I said.

"Right, Dave, go along with Willie and he'll show you where to stand."

It suddenly occurred to me that the Vicar must be captain of the team. I said, "Well, now, wait a minute. What am I supposed to do?"

"Not to worry," said the Vicar with a wave of his hand. "Just stop any balls that come to you and sling 'em back, you know." He hurried off.

The first few minutes after Brock had planted me somewhere in what I'd have called center field were dark. I couldn't make out what was going on, and I felt like the worst kind of a fool—the kind who knows how foolish he is but can't stop. After a while, however, I gave up trying to do anything and instead just watched and listened. And as the Vicar had said, I began to get the hang of it. It wasn't all that complicated, basically.

The wickets consisted of upright sticks, three of them set fairly close together, a couple of feet high. They were called stumps, and they had two wooden spindles laid across their tops. The bowler tried to knock the spindles off with a ball; the batsman tried to keep the ball away. He could hit it or not, as he chose, nor did it matter if he missed it so long as the wicket was unharmed. But if he did hit it, he could choose to run to the opposite wicket, where a second batsman was waiting; in this case, they passed each other and kept running back and forth as long as they thought they could get away with it. They had to touch the ground in front of the wicket, generally reaching out with the tips of their bats to do so, and they could be put out if the ball was caught before it hit the ground, or if it was thrown back before one of them made it to the crease. At the end of six balls, an umpire wearing a long white coat like a mad scientist in a movie called, "Over!" and then it was the turn of the second batsman. Obviously, however, I wasn't getting all the fine points, because just about when I thought I knew what was going on, there was a flurry of movement and a slow, measured clapping from the clubhouse where the opposing team were sitting, and one of the batsmen walked slowly away. "Is he out?" I asked one of my own team, who was near me in the field. "Yeh," he said. "Well, why?" I asked.

"Ah, nobody knows that," he replied. "However, the object of the exercise is to go on playing as if we did."

Well, Spendwell was right, I began to enjoy myself. The smooth green turf, the white-clad men, the puffs of white cloud leisurely drifting across the bluest of skies, made a pretty picture. It was quiet, too, unlike any game I'd ever been in. People spoke in low voices, there would come the *pock!* of the bat, and sometimes that languid applause. Now and then, when something was challenged—a batsman putting his leg in front of the wicket, for instance—you'd hear someone call, "How's that?" But the general feeling was one of relaxation and hush, as if we were all the votaries of some rural god, going through the casual, good-humored movements of a well-known ritual.

My team-mate in the field explained where to throw the ball if I caught it. Once in a while, a ball would come spinning along the grass in my direction, and I'd grab it and toss it back, feeling like a veteran.

I had at least one moment of excitement. One of their batsmen was very skillful and couldn't be put out. Time after time, he'd slam the ball into one of the adjoining meadows, and our boys would have to climb warily through the barbed wire to retrieve it. When he did this, it scored six runs and he didn't even bother to move. Since a batsman stayed in the game until he was put .out, it looked as if this man was there for the rest of the afternoon. By the time he'd made about sixty runs, I shared the common hatred for him and the easy-going mood of the day changed to one of bitter tension. More than anything else, we wanted to get him out, but it began to seem that if this happened it would come as a Christmas present.

Several times, he had hit balls my way but I could never get to them fast enough to do any good. Then, he snicked one off the edge of his bat that came steaming along the ground right at me. I rushed for it and scooped it up. I could see him sprinting for the other wicket, and I threw it blindly in that general direction, hoping with all my heart that the ball would get there at the same time he did, and kill him. As it left my hand, my feet slid out from under me and I fell over backward. I landed with a thump that jarred the breath out of me. When I scrambled up, I heard that lazy clapping and, looking wildly around, I saw the Enemy walking slowly, with his bat under his arm, towards the clubhouse. Our wicket keeper had the ball.

My team-mate nodded at me and said, "Good show. Still in one piece?"

"I'm okay," I said. "What happened?"

"Run out," he replied.

"Is that good?"

"Well, we're finished with that lad," he said, with a grin.

I went back to my position, feeling I had served my country well.

At last the innings was over, and we adjourned to the clubhouse for strong-mud-colored tea in thick mugs, served by the wives of some of the team. The Vicar clapped me on the back and said, "Bearing up, Dave? Well done. You'll bat ninth. Follow that chap there," and he pointed to a young man with an enormous mop of yellow hair.

"All right. Now about this batting, what do I do?"

"Not to worry. Just take hold of the handle and bash away." And he was off again.

Not to worry, I thought wryly. Ah, well, what's to lose? Only after this I wouldn't even trust the Vicar of Wakefield.

Around me the talk pattered on, the curious, funny, sometimes incomprehensible speech: "No cigarettes? You bloddy Heronwick shower." "It's been so wet they've to cut when they can." "Instead of having a real crack at it, he'd push and with two men posted around gully. . . ." I rode with it in a slight fog, but, as my Uncle Frank used to say about the race track where he spent most of his time, win or not I enjoyed the place and the show.

When it was my turn to bat, they buckled me into a pair of pads—leg protectors which came up over the knees—and I waddled out to the pitch. Their wicket keeper was a short man with a droll clown's face.

When I came to the crease, he said, "Now, me lad, ask the umpire in your best English accent, 'May I have a guard, please?'"

I said, parodying him, "May I have a guard, please?"

The umpire called, "Hold your bat upright, please."

I put the tip of it on the ground and held it straight, as I'd seen some of the other batsmen do.

"You want a center guard, don't you? A bit more towards you, please."

This was to show me where to stand in relation to the wicket.

The bowler walked back some distance. Then, in the terrifying way they have, he charged forward and, with his arm whirling like a windmill, shot the ball at me. I watched it bounce and saw that it was going off to the side, so I let it go. A fine sweat broke out on my forehead.

He bowled again. I swung and missed. However, the wicket was untouched.

Oh God, I prayed silently, I've always tried to be a good boy, just let me hit it once.

He sent a fast ball down. I took a step and flailed out at it with all my strength. My arms jarred, and I heard a loud crack, the most satisfying of sounds. I started to run.

"Never mind," said the wicket keeper. "You've done it properly. Stay where you are."

Above the languorous applause, a voice yelled, "Hit the clock!"

A burst of laughter went up, and I looked around at the wide grins of the Nottswood team.

"What'd I do?" I asked.

"You've been and smashed your clubhouse clock with that six," said the wicket keeper.

"Oh, my God," I said. "I'm sorry."

He cocked his head on one side with a peculiar look, but he said nothing.

I stood before the wicket again. Anyway, I said to myself, it was a six. One more like that. The ball came; I swung at it, hit empty air, and almost lost my balance. The stumps were spreadeagled.

"That's it, eh?" I said.

"Ah, you've been clean bowled, lad," said the wicket keeper.

I took the long walk back to the clubhouse, and the Vicar slapped me on the back. "Well done," he said. "Oh, well done. You see? A six! Nothing to it, is there?"

"Well, yeah, but I hear I busted your clock," I said. "I'll pay for it, of course—"

He began to laugh. Several of the other men gathered round, and one of them said, "Why, Yank, I know men would give a week's wages to a done that."

"Are you kidding?"

"Not at all," said the Vicar. "You'll hear many a good batsman bragging about hitting the clock, but most of them only wish they'd done it."

"Up to now, nobody but Brock's done it in this club," said the tall man, Jeffrey Parry. "You'll want to watch yourself, Slasher."

Brock's heavy face was sullen. He nodded to me, and said, "You done well. Too bad some chaps can't do better with their bloody comedy."

He turned abruptly, and strode away to the clubhouse.

"Gloomy, he is," said Parr.

"He certainly wasn't in form today—not even a double figure," said the Vicar. "Something's bothering him. I'll have a talk with him later."

The game ended not long afterward, when the last of our men was put out. Our shadows stretched across the grass, and the sun was cutting the tops of the elms that fringed the next field. Birds flew up out of the trees as if they had been thrown away across the golden sky.

The Vicar said, "Lovely, isn't it?"

"Did we win?" I asked.

"Only spiritually."

"Huh?"

"Didn't you listen to my sermon? He who does his best, wins."

I looked at him, but fortunately he was grinning. "I'm afraid they walloped us," he said. "Coming along to the pub?"

The Falcon was smaller than the Goat & Compasses, and was at the other end of the village, at a fork in the road. It had immensely thick walls and a low ceiling with heavy beams, and when we were all jammed into the public room it was difficult to get your pint up to your mouth. After some argument, the Vicar agreed to let me pay for fixing the clock, and then he bought me a drink. The captain of the other team squeezed over and exchanged a few words with Spendwell. "This is your surprise batsman, is it?" he said. "A dirty trick, Jack, sneaking in a Yank baseball player." Several other men bought me drinks. Jeffrey Parr, winking at me, said, "Well done. Why not settle here, eh? We'll make a cricketer out of you. Have another go at Nottswood next summer." I bought a round of drinks, fighting my way to the bar and passing the dripping pints back over my shoulder. Somebody, somewhere, began to play a piano and people were singing, earnestly and discordantly, "Don't fence me i-hin."

I began to feel a little woozy, what with the load of drink I had taken on, and the smoke and stuffiness and the standing in one place. My right shoulder was damp and smelled of beer. The Vicar had disappeared, and I pushed my way slowly to the door.

Well, I thought, taking in a deep breath of fresh evening, there was only one thing lacking and that was Lucy. My disappointment was unexpectedly strong. I hadn't thought about her all afternoon, and yet the hope that she would somehow get to the cricket game had been lurking in the back of my mind. Now that it was all over I knew a sense of frustration and emptiness. But how stupid of me! I thought, with some irritation, as I set out to walk back to the Goat. I'm building this girl up in my mind, and there's no point to it. Another day or so and I'll have that manuscript, and I'll be gone. What difference does it make whether she sees me play cricket or not? She's nothing to me, and what's even more to the point I'm nothing to her.

But instead of pulling me out of it, that thought only made me more depressed. I should have been full of elation, but I went to my dinner as if I were going to my execution.

4

I had a satisfying amount of attention from the Davieses. Young Ted had been watching the match from the sidelines with some of his friends, and had told his parents about my clock-breaking feat. After he closed up, Sunday night, Mr. Davies brought out a bottle of Armagnac from his private store and solemnly gave me a drink. I sat up late, talking and drinking with him and his wife, and Monday morning I didn't feel like getting up at all. It didn't have to be early, however. My appointment with Mrs. Herne was for eleven.

It was an on-again off-again sort of morning, now with great dark clouds sailing up before the gusty southwest wind, then clearing to let an almost summery sun pour down. The mail had come by the time I got downstairs but there was no word from Bob. Mr. Davies assured me that any telegram would be delivered, not phoned, so there was no chance of a message being garbled. It was after ten when I finished breakfast, and I decided to walk to Herne House by a footpath he pointed out to me. It began not far from the Goat, crossed a couple of fields and then went through a wood, entering the estate from the rear.

"It was like the Motorway to Birmingham for the local poachers, in the old days," Mr. Davies said. "A traffic problem like that of London, with the pushing and jostling of men setting snares and pulling out fish. But there is not much game there now, except a rabbit or two who have been passed over because of extreme age and decrepitude. It shows you how the Hernes have come down in the world, doesn't it, when there is nothing left worth stealing on their land?"

I walked down the lane from the Goat and climbed a stile—the first real stile I had ever seen, like the one the crooked man found a sixpence at. The path was little more than a shadowy line along the edge of the field; there was another stile in the hedge leading to the next field, and beyond that, up a steep slope, were the tall grey-green stems and thick crowns of the trees, just beginning to go bronze with autumn. Near the top of the slope I turned and looked back. The village was laid out below me like a toy. Its mossy stone-tiled roofs shone warmly in the sun. Then, as I watched, an immense sheet of grey cloud like a wing was lifted over it, and a shadow sped across it and rushed up the hill toward me. In an instant, I was beneath the cloud and the wind under it was chill. I turned and began walking again, and was aware of a man coming toward me from the wood, walking with long strides down the slope.

I stopped, for there was something urgent, almost ominous, in his haste. When he came closer, I saw that it was the big, hefty cricketer, Will Brock. He recognized me, and slowed suddenly.

"Hi," I said. "Nice day."

He grunted something. His face had the color and immobility of a piece of sandstone. The wind cutting into it didn't even make him blink.

I said, to remind him in case he didn't remember me, "That was great fun, that cricket match." Then I remembered the Vicar saying that Brock was off his game, and I added, "Of course, my getting that hit was a pure fluke."

"No. It was well done. You put your back into it," he said.

"Well, if I come back here someday you can show me how it's really done," I said, with a laugh.

His hard faced cracked very slightly.

I felt a sense of camaraderie, of no longer being a total outsider, being a team-mate of his so to speak. I said, still grinning, "And where've you been? Poaching up in the woods? Mr. Davies tells me—"

His expression hardened as suddenly as if a new and darker cloud has passed over it. He said, "I've been fishing. Got to get to work. Morning."

He thrust past me and went off down the hill, almost running.

I stared after him, a little hurt, figuring I shouldn't have said "poaching," maybe. Then I shrugged. After all, New England farmers were as abrupt and dour. And in any case, it meant nothing to me. I'd be finished here in a day or so, and the whole thing would be nothing but a memory.

I walked on and entered the wood. The absence of real undergrowth struck me: there were few bushes, and mostly it was ferns and shrubs, with the trees rising up all about me, smooth, silvery, thick-rinded beeches like elephants, and here and there a gnarled massive oak or horse-chestnut like an ancient herdsman watching the flock. A little way in, I came to a high stone wall. It had been dry-laid and was falling apart; in one place a whole section had tumbled outward and lay scattered on the grass. The footpath led me to a stone stile—two upright flat stones set just wide enough apart to let a person pass but keep cattle out. I guessed this must be the boundary of Herne Park. Beyond, the wood was thicker, and, now that the sky was grey, darker. I crossed a stream bridged by a couple of rotting planks. It ran downhill, to my left, and I recalled a stone bridge next to the Goat and suspected that it came out there.

I followed the path until the wood ended, and I found myself at a wooden fence, green with moss and, like the stone wall, dropping to pieces. The castle-cloak of Herne House rose up beyond, with lawns between me and it, and a vegetable garden on the right.

I went round to the front. I was looking forward to seeing what I already thought of as *my* manuscript. Maybe, I thought, if I had to I'd go up to eight thousand dollars. I could raise another thousand somehow, and I was certain to double it, at least, even if the Chronical wasn't what I hoped it was.

I knocked and waited, fidgeting. I wanted to study it some more, to finger that thick, rich parchment and examine the lovely pot-hooks of the writing. Nobody answered the door.

Could she have forgotten, I asked myself, with mounting annoyance. No, surely not. She wanted that money as badly as I wanted the manuscript. Could she, then, have had another offer from somewhere? Was she going to play hard to get? I knocked again, more loudly. The servant, I remembered, was pretty deaf.

Then I thought, after all, she's an old woman in spite of the way she holds herself. Maybe something's happened to her. Oh, baby, I thought, rather cruelly I suppose, just my luck, she's fallen downstairs and broken her neck or something and there goes my chance at the *Raimond*.

I tried the door. It opened under my hand. I stuck my head in, nervously clearing my throat and with a false smile on my face. The hall was dim and quiet. I edged in, with words all ready: I'm sorry, the door was open, I thought you had forgotten, or didn't hear me. . . .

And then my heart gave a bump which shook me. Something—somebody— was lying at the foot of the staircase. All I could think of was that that sudden, impatient, utterly irrational idea of mine was true, and she had fallen down the stairs.

I ran over. It wasn't her. It was the Yob.

He was lying on his back, and there was a good deal of blood under his head and knotted ropes of it coming from his ears. His forehead was deeply dented as if a giant thumb had been pressed there. But the thing that got to me was his expression. His eyes were wide open and he was grinning, showing all his teeth.

A wave of nausea welled over me, sweeping away any concern or curiosity I might normally have had. I started for the door, and fresh air.

I heard a door open somewhere up above. Mrs. Herne's sharp voice called, "Who's that? Is someone there?"

I almost jumped out of my skin. Then I took hold of myself, and replied shakily, "It's me. Dave Cannon. Don't come down."

But she was already on her way.

She stopped halfway down the stairs. She looked at the body, then at me.

"What have you done?" she said, sternly.

The question knocked the wind out of me. "I just came in," I protested. "I found him like this."

She came down the rest of the way and, automatically drawing her skirts aside, bent over the Yob and studied him for a minute.

"I think," she said, "I had better ring up the police."

With that, the whole thing suddenly became real.

When she had made the phone call, she came back and glanced again at the body.

"It reeks of drink here," she said.

I had been smelling it for some time without being conscious of what it was. "Maybe," I said, "he got drunk and fell down the stairs."

She said, "It's idle to speculate."

She crossed to the door which led into the kitchen passage, pulled it open, and called, "Sarah!" There was no answer.

"Do you think something's happened to her?" I asked.

"I doubt it. She is still at the Falcon," Mrs. Herne replied. "I see no reason to stand about here as if we were mourners. Come into the drawing room. We can wait there for the constable."

The young policeman I had already met turned up a few minutes later. He got on the phone at once, without asking us any questions, saying only, "Not my pigeon, madam," to Mrs. Herne. When he had made his call and reported, he asked us politely not to touch anything, nor to leave the house. "Just a formality, you understand," he said. We remained in the drawing room, sitting silently opposite one another, while the policeman waited in the hall. Only once did Mrs. Herne speak to me.

"I am sorry that this should have happened, Mr. Cannon," she said. "However, when the police have done what they must, and taken him away, perhaps, if you feel up to it, we can continue with our discussion of the manuscript."

"Okay," I said. At the moment, I found it hard to get the Yob's unnatural grin out of my mind, or the memory of the blood looping out of his ears. I admired Mrs. Herne's self-control. She sat bolt upright with her hands in her lap, and I reminded myself that her ancestors had governed this village for hundreds of years and that her poise came naturally. This was no easy screamer in the face of emergencies, this tough old lady, and she had a composure that went deeper than anything I had met before. I didn't like her any more than I had, but I had to respect her.

Eventually, we heard a car drive up, and then a murmur of voices. Mrs. Herne stood up, and after a moment's hesitation pulled open the door and went into the hall. I followed her.

A round-faced man with thinning hair, combed from left to right across his pink scalp, was bending over the body, hitching up his tweed topcoat in a way that reminded me of Mrs. Herne's holding of her skirts. He straightened when he saw us, and from the business with the coat and the innocence of his blue eyes, I thought, This can't be a detective!

"Mrs. Herne," he said. "How do you do? I'm Detective Inspector Codd."

She nodded, making no attempt to shake hands. He turned to me.

"My name's Dave Cannon," I said.

"An American? Or Canadian?"

"I'm an American."

"Here on holiday, are you?"

"I'm visiting Mrs. Herne on business."

"I see. Now, madam, if you'll allow me, I must use your telephone."

She motioned to the stand in one corner of the hall. As he was crossing to it the door to the kitchen passage opened and the slatternly maid appeared.

"Thought I heard voices," she said. Her eyes skimmed the detective and the constable, and lit on the Yob. "Who—?" she began. Then, recognizing him, she said, flatly, "Done for himself at last, has he?"

The Inspector looked a question at Mrs. Herne, who said, "This is my cook, Sarah."

"Have you been in the kitchen all morning?" he asked.

"No, not all morning," Sarah replied. "I only just come back from the village. Shopping," she added.

I heard Mrs. Herne sniff.

"Very well," said the Inspector. "Is there anyone else in the house? No? Then will you all go into the sitting room and wait for me, please? If you'll just post yourself outside the front door, constable," he said, to the village policeman.

"Thanks very much. And tell the DC outside to step in here."

He went to the phone, and we three returned to the drawing room, where Mrs. Herne and I sat down and Sarah stood with her arms folded, leaning against the wall like a used mop. The Inspector joined us very shortly. He left the door open behind him, and I saw that there was another man, in plain clothes, standing unobtrusively outside with a pencil and a notebook ready.

"Now, then," the Inspector said, "can any of you tell me anything about what's happened? Did anyone see him fall?"

We shook our heads.

"Who was the first to find him?"

"I guess I was," I said. "I came here for an appointment with Mrs. Herne. I knocked at the door, and when nobody answered I opened it and looked in, and there he was."

The Inspector eyed me. "You opened the door? Why? Had you heard any noise?"

"No," I replied. "It just seemed funny to me that nobody should answer when I was expected. And I got this peculiar feeling that maybe something was wrong." As I said the words, I got a peculiar feeling right in the pit of the stomach that something was indeed wrong. Just as one feels inexplicably guilty when a Customs man asks, "Have you anything to declare," so I now felt guilty without having done anything.

The Inspector, however, went on, "What did you do then?"

"Well, I went in and looked at him. I couldn't believe my eyes. And then Mrs. Herne called from upstairs and I told her not to come down but she came anyway."

He pursed up his lips. "Why did you tell her not to come down?"

I shivered. "Are you kidding? You saw him."

He nodded. "Mrs. Herne, had you heard anything? Any sound of a fall, or a blow?"

"No," she said. "Nothing."

"Where were you, exactly?"

"In the library, upstairs. I was setting out a manuscript in which Mr. Cannon is interested, and making some notes of points I wished to raise with him. I thought I heard the front door close and someone moving about. I called out, and Mr. Cannon answered and told me not to come down."

"Yet you came anyway."

"Certainly I came," she snapped. "This is my house."

"Of course," he said, smoothly. "What did you do then?"

"My first rather confused impression was that perhaps Mr. Cannon and Neville had had a fight."

"Neville?"

"The dead man's name is Charles Neville. He is—was—my gardener."

"I see. You thought they'd had a fight?"

"I saw Neville lying there, and Mr. Cannon standing over him. Mr. Cannon then told me that he had just arrived. He suggested that Neville might have become intoxicated and fallen down the stairs. I then telephoned the local policeman, Constable Baker."

"Mm. I noticed the smell of whisky. Was Mr. Neville in the habit of taking a drop too much, now and then?"

"I was not an intimate of his," Mrs. Herne said, coldly. "However, I have had occasion once or twice to speak to him, when he arrived here not quite sober."

The Inspector grinned, and at once stifled it. "And you—er—Sarah? You heard and saw nothing?"

"I told you, I was in the village. I had just come back to my kitchen and had no sooner got to my work than I heard the talk and voices."

"Very well," said the Inspector. "The Detective Superintendent and the pathologist should be here shortly. We'll have to inconvenience you a bit, Mrs. Herne. Mr. Cannon, are you stopping somewhere in the village? I'd be most grateful if you would go to your inn and keep yourself available. I shall have to ask you—all of you—a few more questions. Purely routine, nothing to be disturbed about."

I didn't feel much liked looking at the manuscript right then. I told Mrs. Herne I'd be in touch with her after the police had finished, and then I walked back to the village. The sky was low, heavy, and wet, and as I got to the pub it began to rain. A hell of a day, I thought. Just the kind of day to get killed on.

I told Mr. Davies what had happened. With his hands behind his back, rising on his toes, he replied to the House of Lords, "I cannot honestly say that I am sorry, for he was a thoroughly disagreeable fellow. But it is only Christian to hope that he is at rest and in a better place, poor lad. A nice pint of keg, sir?"

I had a pint, and discovered that it was lunch time and that I had an appetite in spite of everything. After lunch, I went up to my room and read for a while, and then sat looking out the window at the wet, wondering what to do, and how this would affect my business with Mrs. Herne, and whether there'd be trouble, until I dozed off. A knock at the door woke me.

A solemn man, who looked vaguely familiar until I remembered that I had seen him taking notes at Herne House, said, "Detective Inspector Codd's compliments, sir, and would you mind stepping next door?"

I gaped. "Next door?"

"Just along the passage, sir."

The Goat had three bedrooms for guests. The plain-clothesman led me to the one at the other end of the hall. There was just barely room enough in it for Inspector Codd and me, and another man, a tall, beaky, morose chap who was sitting on the bed.

Codd smiled at me in a friendly way, and said, "Take a seat, Mr. Cannon. I think you'd better have the armchair. This is Detective Superintendent Gough."

I said hello, and the beaky man grunted.

Codd sat himself on the edge of a straight chair and said, "Now then, Mr. Cannon, there are a few points we want to go over with you, if you don't mind. You are a dealer in rare books and manuscripts, I understand."

"That's right."

"And you came to Heronwick in order to get a medieval manuscript from Mrs. Herne."

"To look at it," I amended. "I couldn't make an offer until I'd satisfied myself that it was what I wanted. And I have to wait until I hear from my partner back home, giving me an okay on the price."

66

"Yes, I see. You came to Herne House this morning, then, to look at the manuscript once more?"

"Yes."

Codd glanced at a piece of paper in his hand. "You knocked at the door, no one answered, and then you went in. Is that right?"

"That's right."

"Doesn't that seem like an odd sort of thing to do?" put in the Superintendent, harshly.

I felt my face redden. "Yes, I suppose it was. But you know, I was anxious to see the manuscript—it could be valuable and just what I want—and I began to have all sorts of ideas. The maid is deaf, and I thought maybe she didn't hear me. And then I thought, what if something's happened to Mrs. Herne? You know how crazy ideas can come into your head when you're waiting for something."

"And are you sure, Mr. Cannon," said the Superintendent, "that you didn't have some sort of crazy idea, as you put it, that if no one was home you might just nip in and help yourself to the manuscript?"

I stared at him. "What the hell would I do that for?"

"I don't know. That's what I'm asking you," he returned. "I'm wondering whether you might have met Neville in the hall, and perhaps he tried to stop you—"

"Now wait a minute," I cried. I was so confused and angry that I could barely get the words out. "Just a damn minute. I'm a reputable dealer. We don't go around stealing things from customers. How could I get away with it? What do you think I'd do, sneak out of the country with the manuscript hidden in my socks?"

"Don't get excited, Mr. Cannon," Codd put in, gently. "Now, Superintendent, I'm sure that was uncalled for. Please let me handle this, sir."

The Superintendent seemed utterly unruffled. "Go on," he said.

"You see, Mr .Cannon," Codd said, looking at me with wide mild blue eyes, "we are a little troubled by one or two things. Mrs. Herne said her first impression was that you and Neville had been fighting."

I was still upset but I tried to pull myself together. "That's ridiculous," I said. "It's the same kind of irrational first thoughts I was just talking about. She came down and suddenly saw him lying there and me standing over him."

"Yes." He cleared his throat. "You did, in fact, know Charles Neville, didn't you? I mean, you had met him before?"

"That's right. In her library."

"And you didn't much like him. You met him somewhere else, I believe." Again, he referred to the paper. "In this pub, on Saturday night."

I couldn't help a grin. "I guess you could say we met. He and two friends of his jumped me outside."

"You had a fight over a girl, isn't that so?" the Superintendent put in, suddenly.

"Why do you keep twisting things around?" I demanded. "Miss Nicholson and her brother were having a drink with me. I went to the bar and when I got back to the Yo—*Mr.* Neville was making a nuisance of himself, and I busted in and told him to quit it. He left, and when I came back from seeing Miss Nicholson and her brother to the road, he and his friends attacked me. So don't make it into a big thing—'a fight over a girl.'"

They exchanged glances. Then Codd said, "You say you met him in Mrs. Herne's library. Mrs. Herne has told us that you asked to be left alone to examine the manuscript, and that Neville went into the library with some firewood. Shortly afterward, she heard your voices raised as if you were quarreling. She started to go up, and then you rang the bell in a prearranged signal to summon her. Is that right?"

I opened my mouth. Before I could say anything, the Superintendent barked, "Were you, in fact, quarreling?"

He certainly put my back up. Codd must have seen it, too, for he shook his head sympathetically. I turned to him.

"I don't know what this is all about," I said, "but I don't see why I should hide the fact that I didn't like Neville's appearance or his manner or anything about him. I actually first met him on the road outside—he bummed a cigarette from me, and I didn't like him then. He came into the library while I was studying the manuscript—and you must realize that this is pretty important to me, a lot of money could be involved, and I wanted to concentrate—and hung over me, and bothered me, and then—"

"Go on," Codd said, encouragingly.

"Well, this sounds peculiar, but he suggested that I should help him steal some books from Mrs. Herne's library. Some of them are quite valuable."

"What did you say?"

"I told him to drop dead."

Codd blinked. "Ah, yes. I've heard the expression," he said. "Under the circumstances, however, I don't think that's quite the way I would have put it."

"No, of course. I forgot. I'm sorry. Well, you know what I mean. I did get angry, and I suppose I did raise my voice. But it's Mrs. Herne's house and I was a guest in it, so I rang the bell for her and I thought that would put an end to it."

I sat back, looking from one to the other. "Now really," I said. "You're not seriously suggesting that we had a fight, and that I knocked him out and killed him? I don't go around killing people just because I don't like them. It's not the American Way of Life." I laughed, rather nervously.

Codd shook his head. "Nobody's suggesting anything, Mr. Cannon," he said, soothingly. "However, there are some curious aspects to the matter. . . . For example, Mrs. Herne said, as I remember, that you intimated Neville might have got drunk and fallen down the stairs."

I thought about it. "I suppose I did. He certainly stank of whisky. You said so yourself."

"Detective Superintendent Gough and I have just come from the post-mortem examination," Codd said, his voice soft and his expression apologetic. "There was no trace of whisky in Neville's stomach. There was quite a lot of it on his clothing, but he hadn't had any to drink. Not recently, at any rate."

"What of it?" I asked. "I don't get it."

The Superintendent stood up. There wasn't much room between his legs and mine, and he loomed over me as if he were about to fall on me. "What of it, Mr. Cannon, is that somebody threw whisky over him to make it look like an accident."

It took a while for that to sink in. Then I said, stupidly, "*Look* like an accident?"

The Superintendent sat down again, took out a pipe and began filling it from a small, round tin of tobacco, as if he had said all he meant to and were now withdrawing.

I said, "Somebody shoved him down the stairs. Is that what you mean?"

"We don't know, Mr. Cannon," Codd said.

"But you do mean that—somebody deliberately killed him."

Codd carefully joined his fingertips, one after the other. "We are hoping that's not the case. We'd be a great deal happier if it were an accident. But there are some things that have to be explained."

I began to feel very cold. "Look here," I said, "I couldn't have done it. You don't think I came in and went up the stairs, and met him, and flung him down and broke his neck—why, Mrs. Herne would have heard me, for God's sake! Do you think I'm the kind of man who could do such a thing, anyway? What for?"

"Take it easy, Mr. Cannon," Codd said. "I don't know what I think. We usually approach cases like this with what a friend of mine calls 'masterly inactivity.' We have to ask questions; it's not pleasant, but it's necessary.

"One thing's certain, however. Neville wasn't killed by the fall downstairs. Somebody smashed in the front of his skull with a good, hard blow of a club or a hammer or something of that sort."

I said, thickly, "Are you—are you accusing me of murder? Are you going to arrest me?"

Codd shook his head. "Mr. Cannon, we're not accusing you of anything. We are certainly not arresting you. But we'll need your help. We will probably have further questions to ask you. I hope you won't mind. We're as much in the dark as—ah—as you are. I am staying here at the Goat, as it's the only inn in the village. I hope you'll continue to stay here, too, for the time being."

"I see. You're telling me not to leave, is that it?"

"Well, it's what you want yourself, isn't it? After all, your business with Mrs. Herne isn't concluded yet."

I sighed. "I don't feel much like business right now. Are you finished with me? Or is there something else?"

"Nothing more just now."

"Okay," I said. "I hope you won't mind if I call the American Embassy. I'm telling you right now that I had nothing to do with Neville's death. You don't believe me, do you?"

He blinked at me, with a smile on his pudgy, inno-cent-looking face, and ran his fingers through what there was of his hair.

"I'm a policeman, Mr. Cannon," he replied. "It's not my job to believe or disbelieve. Only to find out."

5

The Embassy was very polite and sympathetic, and unhelpful. "I'm very sorry to hear you're in trouble, sir," said the cultured female voice, English to my surprise, for I had expected an American. "However, if you are not actually charged with anything, I'm afraid there's nothing we can do. If you should be charged by the police, we will be glad to suggest a solicitor for you."

I hung up, and wondered whether I ought to call Dr. Crouch. But if the Embassy couldn't help me, I didn't see what he could do. While I was still standing there uncertainly, the phone rang and I answered it. It was Lucy Nicholson.

"Mr. Cannon," she said, "I hope you won't think me a busybody, but I've heard some very disturbing news. It's about Charlie Neville. I'm told he's been killed."

"It looks that way," I said.

"Yes, but—well, I hear that there's some—well, that you've been mixed up in it by the police."

"In a way. They don't actually think I did it, but they don't actually think I didn't, either."

"Mr. Cannon," she said, stammering slightly, "I'm frightfully sorry, and I hope their suspicions aren't the result of your standing up to him for me on Saturday. We've been away—Daddy took us to visit some cousins in Somerset, Sunday morning, and we got back quite late. And I only heard today about the fight you had with Charlie and the others after Alan and I left you. And then, just a little while ago came this other news. I couldn't help wondering if they were connected."

"No, they're not," I said. "If I could have killed him, I'd have done it Saturday night. It's nice of you to be concerned about me, though. I appreciate it."

"*Are* the police holding you?" she asked.

"No, but they've asked me not to leave Heronwick."

"I think it's disgraceful," she said. "They've no right even to suspect you. I've talked it over with Father and he agrees with me. He says he'll put you in touch with his solicitor. And he wants to talk to you. And so do I. Could you come round to us for a drink this evening?"

"Well, sure," I said. "But don't feel that you have to—"

"Nothing of the sort. We want you to come. It's five o'clock now. In about an hour. Is that all right? And don't worry," she added, hurriedly. "We're—we're all on your side. Goodbye."

There was one more thing I felt I had to do. I went into the kitchen, where Mrs. Davies was peeling potatoes and Mr. Davies, since the bar didn't open again until six, was drinking tea in a corner.

"You've both been very friendly to me," I said. "I think I ought to tell you that the police don't want me to leave town, on account of the death of that Neville fellow."

"Yes, love, we know all about that," said Mrs. Davies, complacently.

I was somewhat taken aback.

"It is hard, Mr. Cannon, not to know what goes on under one's own roof," Mr. Davies said, unbending sufficiently to chuckle.

"Well," I said, awkwardly, "I want you to know that I—I had nothing to do with his death. I just found the body."

"We are certain of that, Mr. Cannon," said Mr. Davies. "Don't think twice about it. You are welcome here."

"What about a nice cup of tea?" Mrs. Davies said.

"You're very kind, both of you," I said. "And you always seem to be offering me something to eat or drink—"

"Bless you, of course!" cried Mrs. Davies. "It's always been a form of welcome, and we're great ones for tradition, we English."

"The Welsh also," said Mr. Davies, solemnly, "although we have had so little food in Wales because of the English oppressions that we have more often had to offer companionable sniffs at the aroma of yesterday's cooking."

"Get away with you, you wild druid," said his wife fondly. "Sit down, Mr. Cannon, and try one of my nice wholemeal scones."

By a quarter to six, it had stopped raining so I set out walking. The Nicholson's house was a little way out of the village, on the edge of a common, an open stretch of grazing land where by ancient right the villagers could pasture their horses or cattle. Heronwick Common was cropped short by the beasts so that it looked like the smooth pelt of some kind of green creature itself. Here and there grew clumps of tangled hawthorn, and at the edges a line of graceful elms reared up, like a feathery mane. A high wall of the grey local stone enclosed the Nicholson's many-gabled stone house. I crossed over a grid of metal bars laid down to prevent the intrusion of cattle, and followed the driveway to the front door.

Lucy answered my knock and shook hands so warmly that I felt it was worth being a suspected murderer. She led me into a cozy sitting room with small-paned windows that looked out towards the Common, and as she was pouring me a whisky her father came in.

I knew a little about Brigadier-General Nicholson from the Davies, and that little had fixed an imaginary image in my mind. I knew he was "County"—his people had been landowners in Gloucestershire for centuries and had once had something to do with the flourishing wool trade near Stroud. Like his father, he had been a professional soldier all his life, and then on his retirement, being in his mid-fifties and incapable of relaxation, had gone into partnership with a cousin who owned a factory in Gloucester that made electric heaters. I imagined him as small and peppery, with a fierce military moustache, red-faced and white-haired like someone in a Peter Arno cartoon. Perhaps, I thought hopefully, he would even have a monocle.

The man who greeted me, however, was tall and solid, with an air of controlled energy. He moved slowly, but with an impression of irresistibility like a tank going into action. His large, rather meaty face glistened with health and close shaving, and the narrow little eyes set level on either side of his long, thin, high-bridged nose were full of humor. Only when he spoke did I hear the gruff note of accustomed military command which broke through, from time to time, as if against his will. If anything, he reminded me of a more alert, more active, and more self-assured Mr. Davies, a Mr. Davies who had made good.

76

"Glad to see you, Mr. Cannon," he said. "My daughter's told me all about you. I see you have some whisky. Right! One thing you Americans have, whatever your faults, is a sensible notion of drinking. I've had some damn good American whisky. Bour-*bon*, is that it? Sorry I can't offer you any."

He motioned me to a chair and helped himself to a drink. "I must apologize for my rudeness in not coming to see you, to thank you for your courtesy to my daughter. I hear you had a bit of a scrap with young Neville, afterward."

"It was nothing," I said. "I was glad to do it."

He beamed shrewdly at me. "Wouldn't have done it if Lucy'd been an ugly old woman, I dare say. Well, now. You're in trouble with the police as a result, are you?"

"Not actually as a result of that, sir." I explained what had happened. "I don't know whether the cops seriously suspect me or not," I finished, "but obviously they're not going to cross me off their list until they've got whoever did it."

"Naturally," the General agreed. "Makes sense from a policeman's point of view. They can't let anything pass at this stage, no matter how damned silly it may seem."

"But it *is* silly!" Lucy put in, indignantly. "Why on earth should Mr. Cannon kill him? Aren't they always searching for motives?"

"He had as much reason as anyone in Heronwick," said her father, with a grim smile. "I'd have done it myself, if I hadn't been so busy the past three or four years."

"Oh, be serious, Daddy. Mr. Cannon's in real trouble. What is he to do?"

"Turn the matter over to my solicitor," said the General, promptly. "Leave everything in his hands and in mine, Mr. Cannon. Finish up your business here, and go whenever you like. They haven't arrested you, have they?"

"No," I said.

"Well, then. They can't keep you here. Think no more about it."

"I don't think it's that easy," I said, slowly. "You're going to think I'm nuts, but I don't see how I can run away from it like that."

General Nicholson swirled his drink thoughtfully. "Ah, yes," he said. "I see."

"I don't," Lucy said. "What do you mean, run away? You haven't done anything to run away from."

"It's hard to explain," I said. "I'm a foreigner, an American. People around here will be looking at me that way. If I duck out, they'll say, 'What did you expect? Special treatment for him.' They'll say that Americans don't consider themselves bound by anything. You see—hell, I don't know how to say it without sounding like a flag-waver, but I'm not here just as me, but as a representative of my country."

Lucy cocked her head. "You're a frightful romantic, you know," she said. "I thought you people were all hard-boiled and ruthless."

I grinned. "You've been seeing too many movies."

"And you're living back in the nineteenth century or somewhere," she retorted. "It may be honorable and all that sort of rubbish, but it isn't very practical."

"Well, let me put it this way, then," I said. "I'm kind of enjoying this town and the people in it. I'm in no hurry to leave. I was hoping to see more of you—and your father, of course."

"Thank you," chuckled the General. "Most complimentary to me." He put his glass down with a decisive thump. "Right! In that case, what can we do to help? Have you anything in mind besides passively keeping your head in the lion's mouth?"

"I haven't thought that far," I admitted. "Maybe I

78

could try to find out what Neville was doing this morning, whether anyone might have seen him or met him—" I broke off, and snapped my fingers.

"What is it?" asked the General.

"I just remembered something. A farmer named Brock, Will Brock. Do you know him?"

"Yes, of course. What about him?"

"I met him this morning on my way to Herne House. He was coming down from the woods and when I asked him what he'd been doing, he said, 'Fishing.' Then he pushed past me and left. I thought it was rather sudden—you see, we'd been in that cricket game together and he'd been friendly up to that point—but I put it down to the way farmers are."

General Nicholson raised his eyebrows. "You said, as I recall, that your appointment with Mrs. Herne was at eleven. This would be half an hour earlier perhaps?"

"That's right."

"Funny time for a man to go fishing, wouldn't you say? Unless he was a tourist, perhaps. It wasn't raining this morning, and by ten-thirty he should have been harvesting. It's been so wet, the farmers have to cut when they can."

"In any case," I said, "it never occurred to me until now, but you know, he didn't have a rod or a line with him. Not unless he had his line stuck away in a pocket."

"Aha!" cried the General. "He's your man. Depend on it. I've known Brock since he was a child. His grandfather once gave me a hiding for stealing apples: scrumping, we used to call it—picking up windfalls. A good man, but hot-headed as the devil. Lose his temper at something you said and knock you down as quick as look at you."

"His grandfather?" I asked, in some confusion.

"Not at all. He was a quiet sort of chap. Willie

Brock, of course. Hates all these spivs and yobs as much as I do. Had a better reason for killing Neville than you had, I dare say."

"But I didn't have any."

"There you are, then."

"Oh, Father!" Lucy put in. "You're talking just like the police, now. Jumping to conclusions just because Willie said he was fishing when he wasn't. He was probably poaching, or setting snares, and didn't want to be found out."

"Nonsense! You sound like a Victorian manual for the landowner," cried her father. "Poaching, indeed! What the devil would he find to poach on Elizabeth's land? Got plenty of land of his own, hasn't he?"

"I suppose so."

"Very well. Then what was he doing up there at that hour? Find that out and we'll be getting somewhere."

Lucy shook her head. Her bright hair almost flashed like metal in the darkening room. "That's all very well, but what's Mr. Cannon to do—march up to him and ask him?"

"Oh, no. I'll do that myself," said the General, with a belligerent air. "I'll get the truth out of the fellow."

"Don't do that, sir," I said, quickly. "If he was really up to something, he wouldn't tell you about it. And you'd just frighten him off—warn him."

"Something to that," the General agreed. "Well, what then?"

"Let me think about it. Maybe I'll figure something out." I stood up. "I'm very grateful to you—to both of you—for your help. I guess I'd better be getting along, or Mrs. Davies will be wondering where I am. She makes dinner specially for me, you know."

"I'll walk to the village with you," Lucy said. "I want some cigarettes."

She slid into a short green suede jacket, while I shook hands with her father.

"Don't hesitate to call on me if you need anything," he said. "Like you to come and lunch with me one day, if you can spare the time. Perhaps you'd like to look at our plant? We're very proud of it—small, but flourishing. Giving the big boys something to think about."

"I'd like that very much," I said.

"In any case, you'll be seeing my daughter from time to time, I imagine," he said, with a glint of the same wickedness she so often showed.

Out on the Common, the sun was dipping behind the filigree of trees and, above, a fan of purple-grey cloud edged with gold went up like the tail of a fantastic bird. Lucy and I stood in silence for a moment, looking. Then we began to walk towards the sunset.

I said, "It's hard to believe it was only this morning. It seems like a year."

"It's a good deal to happen to you in one day."

"I liked your father."

"He was really being very well behaved. I was afraid he was going to get off on one of his favorite subjects—the nature of the modern world, or the New Elizabethan businessman, or something like that."

"It wouldn't have mattered. I don't know the first thing about it. Uh—Lucy. You don't mind if I call you Lucy?"

"I don't mind."

"Is your mother . . . ?"

She laughed. "Not dead, not divorced. She's in Torquay, visiting Granny. She gets spells of intense filial devotion when she frets about Gran being all alone in Devon with no one but Mrs. Kynaston to look after her. They usually coincide with battles with Daddy over expenses, and off she goes for a week or two. There's really nothing wrong with Granny either, except that she has a sweet tooth for porcelain, and if she isn't watched she can spend her way through any amount of overdraft. Anyway, it means things are rather at sixes and sevens at home. Otherwise, I'd have asked you to stay to dinner."

"Maybe when this is over."

"You're worried, aren't you?" she asked.

I tried to grin. "Worried? Why should I be worried? I'll just cut my throat, that's all."

She put her hand out, shyly, and touched my arm. "Poor Dave," she said.

"Thanks," I said. And this time, it was no effort to smile.

I felt a little shy about sitting in either of the public bars that night, but I had nothing to do with myself so in the end I went into the lounge, which was empty. Not for long, however; I had barely tasted my beer when Inspector Codd came in.

"Mind if I join you?" he said.

I shook my head. He got a pint from Mr. Davies, and brought it to my table. "We're neighbors here, you know," he said.

"Neighbors?"

"I've taken that bedroom upstairs."

"So you can keep an eye on me?"

"Not quite as villainous as all that," he said, with a smile. "There's a good deal of investigation that can only be done on the spot."

"Is your buddy staying here, too? The one who played that game with me of bad guy against your good guy?"

"You guessed it was a game, did you?" He ran a hand over his head. "It's what we call 'wicked uncle.' Still, it works, you know. People do tend to blurt things out, between the two of us."

I liked him. It was quite clear that underneath that

guileless front there was a very hard guy, but there was also something very good about him. He was—well—*wholesome*. It may be a peculiar word to use about a detective, but men surround themselves with an atmosphere made up of subtle things: the intonation of the voice, the movement of the eyes, the chemical composition of their own personal planets. His air was fresh and breathable. It suddenly occurred to me that for some men being a policeman might be a calling that could draw them for the same reasons that make others priests or country doctors. It was a novel and interesting idea.

I said, "Okay, I'll blurt. Maybe I've found out something." I told him about my meeting with Will Brock.

When I had finished, he sat thinking for a while, and then said, "So you played cricket yesterday, eh? Did you enjoy it?"

I couldn't see that that had any relevance to what we were talking about, and said so.

"I know," he said patiently, "but did you? It was your first time, after all."

"Well, I won't say I had a ball, but it was fun."

"What kind of cricketer is this chap, Brock? Pretty good? Or couldn't you tell?"

"I gathered from what they said about him that he's generally one of their star players, but his game was off that day. Let's see, he made nine runs, I think. They were ribbing him about it."

He nodded. "Powerful sort of man, is he?"

"Oho," I said. "Crafty! I see what you're getting at. Strong enough to bash a guy's head in? Yes, he's pretty hefty. He's a farmer, and he looks as though he could lift a tractor by himself."

"I didn't say anything about bashing in heads, Mr. Cannon. I'm only trying to gather information."

"Okay. Sorry."

"Not at all. But you can see from your own situation how dangerous it would be for us to jump to conclusions."

"I understand."

He fiddled with his beer mug. "I appreciate your telling me about Brock. If you should remember anything else, or if you should happen to learn anything . . ." He glanced up at me. "There may be things that don't seem very important to you but which, put together with what I know, might have some bearing. But I can't emphasize this too much—please don't try to play private detective. I know it must be very tempting, since you can't help feeling yourself to lie under a certain cloud. Nevertheless, don't do it."

That put my back up, a little. I was saved from answering, however, by the door opening. The Vicar put his head in.

"Mr. Davies said you were in here," he began. "Um . . . I wanted to talk to you, Dave, but perhaps another time if you're busy."

"Come in, Vicar," I said. "This is Detective Inspector Codd. I guess you could say I haven't any secrets from him."

The Vicar hung there for a moment, undecided. Then he came into the room and closed the door firmly behind him.

"Yes, I will come in," he said. "Inspector, I don't know Mr. Cannon very well, but he was good enough to play cricket for Heronwick yesterday. I've heard that you suspect him of having something to do with the death of Charles Neville, and I wanted to tell him that he can rely on me for any assistance he, as a stranger from abroad, may feel he needs."

"Come and join us, Vicar," Codd said, in that gentle tone which I'd come to recognize as his professional voice. "I'm certain Mr. Cannon is grateful. But he is under no graver suspicion than—several other people.

He happened to find the body, which makes him rather important to us."

"He's right," I said. "I do thank you. But of course, until something definite turns up, anybody can be suspected."

The Vicar hesitated, and then sat down. "I see. I'm sorry, I'm afraid I rather got the wrong impression. My informant was very disturbed. She gave me to understand that there might be a charge against Mr. Cannon."

"She?" Codd asked.

"I called on Mrs. Herne to see if there was anything I could do for her. She was upset because she is hoping to sell a medieval manuscript to Mr. Cannon."

"Yes, I know," said Codd.

"What about that, by the way?" I put in. "Can I visit her? I'm still in business, you know."

"I'll give you a note which will pass you into the house," said the Inspector. "The Forensic Lab people are still at work there."

"Thanks."

"Vicar," Codd went on, "I imagine you know the village fairly well."

"Oh, yes. I was born here."

"I wonder if you can tell me something about Neville."

"What do you want to know?"

"Sorry, I put that the wrong way, didn't I? I'd like to hear what you thought of him. What sort of chap was he?"

"He wasn't exactly a model citizen. Been in trouble with the law once or twice, not too serious—although I suppose you could say that any trouble with the law is serious. I mean, nothing like robbery, or safe-cracking. Once, he was charged with assault. He attacked and beat up a man he claimed insulted him. A couple of times he was hailed before the beak for playing rather roughly with some local girls."

"Paternity cases?"

"Oh, no. Molestation, indecent assault, and so on. He had a cottage in the wood, on a bit of property that belonged to his family, and I understand he called it his chapel." He made a wry face. "Unpleasant things go on there, I'm told. *Used* to go on, I should say. I tried several times to talk to him, but it was no use. Poor Charlie. In spite of everything, I still can't think why anyone should want to kill him. Couldn't it possibly have been an accident?"

"Not much chance of that. Might there have been a parent of some girl in the background? Someone who had a really bitter grudge against him?"

"I can't say. I imagine I'd have heard of it somehow, if there had been. I get to hear most of the rumors and gossip, eventually."

"What about that man he beat up?"

"Oh, no. I shouldn't think so. He's the village chemist, a very quiet man. But in any case, this was long ago, four or five years ago, and Charlie was summonsed and fined."

"No one else?" Codd persisted.

"Not that I know of. With Charlie, it was a matter of most people disliking him for what he represented, rather than hating him for anything he actually did. Do you understand?"

"I think so. A great many people find his type offensive."

"Yes, but it went beyond that. He was one of *us*, here in Heronwick. The Nevilles have been here for ages. His grandfather is still remembered for his benefactions: he helped found a school for blind children. And his great grandfather was a very well-known landowner, and greatly loved; he had a reputation for honesty that was county-wide, I should say. He was by all accounts a generous, kindly, sweet-tempered gentleman who loved nature, and preached conservation and land-management, and opposed blood sports. Sometime in the eighteen-eighties he even attracted considerable national attention for a spirited attack on fox hunting. You see, his close friend, Sir Francis Herne, had been permanently crippled by a hunting accident. He wrote poetry, too, I'm told, although I've never read any of it."

"And then came Charlie."

"That's right. Charlie's father was well liked but he was careless with money. He 'married beneath him,' as they like to say. She was the daughter of a Gloucester publican, a rather frail, silly woman. I remember her as wearing far too much makeup. Ridiculous thing to remember. But her pinched, pale, small face couldn't take it. Well, Harold Neville was killed in the North African campaign, and I don't think he left very much of an estate for his wife. Young Charlie would have been about four, then. He grew up rather wild, as so many kids did after the war, with no fathers to keep them in check. In his case, his mother didn't help much either. I understand she was rather loose in her ways—casual men, drinking, and so on. Of course, I wasn't here, then. At the end of the war I was seventeen, and I had determined to become a priest. I didn't come back to Heronwick until eight years ago, when Mrs. Herne offered me the living. By that time, Mrs. Neville was dead—cancer, I think it was—and Charlie was spending the little he had as rapidly as he could. Didn't take him long. The house in the village went, and he moved into the cottage I told you about— his great grandfather had written poetry there, but Charlie put it to other uses.

"People felt sorry for him and gave him work, but it always ended in a quarrel, or worse. That was the case with the chemist. I suppose he'd have drifted away to Gloucester or some other town, but Mrs. Herne took him on as gardener and odd-job man and so he remained here. She's like that, you know. She still feels she's the lady of the manor, and that she has a certain responsibility toward her dependents. All of us, you know. That's why I got the living rather than an outsider."

I said, "It was hard to believe, looking at Neville, or listening to him, that he came from a good family. He looked and sounded like a bum."

"Yes, you see what I meant, don't you? Those of us who love Heronwick had him thrown in our faces, as it were. Not simply the question of change—no, because most of us realize that the war put an end to Merry England. We're living in a new age. It has its good, exciting aspects, you know. But Charlie wasn't one of them. He assumed a manner, a way of dress, even a speech that wasn't his, as if he were rebelling against decency and everyday morality. But it was a senseless rebellion, one ending in anarchy."

He sighed. "I think I can understand it. There were young people in the village who thought of Charlie as their leader, as a dashing sort of outlaw—Robin Hood, you might say. He reflected their discontent, or, perhaps more disturbingly, their hostility towards the unsettled, chaotic world they've got to live with. And a good many of them can't come to grips with it, can they? Well, it's hard enough for any of us."

He fell silent. After a bit, he said, "I'm sorry, that's all I can tell you. Not very helpful, is it?"

"On the contrary," said Codd. "I'm most grateful."

The Vicar stood up. "I must get along. Goodbye, Inspector. I'm sorry we've had to meet under these circumstances."

He shook hands with me. "Remember, Dave, if you need me—Don't feel you're a stranger and alone here."

"Nice guy," I said to Codd, after he had gone. "You know, I've been made to feel very welcome, to feel that I've made some good friends even in the few days I've been here. And I always thought you English were supposed to be so cold and stiff and distant."

Codd grinned. "Some of us are very nearly human," he said.

On my way up to bed, Mrs. Davies stopped me. "Oh, Mr. Cannon," she said, "I'm dreadfully sorry—I've had so much to do that it went clean out of my head—Mrs. Herne telephoned."

"When was this?"

"About half-past six. But as I say, I was in the middle of preparing dinner—"

"It doesn't matter. Did she leave a message?"

"Yes, I've written it all down here. 'Mrs. Herne says to tell you that she hopes you will be able to visit her tomorrow morning at ten, to discuss your business in spite of today's unpleasantness.'"

I had to laugh. "Today's unpleasantness!" I said. "What a dame!"

6

I took the footpath up the back way to Herne House, chiefly out of a nagging feeling that since I had met Brock coming that way I might find some sort of clue to what he has been doing. A light ground mist hung about the village, and by the time I got to the top of the slope and came to the edge of the wood I began to think this route had been a mistake. The mist had thickened as I climbed and in the wood it blanketed everything so that I could barely find my way.

I passed through the stile in the wall and once I was among the trees I moved in a world of peculier silence. I went slowly, to be certain of the path, and the quiet was reinforced by the faint dripping of water from the branches. The boles of the trees were like the pale brush-strokes of a Japanese painting, and their upper branches were invisible. The chill struck into me, and the dank smell of the wood was like a cellar.

I stopped, for I could hear the gurgle and rush of the stream. As I stood there, I heard another noise, a soft rustle of damp leaves and ferns. A small animal moving about, I thought. I stepped off the path to try and get a glimpse of it. Then there came a small but startling crack of a twig breaking. That, I told myself, could only have been caused by a weight pressing on it, the weight of a man's foot. The certainty that I wasn't alone in the wood brought with it a sudden leap of fright.

I had no reason to be afraid. Why shouldn't there be someone else walking in the wood, in the mist? Anyone from the village could be there. Or it might even be Codd, who had had his breakfast and left the inn before I came down, and might have come here for the same reason that had brought me. Yet the unreasonable fear persisted. For what I admitted to myself at last was that it might be Brock. Suppose he *had* killed Neville? And suppose he had come back to cover his traces, or to find something he had dropped? If he had killed one man, he wouldn't hesitate to kill another who might be spying on him. I knew that much from mystery stories.

Like most men, I had never thought of myself as either particularly cowardly or particularly brave. I had been in a couple of fist fights and once, in college, in a barroom brawl, but I had put in my Coast Guard service without ever hearing a shot fired except in training, and I had never been in actual danger of my life. Now, at the thought that I might come face to face with a murderer, my muscles turned to jelly. All I wanted to do was run.

Then that impulse passed, or dropped into the back of my mind, over-ridden by curiosity and the thrill of anger. Was it Brock? And if so, what was he up to? And could I catch him at something that would prove his guilt and get me out of trouble?

I stepped behind the trunk of a tree, and listened. I stopped breathing. My throat dried up, and I found that I was holding my mouth open as if that would help me to hear better. The sound had stopped. Suddenly, I heard a clatter as if stones were knocking together. Now I could get the direction: off to my left. I slid over to the next tree trunk, trying to feel the ground under my soles as you do when you're stalking deer, setting my feet down carefully and moving with a slow, light, easy rhythm.

I heard a swishing in the ferns again. It seemed a bit closer. I took a few more steps, peering into the pallid vapor until the skin around my eyes ached with the effort. There was a hint of movement among the trees, no more than a shadow wavering. The next instant, my heart leaped into my throat and hammered there, for I could see a shape silhouetted against the ground.

It was a crouching man. He appeared to be dabbling in the stream, and I could hear the click and splash of stones and water. After a moment, he stood up and walked further off, distorted by the mist so that I couldn't tell whether he was short or tall, nor could I make out his face. I stepped forward, for it looked to me as though I were about to lose him. He stopped at that instant, and I saw him stand as if listening; then he had darted off between the trees and was gone. I heard him running, and, as abruptly as if he had fallen into a hole, there was silence.

It was hopeless to try to catch him in the mist. But at any rate, I felt a lot better for it was obvious that even if it were Brock he was more afraid of me than I was of him. I went down to the stream. It occurred to me that whoever it was might have been setting out a line of traps for muskrats, but I didn't know whether they had muskrats in England or whether anybody trapped for them if they *did* have. There wasn't a sign of a trap, however, or of anything unusual. The water was clear and brown, frothing into bubbles here and there were it rippled around stones or cut into the shore. Over it, the mist rose in curls as if it were boiling hot. I remembered that a plank bridge spanned it, and decided that the easiest way to get back to the path was to follow the water to the bridge.

I kept looking into the stream, as I walked, thinking about fish and *The Wind in the Willows* and how streams had the same fascination for everybody no matter what country they flowed through. I came to a spot where the water went swirling over a lip of stone in a miniature waterfall. Under the creamy foam I saw a light-colored shape, long and thin, some sort of fish. It lay motionless; its apparent movement came from that of the water. I bent over to see it better. It wasn't a fish at all, but a shaped piece of wood. I took off my jacket, rolled up my shirt sleeve, and was just able to reach it and pull it out. It was a hammer.

I dried my arm off with my handkerchief, and inspected my find. It was an ordinary claw-hammer, a little chunkier in the head than ours, so that it felt unbalanced. Near the end of the handle, painted on with one of those felt-tipped ink markers I suppose, and somewhat smudged and worn away by use, was the word PROFFER.

Good! I thought. If I haven't got anything else, I've got a hammer. And who's Proffer? The man I saw prowling, who might have been looking for this in the stream? He might have come through the woods, keeping off the path so he wouldn't be seen, and dropped the hammer in the water and now he's come back to find it. He had been working the other side of the stream, so he had missed it, and I'd shown up and kept him from trying this side. A shiver went up my back, for this was the likeliest kind of blunt instrument for head cracking, and automatically I examined it for bloodstains. But of course, if there had been any the water would have washed them away.

For that matter, I told myself, Proffer didn't have to be a who. It could be a what. It could be the name of a shop, or a firm, or even a farm. Spelled backwards, it was Refforp. And for all I knew, I could be inventing a marvelous fantasy out of nothing because the hammer might have been lying in the stream for a year, and the man I saw might have been a poacher after all, in spite of everybody's insistence that there was nothing to poach in Herne Park.

Just the same, I didn't want to go walking up to the house flourishing this thing. I went on until I reached the bridge, and the path, and close by I found an oak with a gaping hole at the base among the twisted roots. I shoved the hammer inside and with my pocket knife made a little blaze about the size of a half dollar, facing the path.

I neither saw nor heard anything more the rest of the way up to the house. A uniformed cop was at the door. I showed him the note from Codd, and he led me around to the rear of the house and knocked at the back door. When Sarah appeared, he touched his helmet.

"This gentleman can come in," he said.

"I don't need you to tell me that," she retorted, and stood aside so that I could enter.

She took me through the kitchen and into the passage, and turned aside to a flight of steps.

"They have the hall shut up," she grumbled. "Doors locked, no one's to go into it until they've finished with their scraping and stirring and messing about."

The stairs ended in a dark corridor, in the sooty plaster of which were embedded the heavy beams of the old house. She led me to the right and we emerged on the railed landing which ran around three sides of this upper story, with doors opening to the library and, I presumed, to bedrooms. Below was the hall, and there was a man on his knees examining the bannister of the staircase with a magnifying glass like a real detective, while another one who kept yawning stood in a corner fiddling with a Rolleiflex camera. Neither of them so much as glanced up. Sarah rapped at the library door, opened it, and announced, "That American gentleman, madam."

Mrs. Herne was wearing a dove-grey dress which made her look softer, if a little older. It emphasized the grey in her hair and the smudges of fatigue under her eyes. She looked tired, and I realized that she must have had quite a time of it what with a murder in her house, detectives tracking everywhere, and probably a session with Codd and the Superintendent like the one I'd gone through. It would have been hard on a much younger woman, and she, I judged, must be close to seventy.

"I'm sorry you've had all this trouble," I said. "I hope it hasn't been too difficult."

"Not at all," she replied. Her voice hadn't lost any of its snap, anyhow. "I am quite well. From what I hear, it is you who have been having a difficult time of it."

"Yes, they did sort of put me through it," I admitted. "But I suppose it's only to be expected."

"From the police? Certainly. I expect them to make as much of a disturbance as they can with a maximum of rudeness and a minimum of efficiency. So far, they have succeeded in turning my house upside-down without finding anything of the slightest importance."

"Well, I guess it isn't easy to track down a murderer."

She raised her eyebrows. "I'm sure I have no experience in the matter," she crackled. "However, I dare say my father would have tolerated none of this nonsense. But then, things were different in his day, England was different. Policemen knew their place. They weren't infected with Socialist ideas."

I blinked at her. "What do you think your father would have done in a case like this, Mrs. Herne?"

"He would have seen at once what was perfectly obvious to anyone but a jack-in-office like that Detective Superintendent, that young Neville was drunk and fell downstairs and quite properly broke his neck."

Oho, I thought, so you did get the "wicked uncle" treatment and it hurt. Aloud, I said, "But he didn't break his neck, Mrs. Herne. Somebody hit him on the head. And they don't think he was drunk. Maybe they didn't tell you what they told me, that they think somebody poured whisky over him after he was dead."

She didn't actually shrug, because she wasn't the type, but there was a shrug in the air about her. "I am aware that it is fashionable nowadays to conceal one's ignorance in a cloud of technical jargon," she said.

"Uh-huh," I said noncommittally. "But surely somebody could have sneaked in and cracked him one and then left in a hurry? I gather Neville wouldn't have won the contest for Most Popular Kid in Heronwick. There must have been lots of people who didn't like him."

With the merest hint of a smile, she replied, "Mr. Cannon, I didn't *like* him myself. He was a thoroughly disgusting, idle, dirty young brute. I don't expect you to understand—you Americans seem to take pleasure in an excessive tolerance in such matters—but he was like a slug in a garden, leaving a trail of slime on everything he touched. There was a time when England was the greatest nation in the world, and when such old-fashioned notions as honor, fidelity to one's word, a sense of responsibility towards the less fortunate, and a stern respect for order all carried weight.

Now, those virtues are out of date. Lesser races, whom we helped slowly to civilization, have been granted what your countrymen like to think of as the benefits of democracy and have plunged the world into chaos. Is it any wonder that creatures like Neville are not only allowed to shamble about freely, but are fawned over, grow wealthy from jigging about on television, and are even decorated with Orders which were once reserved for benefactors to the nation?"

Her face had become hard, and her voice icy, and even the grey dress took on a tint of steel. "I should think there are still a few of us left who would enjoy seeing, as you put it, someone *crack* the Nevilles one."

I had nothing to say in the face of that majestic wrath. She left me and went to unlock the cabinet. She got out the leather case and laid it on the desk. As she was taking the manuscript out of it, I thought of something.

"Why did you have him working for you if you felt that strongly about him?" I asked.

"What I thought of him had nothing to do with the fact that his family have lived in Heronwick very nearly as long as mine. His great grandfather and my uncle were friends, and after my uncle's death my father continued that friendship. I was brought up, Mr. Cannon, to feel that loyalty is important. However, that is only part of the story. People buy and sell the land now, but my ancestor, Nicholas Herne, held this manor for King James. It was given in exchange for honorable services, and it carried with it a responsibility. We Hernes have been trustees, not owners, and we have given far more to the village than we ever received from it. I am not ashamed to say that although the politicians who have ruled England in the last twenty years have seen to it that I am poorer than most of the farmers who were once my tenants, I feel that I must continue that tradition."

She was no longer angry, but looked thoughtfully at me, even somewhat sadly.

"I think I understand," I said.

"Do you? Well, shall we get down to business?" She tapped the cover of the manuscript. "I've had a talk with my solicitor, not only about the unfortunate occurrence yesterday, but this as well. His opinion is that if I cannot get a reasonable offer from you at once, it would be best for me to send the manuscript to Saxby's for auction."

I said, "Well, you'll do whatever seems best for you, of course. But maybe you haven't realized that if Saxby's sells it for you they'll take a fifteen per cent commission. A manuscript poem of about the same period as yours sold at auction in London last year for a thousand pounds. On that thousand, the owner collected £850."

I could see by her face that she hadn't considered the point. I pressed on. "If you send this manuscript to be auctioned, it may bring in more than I offer you. I may even be the one to buy it in the end. But after they've deducted their percentage you probably won't wind up with any more than I'd have given you in the first place.

"I don't know what your lawyer means by a 'reasonable offer.' You've got to give me credit for knowing the market: I'm fully aware of the current prices being paid. Just remember that your manuscript hasn't any illuminations, none of those handsome gilded initial letters, no drawings in the text. I've got to balance that against its age and its possible—er—historical value.

"You'd like to have things settled. Okay. I've cabled my partner and I'm waiting to hear from him. That should show you I'm serious. I imagine he's been out of town, or I'd have had his answer by now. Give me

98

a chance to examine it again. And if I'm satisfied, just be patient for another day or two.

"In any case," I added, "I can't leave the village until the police let me off the hook. And if you send it to Saxby's, things won't go any faster; they'll just hold it until they have other manuscripts or books to auction. It may be months."

"Very well," she said. "I agree."

She cleared her throat, and a curious expression came over her face. If I hadn't known better, I'd have called it shy. "I hope you won't mind my asking a favor," she said, reluctantly. "Would you object if I were to sit here while you're studying it?"

I opened my mouth, but she went on, quickly. "I know you prefer to be alone. I shall sit in the far window seat. But the police have taken over a good part of my house and I don't like to ask them for anything."

I spent a very pleasant hour with Raimond de Poitiers, not even conscious that she was in the room with me. By the end of that time I knew that I wanted this manuscript no matter what it cost. I knew, too, with a premonitory sinking of the heart, that if I got it it was going to be awfully hard for me to part with it, even though I couldn't afford to keep it. I was in business to make a profit, after all. Raimond's manuscript would, I felt sure, cause quite a stir in the scholarly world: some of its comments on Richard Lion-Heart and his relations with the king of France and the marquis of Montferrat were illuminating, and quite different from the other two extant versions. But what got to me more than anything else was the sense of a direct contact with the distant past: a man had sat over these pages, chewing his pen and getting it all down in just the right words so that I, more than seven centuries afterward, could touch what he had touched and read what he had written.

By the time I left Herne House the fog had lifted and there was a pale yellow light that hinted the sun might come out. I took the woods path back to the Goat, and stopped on the way to pick up the hammer. I stuck it in my belt and buttoned my jacket over it, and felt like a desperado carrying a concealed weapon. I wanted to slink. I hid it under my shirts, in the bureau, and went down to have lunch.

I strolled out to the bridge next to the Goat, afterward, and leaned on the stone parapet to look at the water. I felt heavy and depressed; what the hell was I doing here, and how was I going to get out of it? It might have been my lunch—the suety steak-and-kidney pudding and watery brussels sprouts—that was responsible. On the other hand, I'm told that people who live abroad get waves of this feeling, compounded out of foreignness, distance from home, and a sense of detachment from reality, the reality of one's own accustomed place and people. It was worse for me, with the murder hanging over my head. The fact that I had nothing to do with it, that I wasn't directly accused of it, didn't diminish my sense of involvement, even in some obscure way, of guilt. If only I had never met Neville, had never battled with him, hadn't disliked him so much. In that case, I might possibly have felt no sense of complicity at all.

The more I thought about it, the more I was inclined to agree with Mrs. Herne. The Yob had been a blight on Heronwick. You could understand people wanting to hit out at him. I couldn't say I knew England very well, but even I could see that to a lot of Englishmen the Yob and his type were like mildew, blemishing and defacing what they lived on. And like mildew, it was a passive thing—they didn't *do*, they just *were*. They stood on the sidelines and jeered at everything, new or old, good or bad, on principle you might say, except that they didn't seem to have many principles. Even in death, he had been grinning.

Thinking about Mrs. Herne, I was jolted by an unexpected idea. Suppose she herself had killed him?

That shook me. But was it such a wild idea? Whether anyone else had come into the house was questionable, but she had certainly been there. And alone, because Sarah had been at the pub. Sure, she was an old lady but she was a tough old bird with plenty of spirit. If she had a reason to kill someone, I didn't doubt she'd do it and go to dinner with a good appetite afterward.

Something else occurred to me, something that made the hair on the back of my neck ripple. Thinking over that first interview we had all had with Inspector Codd, I remembered her saying that she had heard the front door close and had then come out of the library to see who was there. But I hadn't closed the front door behind me. I could visualize everything that had happened quite clearly. I had poked my head in, had seen the figure lying at the foot of the stairs, and, full of the thought that it might be Mrs. Herne herself, had run in without a pause, without even thinking about the door.

By God, I said to myself, how about that? She was lying.

And in a flash, I saw it all, the whole scene, tiny but clear before my eyes: Neville is in the library—maybe, as he hinted to me, he's stealing one of the books; she comes in and surprises him; he runs out to the landing; she grabs up—what? some sort of weapon: I'd have to look around the next time I was in the library and see what would serve—and she hits him a powerful bash on the head. . . .

At this point, my imagery wavered. I couldn't see Neville just holding still while she hit him. He might have run, in which case he could surely have outdis-

101

tanced her, or he might have fought back, in which case it was hard to believe she could have overpowered him. If he had been shot, or stabbed, it would have been easier.

Nevertheless, it did seem clear to me that she had lied about hearing the front door. I thought about that old woman, and I could believe that she had been sitting in the library knowing perfectly well that a dead man was lying out in the hall, and she would have gone ahead with writing letters or whatever she had been doing without a quiver. She might have been shielding someone. I remembered the back stair I had climbed that morning, and I remembered, also, how Mrs. Herne had shepherded me into the sitting room to wait for the police. What if she knew who the killer was—had even employed him? After he'd done the job he might have gone upstairs to tell her it was done, and when I came in he might easily have hidden in the upstairs corridor until I was in the sitting room. Then he could have slipped down the back stairs and got away.

I rubbed my forehead. It was all so fantastic: to be thinking about a real murder, and to be considering which of the people I'd met might have killed a man—if simply being in this foreign land was strange, then this was fifty times as dream-like. I had a sensation of light-headedness, as if I had gulped down a drink on an empty stomach.

In any case, it *was* real, no mistake about that. And I had something to tell Codd: maybe, as a detective, he could figure out the reason Mrs. Herne might have lied about hearing the door. The problem was to find him. Mr. Davies said he hadn't seen him since early morning, but he suggested that I try the local constable. So I walked up through the village.

The mellow stone houses leaned this way and that, and the High Street wound between them up to the market square. Here, there was an ancient stone cross, and behind it the Market Hall, which dominated the center of the village. It was a half-timbered building with a roof, like that of most of the old houses, covered with flat stones pegged into place and green with moss. The ground story was open, upheld by thick pillars and flagged with stone: this was where, on Fridays, the market stalls were erected. The upper floor, one big room reached by an outside stair, was used for plays, dances and auctions. A cupola on the top had a clock which was always ten minutes fast, and an iron weathervane in which was cut the date: 1620. A poster on the side of the hall announced in home-made lettering: RAVE WITH MEL CLUFF AND THE MANIACS FRIDAY NITE SEPTEMBER 17 HERONWICK MARKET HALL.

Well, why not? I thought. When the hall was built, local Puritans had undoubtedly frowned grimly on the frolics of young people after a market day. Upstairs, a century or two later, there had been routs and balls. The place had been a social center for so many years that it was natural for it to embrace, cheerfully, the courting couples, and if the waltz and the fox-trot, why not the jerk, the frug, or the gloop?

From the market square, three or four streets radiated: Church Lane which led, appropriately, to the church, Friday Street which squeezed between a chemist's shop and an ironmonger, and Knottswood Road which ran out past the Falcon and eventually reached the neighboring village whose cricketers had given us such a hard fight. A little way along this road, a lane led down to a branch of the stream where there was a house called Kingsmill, and at the head of the lane stood a cottage in a garden. Its small windows were almost hidden by a yellow-flowering vine, and above its low, red door was a neat but slightly incongruous blue and white sign: POLICE.

The young policeman opened the door, buttoning his jacket. "Good afternoon, Mr. Cannon. Something I can do for you, sir?" he said. I had expected him to be cool or reserved, but he seemed as cordial as ever.

"I'm looking for Inspector Codd," I said.

"The Dectective Inspector isn't in now, sir. He was talking to people here all this morning, but he went out at lunch time and I haven't seen him since. Would you like to come in and wait for him?"

"No. I'll probably see him this evening at the Goat. Just tell him I was looking for him, will you?"

"Yes, sir."

I started to go, and turned back. "You told me you were interested in weapons."

"That's right," he said, with a smile. "Would you like to look at some of my bits and pieces?"

I didn't want to hurt his feelings, so I said yes and he ushered me in. Through an open door on the right I could see his office: a table, a couple of straight chairs, a filing cabinet, and a poster which, over a picture of some unidentifiable pieces of explosives, exclaimed hysterically, DON'T TOUCH ANYTHING! He led me into the room opposite, which was crowded with overstuffed furniture. A television set with a flowering plant on top of it filled one corner. Tucked away behind the fat couch was a table with a lace cloth over it, and next to or behind the fat chairs were other little tables. There were coronation mugs, souvenir plates and ashtrays and cups from Brighton and Bournemouth and Wookey Hole. When I lifted my eyes from this cozy domesticity, I felt like a schizophrenic: the walls were covered with weapons, some on brackets and some in tidy clusters.

The contrast didn't bother him. He began pulling them down, displaying the blades and talking enthusiastically about watering, types, and regional characteristics, spouting peculiar names and words—"wakizashi," "katar," "kukri"—and, as he grew more enthusiastic, become more incomprehensible. When at last he ran down, I got to what I'd wanted to ask him in the first place.

"This is very interesting," I said. "But tell me, is there any sort of weapon a person could use from a distance which could, say, break an enemy's skull without the user getting too close?"

He looked puzzled. "A club with a long handle, you mean?"

"No, that wouldn't do because the guy who was being attacked could grab hold of it. I mean, say, a sling which could throw a heavy stone. Only that isn't quite it, either, because you have to be a skilled slinger."

"I see. Something that would take no special practice, but would keep you out of reach. What about a morning star?"

"What's that?"

"Why, it was a type of weapon used by the knights in the Middle Ages, a staff with a chain attached to the end of it, and on the end of the chain an iron ball. Because of the chain, it wouldn't be so easy to catch hold of, you see."

I hesitated. "Could be. I wonder if . . . well, you know in the entrance hall at Herne House there are trophies of arms hanging on the walls. I wonder if there's a morning star among them?"

He shot me a sharp look. "I wouldn't know, sir. Why do you ask?"

"Just an idea I had."

"To do with young Neville's death, is that it?"

I nodded.

"Well, sir," he said, carefully, "I don't think as it's a good idea to discuss this any further. But I could just mention it, say, to the Detective Inspector when I see him."

"Yes, you do that," I said. "And meanwhile you might be thinking about other weapons of that sort."

He gave me a rather wary smile.

7

I was crossing the market square on my way back, when Vicar Spendwell came marching with long strides up the High Street towards me. I hailed him.

"Looking for me?" he asked.

"Yes and no. I wasn't looking for you specially, but now that you're here there's something I want to ask you."

"Something public?" he said, lowering his voice. "Or shall we . . . ?"

"No, it's okay. I'd like to get hold of a history of Heronwick, the records of the town or something like that. I'm curious about the background and the family that produced Mrs. Herne."

"Not impossible. A history of Heronwick was written by one of my predecessors, David Ratliff. I've got a copy. I don't know how much good it will do you, but it's all there is, with the exception of the parish records—dates of birth, baptism, death, and so on. Look here, I'm just going home to have a cup of tea.

What about coming along with me and I'll give you some tea and the book?"

"Sounds tasty."

He lived in a large, ugly house across the road from the church, a place that had been built in the days when country parsons had enormous, active families. Spendwell confessed to me that he rattled around in it a bit, and sometimes found himself yearning for a few ghosts, just so that it wouldn't be quite so empty. "Or perhaps I'll get married one of these days," he added. "If I can ever find the time, between committee meetings, the Young Communicants, the Mothers' Union, and half a dozen other things. One advantage of this house is that they can all meet simultaneously here, in various rooms, without ever actually meeting each other."

He made some tea and brought out a box of sugary biscuits. "I hope you don't mind," he said, cutting slices of bread, "but there's no cake. I rely on Mrs. Fish to do the shopping, and she's not wildly efficient."

"Mrs. Fish?"

"My housekeeper. I really ought to get married, I suppose. Have some bread and butter. One gets the impression that a century ago, when this house was built, an unmarried Vicar was slightly suspect—Roman practices, maybe, or a warped mentality. In my case . . ."

He grimaced. "Well, I won't bore you with my problems. You have quite enough of your own."

"What is it?" I asked. "Can't you find the right girl?"

His smile was lopsided. "Oh, I've found her, all right."

I had a sudden rush of clairvoyance to the head. "Lucy Nicholson!" I blurted.

He blushed, like a kid. "You Americans are extraordinary."

I felt myself getting hot in my turn. "I'm sorry. It was really none of my business," I said.

"No, no," he said. "I didn't mean to be rude. You took me by surprise. Does it stick out that much?"

"I didn't have any idea of it. Her name just came into my head. I guess because she's so—" And I stopped.

We sat looking at each other for a minute. I suppose he was wondering what I meant. I was, too.

"Well, now you know," he said, at last. And with an effort, he added, "Now about that book."

I was feeling confused, and when he handed it over I couldn't at first give my attention to it. I wanted to ask him what there was between him and Lucy. Wouldn't she have him? Was he afraid to ask her? Damn the English, I thought, with their reticence. It was having the same effect on me; I usually said whatever came into my head, but now I was feeling my own strangeness. I kept my mouth shut, and instead opened *A Brief Account of the History and Antiquities of Heronwick, in Gloucestershire*, by the Rev. David O. Ratliff, M.A. The first thing I saw, opposite the title page, was the dedication: "To Elizabeth Margaret Herne, for her fifth birthday."

I glanced at the date of publication. 1903. So I'd been right, she was crowding seventy.

"Take it with you and read it at your leisure," Spendwell said. "Then if you have any questions, perhaps I can help you."

We finished our tea in silence. An odd kind of constraint had fallen on us.

I said, "Any more cricket these days?"

"No. No, that was the last match of the season. It's darts, now."

"Darts? Are you on the team?"

"I haven't the time. Anything new from the police?"

"Not really. I thought I'd try to find out a little about the background of these people. Maybe I can spot something that the cops can't find, something that would help clear it all up."

"Not much chance of that, is there?"

"Maybe not, but I can't just sit around waiting, with this thing hanging over me."

He nodded. "I'd feel the same way." With his eyes on mine, he added, "We seem to feel alike about a number of things."

"That's right." I grinned. "I haven't got time for darts, either."

He saw me to the door and shook hands, repeating that I shouldn't hesitate to call on him if I needed anything. All the way back to the Goat I kept thinking what a nice guy he was, and what a lovely girl Lucy was, and how much of a bastard I was because I was jealous of him, and what I really wanted to do was cut him out with her. And then I had to laugh, because it didn't look as though he was going to get her and, as for me, she didn't even know I was in the running.

Young Ted Davies met me at the door. "There's a telegram come for you," he said. "Mum's got it. Has it come all the way from America?"

"I imagine so. It's what I'm expecting," I said.

He dropped his voice. "You know that detective what we got stopping here? Are you and him friends?"

"Yes, in a way," I replied, uncomfortably.

"Have you ever seen any crooks or gangsters?" he said. "Real ones? Close up, like?"

I didn't want to demolish the kid's illusions, so I said, "Yeah, a few. Mostly behind bars, though."

"Cor! Honest? This paper I read, it tells all about crooks."

110

He fished a comic book called *Whizzo!* out of his pocket and unfolded it. Turning past the first few pages of cartoons, he read out, 'Master Criminals and Their Methods, by a Detective Chief Superintendent.'"

"Sounds great," I said.

"It's smashing." He held out the paper. "If you want to borrow it, you can. It might give you some ideas."

"Ideas about what?" I said, not catching on.

He frowned at my dullness. "*You* know. Finding out the one what knocked off Charlie Neville."

"Oh. Oh, yes. Well, thanks a lot, Ted," I said, taking the magazine. "It should be very useful."

He nodded. "If you need any help, like spying or finding out things," he said, confidentially, "why, I don't mind."

"Thank you," I repeated. After all, even Sherlock Holmes had not scorned the Baker Street Irregulars.

I found Mrs. Davies and took the cablegram up to my room. It said, "SORRY DELAYED BOSTON USE JUDGMENT MANUSCRIPT EIGHT THOUSAND LEVEL TRY FAMOUS CANNON CAJOLERY BOB."

That was a weight off my mind. If Bob, cautious as he was, said we could go up to eight thousand dollars, it meant he must have been delayed in Boston to good purpose and that we were solvent enough for me to venture a thousand or so above that amount. It gave me plenty of leeway around the figure I had thought of as my top. It was just as well, because if I couldn't strike a bargain with Mrs. Herne, and the manuscript went to the sale room, I'd have to be prepared to lose it; there would be plenty of others at the auction who would know what a contemporary account of Richard Lion-Heart's crusade was worth.

I put the cable away, and took up *A Brief Account.* I already knew something about the author: he was the kind of man who would dedicate a scholarly work to a five-year-old girl. He was also the sort who would call a two-hundred-page book a "brief account." I expected to find him prim and pedantic, and also perhaps just a tiny bit servile towards the Herne family. I was right; he never referred to any of them without scattering a handful of rosy adjectives.

I learned that Heronwick had been, originally, Heregythwyc, or the town of a woman named Heregyth, but that this had appeared in Domesday Book as Heriedewic. By the time of King Stephen it had become Heringewic, and during the next century, after vacillating between Herringwick and Heronwick, had turned into the latter, no doubt to everybody's relief. I skimmed over the pages dealing with the number of hides and knights' fees and the changes of feudal owners until I came to the first Herne, Nicholas.

"This industrious and sagacious gentleman, of the ancient and well-known family originating from, it is said, the Danish warrior-poet Heire who settled in Northampton during the reign of Ethelred, succeeded in establishing the not-inconsiderable fortunes of his house during the Netherlands campaigns of Queen Elizabeth," I read. The old boy had bought into a firm of Sussex cannon-founders, and had secured government contracts which made him respectably wealthy. "Forsaking Mars for the Muse, he penned an ingenious booklet which, under the title *The Indian Weed Expos'd,* contained in verses of an exceptional lucidity a polemic against the evils of 'drinking tobacco.' This work, appearing two years after the *Counterblast to Tobacco,* was dedicated to the anonymous author of the latter work in terms of no uncertain admiration. As it happened that the *Counterblast* had been written by the sovereign, James I, himself, Nicholas Herne's booklet drew the king's attention. When, in 1611, money was needed for the Irish wars, Herne was one of the first to respond with donations which won for him a baronetcy. The royal patronage, so graciously extended, became friendship. . . . Being desirous of rewarding Herne's many services and long personal attention, the king cast about for a suitable manor, and hit upon Heronwick with the felicitous words, 'As I have a faithful Herne (heron) it is but just he should have a heronry in which to bide.' "

No mention was made of what happened to the former owners of the manor.

There was lots more of this stuff about the early Hernes, and a slew of antiquities which I skipped: early ring forts, a fragment of a Roman villa, damage to the Norman church by Cromwell's men, and so on. Eventually, Reverend Ratliff wound his way up to the nineteenth century.

"That estimable man, Sir Timothy Herne, having been laid to rest, his son, Francis, succeeded to the title and estate in December, 1873, at the age of twenty. He was a youth in whom every virtue and natural endowment blended to such perfection that all who knew him could not fail to love him," blethered my guide. Sir Francis, it appeared, was a sportsman, a musician, a wise farmer, a provident businessman, witty, graceful, possessed of a pleasing tenor voice, a poet, and the author of scholarly historical essays, "the fruit," as Reverend Ratliff put it, "of much lucubration." However, unfortunately, only three years after getting the title, he fell from his horse in the hunting field and injured his back. At first it was thought to be only a sprain, but it affected his legs and within another year or two he was confined to a wheelchair. He seemed to have resigned himself to a life of relative inactivity, and turned for consolation to his collection of rare books and manuscripts. He had started this in his teens, and as time went on he bought more and more stuff and spent most of his days in the library, cataloguing and cherishing his prizes, and writing more essays which he contributed to various journals.

Happily, he was not always alone. His brother, Alastair, who had been living in London, returned home in 1894. He devoted himself to the care of Sir Francis, looking after him, running errands for him, pushing his chair around in the garden so that he could take the air, and assuming the stewardship of the property. In spite of his brother's solicitude, however, Francis was the victim of another, and this time fatal, accident: while wheeling himself from the library to his bedroom, a wheel came off his chair and he pitched over, fell down the stairs and was killed. This happened on May fifth, 1895.

Alastair became thirteenth baronet. He was thirty-three years old, and there was a photograph of him in the book: a stiff-backed man whose carriage and poise of the head reminded me of Mrs. Herne. He had a wide, thin-lipped, hard mouth and large eyes, out of which he looked sidelong at the camera, which gave him a shrewd and calculating air. According to Reverend Ratliff, he quickly showed himself a worthy successor to a great name, and became justly famous for his many charitable deeds, his careful husbandry, and his regard for his dependents. He married a young gentlewoman named Sarah Goodall, in 1897, and the following year their union was blessed (a favorite phrase of Ratliff's) by a daughter, Elizabeth, a child of exceptional beauty and promise.

And with that, as the rosy sun sank in the golden west, we bade farewell to the lovely and talented Hernes.

There were other families mentioned in the book, some of whose names were familiar to me: the Nevilles, the Brocks the Parrs, the Spendwells, and, yes, the Nicholsons—a Colonel Nicholson was spoken of as owning the estate called "Ramillies" in the village

114

of Littlegate, and an old house on the borders of Heronwick. I guessed he was Lucy's grandfather. But there was nothing else about him, and very little about anybody else, and that little was mostly stuff I already knew.

I went and leaned on the window sill and looked out into the garden. The sun was very low and the grass was golden, barred with long, cool shadows. Starlings hopped about the lawn and a blackbird whistled in the hedge. It was hard to remember that the morning had begun in cold mist; England could give you enough different kinds of weather in one day to supply six other countries.

It was even harder to remember, on this peaceful, quiet evening, that I had been frightened by the figure in the wood. I wondered idly about him, and then turned, once more, to my idea about Mrs. Herne. It began to seem more improbable than ever. Her background was so intensely respectable, her heritage so long and solid, that I couldn't imagine her hitting anyone a mortal blow. It was like trying to imagine Queen Victoria throwing an inkwell at somebody. A cold deadly snub, yes, or cutting words, but someone who was the daughter of a man described as famous for charity, careful husbandry, and all the rest of it, didn't suddenly start swinging a club against a young man's head.

Of course, I reminded myself, I had only Reverend Ratliff's words for it that that was what her father was like. Or her uncle, that chair-ridden recluse who spent his time in nocturnal meditation producing essays and collecting books, and who died so unfortunately.

And suddenly I said to myself, Oh-oh. One brother in a wheelchair, the other one comes back from London to take care of him, and a short time later—I snatched the book and looked up the page: yes, a year later, maybe a little less—the book collector goes flying down the stairs and dies, and the other brother succeeds to the title and the dough.

So maybe Sir Alastair wasn't such a saintly type, after all. Maybe Reverend Ratliff knew it and genuflected so continuously out of terror. If that were the case, Mrs. Herne's background wasn't all sweetness and light. But that wouldn't necessarily make her a murderer. All it did was provide me with a slightly different slant on her.

This was certainly something to ask Jack Spendwell about. I counted on my fingers: it was something over seventy-five years ago that Sir Francis had died. It was possible that somewhere I could still find some more detailed report of his death, of his relationship with his brother, or of his brother's character, than Reverend Ratliff provided. There might be old newspapers around, or someone in the village might recall gossip handed on from a parent.

In any case, it gave me an illusion of activity. It was something to track down, better than sitting still.

And I had to see Codd. What I wanted to show him was real enough, and might be important.

He turned up about nine, knocked at my door and came in. I put aside the letter I'd been writing to Bob and asked him to sit down. He put his hat on the bureau and rubbed his eyes. He looked very tired, his round face sagging and grey.

"I'm told you wanted to see me," he said.

"Yes. You look as though you've had a rough day."

"Oh, one has to chase around a bit. I've had a number of people to interview. And I've been to Bristol and back." He glanced about the room, which was larger and pleasanter than his, with a sigh. "I hope you haven't felt too confined today. I mean to explain to you that although I'd prefer you to stay in the district, you needn't sit here in Heronwick. I wouldn't like your visit to England to be a—er—"

"Form of imprisonment?" I suggested.

He looked a trifle uncomfortable. "I shouldn't have put it quite that way." Then he laughed. "Just so long as I know how to find you if I need you."

"Thanks. Have you found out anything?"

"Quite a bit, actually. We're got a general idea of what went on, although I can't say we're much nearer a solution."

"Can you tell me any of it?"

He tapped his fingertips together for a moment, and then looked up at me. "All right. It appears that someone else was in the house that morning. Someone with slightly dirty boots came in through the kitchen, went along the passage, and then must have taken off his boots. At any rate, the traces of them disappear. We believe he came into the hall in his stocking feet, perhaps so that he'd make no noise. This may have been because Neville was standing on the staircase. He turned round, and his assailant hit him. Then the murderer poured some whisky he'd brought with him, over the body. We found none in the house—Mrs. Herne drinks only sherry. The murderer went back to the passage and put his boots on again. We've found one or two marks which indicate that he went out through the passage and the kitchen."

"I see. But it does tell you something, doesn't it? It tells you I didn't commit the murder."

"Perhaps. You might have gone round and killed him, and then hurried back to the front door, mightn't you?"

"But I didn't!" I cried. "All you've got to do is compare my shoes with the footprints you've got."

"We've done that," he replied, drily, pulling his tweed topcoat more closely over his knees. "All but the shoes you're wearing, and I've been looking at them while we've been talking. They're the wrong shape, and they have smooth, crepe rubber soles. The ones we're looking for are quite different. About the same size, however."

"Oh. You mean that while I was out this morning, you had a cop come and check my shoes?"

"This afternoon, actually. But all it tells us is that we don't know where the boots are now, or who was wearing them."

"Okay what about Brock?"

"Ah, yes. He claims that when he met you he had just come from checking snares he'd set for rabbits in Herne Park. And when you asked, suddenly, where he'd been he felt upset and didn't want to admit he'd been poaching so he was rather abrupt with you."

"Rather abrupt?" I snorted. "Has anybody told you that there's nothing to poach in Hern Park? I've heard that from two different local people."

He raised his eyebrows. "Is that so? That's very interesting. Brock produced the rabbit snares when I asked him. He also showed me a pair of Wellingtons he claims to have worn that morning. Not at all like the boots we want, which would have had leather soles. I have to go into this poaching business a bit further. We checked all his boots and shoes, and couldn't find any that would fit our photographs. Unfortunately, you see, we haven't any clear, complete footprints, only bits and pieces."

"And that's all so far, huh?"

"That's all."

"Now let me tell you something. Do you remember when you first arrived and we were all in the sitting room, Mrs. Herne, Sarah, and I, and you asked us what happened? Do you recall what Mrs. Herne said?"

He shook his head. "Not exactly. But I have a transcript."

"I'll tell you. She said she was in the library, and

she thought she heard the front door close so she came to investigate."

"Yes, I do remember that."

"And you remember what I said? I told you I opened the door—"

"Because you had a peculiar feeling that something was wrong."

"Yes, and that's true, too. And I saw the body lying there and ran in to look at it. Well, I didn't close the front door behind me. So she couldn't have heard it."

"Mm. Very interesting."

I began to feel annoyed. "Isn't it interesting, too, that although she was sitting up in the library she didn't hear me knocking? And although she could think she heard the front door close, she didn't hear Neville go crashing down the stairs when he was hit?"

"Yes, it struck me as odd at the time," Codd said, gently. "But you see, now we aren't absolutely sure Neville *did* go crashing down the stairs."

"Oh? How come?"

"It's very difficult to establish this sort of thing on a steep, wooden stair like that one. But the only blood we've found, except for that on the floor where he was lying, is three steps up from the bottom. Only a drop or two. We consider that it's possible he may have been seven or eight steps up when he was hit."

"It would have been difficult, then," I said, "for anybody but a tall man to get at him. Right? Or else, somebody who was using a peculiar kind of weapon."

I had the picture in my mind of somebody swinging that ball on the end of the chain, the morning star the young policeman had been talking about.

Codd was saying, "Yes, the weapon. I've had a suggestion about that. It's all very difficult. The nature of a wound such as Neville received is that it needn't begin to bleed instantly. There's no spattering, as would be the case if the skin had been broken. The bone was crushed in—it was quite a whack. It knocked his upper plate loose."

I stared. "You don't mean he had false teeth? Neville? Why, he was only about thirty."

Codd chuckled at my expression. "It's not as unusual here as it might be in the States, Mr. Cannon."

I snapped my fingers. "So that's why he was grinning in that horrible way!"

He nodded.

"Well, listen," I said, "suppose Brock had some kind of weapon that would allow him to stand in the passage and still kill Neville at a distance. Maybe, if he could hit him with it while Charlie was at the foot of the stairs, Mrs. Herne really wouldn't hear anything."

"Mr. Cannon, it's as possible as anything else," said Codd. "But we haven't a clue as to why Brock would want to kill Neville. And this is a terribly dangerous business, this speculating as you're doing. Suppose this, suppose that—you can involve anyone you like that way, in any way you choose."

He leaned back. "We've rather lost sight of something. What did you want to see me about? To tell me about Mrs. Herne not hearing the front deer?"

"Not altogether. I've got something for you which may or may not have a bearing on the killing."

I fished the hammer out from under my shirts and handed it to him. His face lost some of its weariness, and he sat up straight. But his voice, when he spoke, was as soft as ever.

"What makes you think it may have something to do with the murder?"

I told him about the man in the mist, and how I had found the hammer in the stream.

He said, "Did you get a clear view of him?"

"No. I was some distance off, and the mist was too thick."

"You couldn't identify him at all?"

"No, I don't think so. I couldn't even tell whether it was Brock or not, by his size."

He had pulled out his handkerchief to take the hammer. He turned it about in his hands, and said, "Have you any idea who Propter is?

"Propter? I thought it said Proffer."

"Difficult to say. The letters are worn and smudged, but it looks like Propter to me."

"I thought it might be the name of a place."

He folded the handkerchief around the hammer. "Mr. Cannon," he said, and heaved a deep sigh. "Mr. Cannon, look here. I told you not to play detective, didn't I?"

"Now, wait a minute. Maybe it's got nothing to do with the case, but it *could* be the weapon that crushed in Neville's skull. Couldn't it? A guy prowling around in the woods near Herne House—looking for a hammer he may have dropped—hell, it looks to me as though I'm doing you a favor. You don't sound very grateful."

"It doesn't seem to have occurred to you that you might have done me more of a favor by leaving the hammer where you found it. You could have told me about it later. There might have been footprints or marks of some kind nearby. Something about the way it was lying in the water might have given the Forensic Lab people an idea which might have been helpful."

"I didn't think of that. But suppose I'd done what you say, and gone off. The guy might have come back, found it, and then you wouldn't have had it. What about that?"

"Possible, but I doubt it. I think you frightened him off."

"Yes, but you don't *know* that."

"I don't know anything, Mr. Cannon," he said, in an exasperated tone. "I don't know about you, for a start.

121

If you had killed Neville, nothing would be more plausible than for you to turn up with a cock-and-bull story about a strange man in the wood, and a hammer which you might have picked up anywhere. It would certainly distract attention from you. And it makes you look quite innocent, turning over a possible murder weapon to me, doesn't it?"

I didn't know what to say. I shoved my hands in my pockets to keep them from waving hopelessly.

"For Christ's sake!" I exclaimed at last. "Do you really think I'm guilty? Or is this another wicked uncle game."

"Not a game," he replied. "You'd better put that notion out of your head. A man's been killed. I intend to find out who did it."

He said this in a firm but quiet voice that calmed me down.

I sat on the end of the bed. "Okay. I'm trying to see your side of it, Inspector. But you've got to see mine. I don't have any intention of being the clever civilian who outsmarts the police. It's not my line. At the same time I can't just sit around twiddling my thumbs. You told me yourself to keep an eye open. Put it down to my being one of those headstrong, nutty Americans, okay, but I feel I've got to do something to help myself. I already have a couple of friends in Heronwick, and if nothing else they may be able to fill me in on some background stuff about people involved in this murder."

"I've no objection to that, Mr. Cannon. The trouble is, you see . . . well, people have such a curious notion of how we work. The word 'detective' is one of those fuses which set off the film images: they see us busily collecting clues, conferring with a nark in some deserted warehouse with the collar of a trench coat turned up and the brim of a soft hat pulled down, and finally shooting it out toe to toe with the villainous

122

gang leader. But you know, we don't even carry pistols. It's mainly slow, methodical, unromantic legwork, asking hundreds of questions, putting bits and pieces together and trying to make some sense of them. Dull and dreary for the most part. Tiresome drudgery. I often find myself wishing I *could* have one of those lovely secret agent kits complete with throwing knife, hand grenade, and collapsible rifle, and shoot it out in a dark alley with a gang chief. What a lark! But I'm afraid the last time I went to pistol practice, I barely knew which end of the thing to point."

He lay back in the chair with the wrapped-up hammer across his lap, and laughed, sleepily. "Do you know what my hobby is?"

"Raising orchids?"

"I wish it were. No, dreaming that one day I'll have a lovely dramatic case, which turns out to be as neat and precise and mathematically solvable as the ones you see on telly. Those we get are generally sordid, petty, or downright nasty, which is what crime really is when you come down to it. As for solving them . . . I had one only last month in which we all knew who the guilty man was, but we couldn't pin a thing on him."

"How did you ever get into this business?" I asked.

He looked sheepish. "I'm afraid I—ah—had some rather romantic notions about it myself. I was the victim of, well, let's say, of too much reading. But I don't think we'll go into all that just now, if you don't mind."

He stood up, easing his shoulders. "It's an extraordinary thing, you know," he said. "No Englishman would dream of asking me a question like that."

"Do you mind?"

"Oh, no. I don't think so. Good night. And for heaven's sake, Mr. Cannon," he added, at the door, "before you pin the murder on anyone else, come and talk it over with me."

I thought about him, as I undressed before the single, glowing wire of my electric heater, trying futilely to keep warm. All my ideas about policemen were upset by him. If he had played rough, I could have exploded—called a lawyer, raised hell, I don't know what. But he put me off with that round, boy's face combined with a sense of authority that was more crushing somehow than violence would have been. No concealed shoulder-holster, no gun, no blackjack, probably not so much as a pocket knife, it was the way cops had always been in this country. I'd seen antique truncheons: a baton about a foot long with a royal crown on one end, the symbol of the policeman's authority. Certainly not big enough to serve as much of a weapon. Armed with nothing but this, a cop would bring the toughest crook meekly to heel— or so I'd heard. That's how it appeared to be with Codd. He relied on his assurance that the law was right and the criminal was wrong. It gave him a power I'd never met with before.

In a way, it was reassuring. I knew I hadn't killed anybody. And I had the feeling Codd was going to be damn careful not to make any mistakes about it.

8

There are some days which begin amiably enough and end horribly, and others which launch themselves on a fleet of tiny disasters but relent later on. This was going to be one of the latter. My shoelaces broke. My toothbrush slipped out of my hand and vanished into the sink drain. I cut myself while shaving: not on the jaw but more painfully on the finger while trying to change a blade. I took the rubber band off my address book to look up the Vicar's number and the rubber snapped and hit me in the face. By the time I went down to breakfast, I was ready to dive for cover at any unusual noise.

When I got Jack Spendwell on the phone, he said, "I'm sorry, Dave, I can't see you this morning. I've got a meeting of the Harvest Festival Committee in about ten minutes. It's always a problem because I have to mediate between Mrs. Herne and the other members. Try me this afternoon, will you?" So that was no good.

I phoned Mrs. Herne. I wasn't surprised to hear from Sarah that she was out, obviously on her way to the meeting. I'd have to wait for her, too.

I remembered that Lucy was on that committee and for a minute I toyed with the idea of crashing it as a foreign observer. However, before I could make any rash decisions, she phoned me.

"I just wanted to find out how things were going with you," she said.

"I'm not in jail yet."

"Good. Look, I've got to dash—"

"I know, you have a meeting of the Harvest Festival Committee."

"How on earth—? Well, yes. Anyway, Daddy asked me to ring you to see if you can come to lunch with him today. Would you like to? He wants to show you his plant. I can't promise you a marvelous feed, but it might be fun. Will they let you leave Heronwick?"

"Oh, yes, no problem about that," I said. "I'd like to go very much. Shall I phone your father?"

"No, I'll tell him. Got a pencil? You go to Gloucester, and ask someone to show you where the Bristol Road is." she gave me the address, and told me to be there at noon. "Now one more thing," she added. "Are you free Friday night?"

"Unless I'm arrested by then, I am."

"There's a dance in the Market Hall. Would you like to take me?"

"You mean Mel Cluff and the Maniacs? I thought that was going to be all teenagers and imitation Beatles."

"Oh, no. It'll be all sorts of dancing. Of course, some of the village yobs will be there, but so will some of my friends. What do you say?"

"I'd love it," I said, so fervently that I thought I could feel the glow of her blush.

"All right," she said. "I'll be in touch with you before then, to arrange when and where to meet. Good luck. And don't let Daddy intimidate you if he starts off on his 'damned American competition' kick."

I took my maps into the bar and studied them in consultation with Mr. Davies. It wasn't going to take me more than half an hour to get to Gloucester, so I had nearly two hours to kill. I didn't feel like sitting around and it was a mild day, if overcast, so I decided to walk up through the village to the other pub, the Falcon.

It may have been only my imagination, but this morning I felt more noticeable than I had before. People fell silent as I passed them, and seemed to look after me. I thought I saw faces turn towards me through shop windows, and then turn back again as if whispering together. Three or four young men were loitering at the Market Hall and they stopped talking and watched me come towards them, looking me silently up and down so that I became very self-conscious. I could feel my arms swinging, and wondered if my fly was open. One of them was the short youth with the permanent wave who had been in the fight at the Goat. I smiled straight at him and said, pleasantly, "Good morning. Nice to see you again." He was taken by surprise. His mouth opened, but then he quickly shut it again and pulled out a comb and began combing his hair sulkily. I felt a little better.

I took the Knottswood Road, passing the policeman's house, and looked for any sign of Inspector Codd. The dusty Vauxhall in which he traveled was parked at the head of Kingsmill Lane and I assumed he must be in the house messing about with clues and things. Someone hailed me, and I turned around.

It was Jeffrey Parr, the tall, lugubrious-looking man who had bowled for our cricket team. He was carrying a brown paper parcel, and came towards me glancing from side to side as if he didn't want to be observed.

"Good morning," I said.

"Hallo, Yank. Dave, is it? Been keeping well?"

"Not bad."

"Practicing your batting?"

"I'm staying away from clocks."

He grinned. Then growing serious, he said, "About this murder—"

I bristled. "You want to know if I had anything to do with it?"

He shook his head. "I don't wonder you're feeling edgy. No, I don't mean to be nosy. You did us a favor, going in for us last Sunday, and I wanted to do one for you, that's all."

"I'm sorry. You're right, I am sort of jumpy."

"I don't blame you, mind. And I know you'd nothing to do with it. But not everybody in the village feels that way."

"What do you mean?"

"Look here, Dave," he said, earnestly, "Will Brock's lived here all his life. You come along, an outsider—meaning no offense, you understand, I'm just trying to explain—and the first thing that happens is you put the police onto Willie. You see? It's only natural some of his friends might feel resentful."

"Put the police onto him? You mean because I told them I met him that morning? It was true."

"Doesn't matter if it was. And I'm not saying it wasn't. But there are some who are saying you did Charlie in and now you're covering up by trying to involve Will."

"That's ridiculous," I said. "It's—it's a—Jesus, I don't know what to say. I didn't have any choice. The police questioned me, just as they did everyone who was there. I had to tell them what I knew, didn't I?" I hesitated, a little confused. "I don't see how I could have kept quiet about Brock. I was being suspected of something I hadn't done. For all I know maybe he *was* up to something that morning. If he's innocent, he's got no more to fear than anyone else."

I stopped, conscious that the more I talked the more it sounded just the way Parr had put it: that I had tossed Brock to the wolves to protect myself.

He said, "Maybe so. That's not the point. This is only a small village, and maybe villages here are different from what they are in the States. Not all country people take kindly to the police. Nor to strangers. When it comes to a crime they'd sooner suspect you than one of their own. You see?"

I rubbed my forehead. "I guess so."

"I'm sorry," he said. "It's no joke. Some of Brock's friends are rather rough. One of them works for me, look, and I had to bring along this parcel to pretend I'd an errand, so I could go after you. I don't want any trouble in my shop. But I felt I owed you something. After all, it's not everybody can hit the clock—specially," he added, with a smile, "a bloody foreigner."

I said, "Thanks, Jeffrey. I mean it, I'm very grateful."

He nodded. "I'll do what I can to help. But it won't be much. So long."

When he had gone, I felt for a moment the chill of vulnerability, as if suddenly attackers were going to come swarming out of the neat, quiet houses. I shook it off. If I let myself go, I could easily scare myself to death so that I'd be afraid to set foot out of doors. Obviously, whatever any of Brock's friends felt they weren't going to do anything, and there were some people who were on my side—the Davies, Spendwell, the Nicholsons, and even Parr. I wasn't wholly alone by any means. I lit a cigarette and went on.

The public bar of the Falcon was empty. I rapped

on the counter and after a bit the elderly, rather haggard woman who ran the place appeared. I got a half pint and sat down on one of the well-polished benches in a corner where I could look out the window at the road and the ugly, tan stone, modern cottages across the way.

The woman said, "Just call if you want anything more, love," and left me.

The grey day made the low-ceilinged room dusky, and I had already noticed that the English never turned on any lights until darkness forced them to it. They have a kind of horror of the electric light, even the most up-to-date of them. I have never been in a private house or a hotel room in England where there was such a thing as a proper bed lamp, and even in the Nicholson's study where I had met the General, there hadn't been a lamp for each easy chair as there would have been at home, but only one monstrous floor lamp standing as remote from the chairs as if it had a communicable disease. However, I didn't mind it so much today, in this pub. Feeling as I did, it seemed safer to be in gloom, and it matched my mood. My finger was throbbing where I had cut it that morning, and the knot I had had to tie in my shoelace hurt my instep. I made a mental note to stop somewhere and get a new pair of laces.

A hoarse voice said, "Look sharp, Jarge."

I jumped. There was nobody in the room with me, yet the voice seemed to come from the far corner.

Another, higher voice said, "Pint o' mild and a smile, please, Mary."

The hoarse voice said, "Look sharp."

The hair on the back of my neck waved to and fro like grass before the wind. Ghosts, I thought. That's all I need.

I got up bravely and peered around the room.

Somebody began whistling "Tipperary," off-key. I

walked towards the music. if you could call it that, and discovered that behind the bar counter there was an alcove. On the other side of it, another, smaller counter served the lounge, where there was a piano. That was where they had been singing on Sunday evening after the cricket match. And in the alcove between hung a large brass cage in which there was the moldiest, most miserable-looking parrot I had ever seen.

Except for his head and the secondaries of his wings, he had almost no feathers. A few still clung here and there to his grey skin, and his wings and head were a dusty green, a wan mockery of former brilliance. He cocked a filmy eye at me. In a deep growl, unlike the other two voices, he said, "Good night all."

This parrot could have been a hundred years old. And I realized with a shock that I must be hearing ghosts indeed: the voices of customers long gone, registered on this avian tape recorder.

"Pint o' mild and a smile, please, Mary," the high voice insisted. A fourth voice, thick and drunken, said, " 'Oos for a moonlight swim?" and followed it with a dying chuckle.

I went back to my drink. The voices continued, interspersed with other noises which I recognized as the clink of glasses or the sound of a door closing. The whole eerie pageant of the last God knows how many years went on until a new voice said, "Good morning, love. Who's a good boy?"

The parrot fell silent. Then, in a coy, childish voice, he said, "I'm a good boy."

The manageress appeared, crossing behind the bar counter to the lounge bar, and I heard her say, "Late again this morning, Sarah?"

"Oh, everything's topsy-turvy at the house."

"Are the police still there?"

"No, thank goodness, they've all gone. But now I've

to clean up after them. A proper mess they've left me, too."

"What about *her?*"

"Not a bit put out, not her. As usual. She went off to her committee this morning, ready for the fray. She was troubled enough Monday night, though. Those two detectives had been on at her nearly an hour in the afternoon."

"Wicked, they are. I've seen them on the telly, interrogating prisoners, like in *Softly, Softly*. Was it like that?"

"I've no doubt, They was in the library, and I couldn't get near the door for the coppers scrambling about below, measuring and photographing, but I saw her face when they all come out. White as a sheet with anger, she was. *I* know what she was worrit about. She was afraid what's happened might make difficulties for Mr. Lionel. Like that last time. You know."

"You think it might have something to do with him?"

"I'm not telling all I think, love. They questioned me, too, but they didn't ask me much. If they'd asked me, I could have told them a thing or two. They've left off their snooping now, and a good riddance, too. They'll get no volunteering from me."

"I should think not, indeed."

"All I'd say is, I'd say why did Mr. Richter come up to the house Sunday night? And especially if it didn't have nothing to do with Mr. Lionel?"

"Did he, now? You didn't tell me that."

"Ah. I was just off to Eunice's house, about eight it might have been, when he come to the door. 'Medicine,' he says, 'I've come to bring Mrs. Herne some medicine.' Oh, yes, I knew she'd telephoned him all right. But there's nothing wrong with *her*. Medicine? I ask you."

"What do you think it was?"

"Well, it's not my place to talk, is it now? But if they'd asked me, I'd have said some more of that stuff —*you* know—like what got Mr. Lionel into trouble the last time."

"Ooh, yes, I remember your telling me. Have another shandy, dear?"

"I don't mind."

After that, they began talking about Eunice and her rheumatism, and how wet it had been although it was looking as though it might clear a bit, and how dear things were getting, all in the same loud voices because of Sarah's deafness. I realized that although they might get back to the fascinating subject of Mrs. Herne and Mr. Lionel and Mr. Richter, it wouldn't be for a while. I put my tankard on the counter, making a thump so that the manageress, who was leaning on the counter to the lounge bar, turned round.

"Will there be anything else?" she said.

"No, thanks. This is quite a parrot you've got here," I said. "He was talking away to me before."

"Yes, he does that," she smiled. "Been here for ages. I got him with the pub, and he was talking then. Pulled all his feathers out during the war, when we couldn't get the proper feed for him, poor thing."

I could see Sarah in the lounge, and as I had hoped she looked up at me when she heard my voice.

"Good morning," I called.

"Good morning, sir."

"Do you come here every day?" I asked.

"Them days I can get away," she replied, sourly.

The manageress laughed. "What should I ever do without you I'm sure I don't know, love. Thank goodness, the days you can get away are from Monday to Sunday."

I glanced at my watch. It was ten-thirty.

"It's nice to have regular habits," I said. "At home, I

always like to hit the same counter joint for coffee at the same time."

"Sarah's the same," the manageress said. "Ten minutes after I open, she's here to keep me company."

Sarah was looking very dark by now, and I guessed she didn't like this prying into her habits, so I said, cheerily, "Well, nice to have seen you."

"Bye bye," said the manageress. Sarah said nothing, but gave me a curt nod.

This was very interesting information I now had, although I didn't quite know what I was going to do with it. I did know, however, that Sarah came regularly to the Falcon at about ten past ten. Maybe whoever had killed Neville would have known that and would have counted on nobody being in the house. Of course, this might leave a wide field: it was possible that everyone in the village knew her schedule. Somehow, though, from the grim way she had acted, I didn't think so. Like a lot of people who needed a morning nip or two, she probably preferred to keep up the pretense that she was marketing or just visiting. And from what the manageress had said it seemed possible that there were rarely customers in that pub in the morning. Most of the daytime custom went, I judged, to the Goat.

And then there was Mr. Lionel and Mr. Richter. Who were they? What was the "stuff" which got Mr. Lionel into trouble? And why should it seem to Sarah that Neville's death might be connected with them? Mr. Lionel and Mr. Richter. A team of lawyers? A pair of fences?

I came into the market square, noting that the idlers were gone from their post, and remembered shoelaces. The question was, where to get them? This was not so foolish as it sounds, because even in this short time I had learned that there was a whole special mystique of knowing where to buy certain things, in English villages. For instance, you could not buy cigarettes in a drug store, but you could buy them almost everywhere else. For paper napkins, toilet paper, and the little pleated paper cups you bake muffins in, you went to a stationer; you didn't get bacon at the butcher's but at the grocer's; and a shop labeled "Undertakers" did not necessarily supply coffins but did carpentry repairs. Consequently, I pondered the question of shoelaces. Not an ironmonger, certainly, although I knew I could buy a corkscrew there. Maybe a chemist? Then, to my surprise, I saw a shop which bore the sign, Shoe Repairs.

I was even more surprised when I went in and found myself facing Jeffrey Parr. I began to say something amiable, but he cut me short with a "Yes, sir? What can I do for you?"

I blinked at him. He had his back to the rest of the shop, and without a word he rolled his eyes sideways. I caught on. There was another man in the shop standing at the workbench cutting a piece of leather and watching me with a grim expression. This must be that friend of Brock's. I got my shoelaces and paid for them. As I was picking up my change, he lifted his shoemaker's knife and, with a short, deliberate gesture, pretended to slit his throat with it. Then he gave me a wicked smile and bent to his work.

"Nice—day," I gulped, and took my leave with an uncomfortable feeling between the shoulder blades.

Gloucester, except for its magnificent cathedral, was something of a let-down: it looked like Bridgeport. I parked the car and found the Nicostamp Mfg. Co. Ltd., a glum brick building dominated by its next-door neighbor, a mammoth plant which proclaimed England's Glory—not ships, nor even flags as I

135

thought when I first saw it, but matches. Nicostamp
was a little more cheerful inside than out, with pop
music blaring from loudspeakers, bright whitewashed
walls, busy workmen, and the clang and rattle and
thump of machinery. I found the General in a tiny office decorated with a brass rubbing of a knight in
armor, across the top of which someone had lettered,
"Early Nicostamp metalwork. Guaranteed moth-
proof."

The General got up from behind his desk, and at
once the office became overcrowded in the most
alarming way.

"Good to see you, Mr. Cannon," he boomed. "I've
just cleared away the last of my morning, and I'm all
yours. We're keeping busy these days, I'm happy to
say. Like to see the plant first? Right. Then we can
have a spot of lunch at my club."

Walking behind me, he propelled me out of the office and through the plant, not by touching me but by
the sheer force of his bulk. He moved slowly but with
powerful smoothness so that I felt a little as though I
were riding on the bumper of one of those big, old-
fashioned limousines. He seemed popular. Workmen
greeted him as he passed, and exchanged jokes with
him, and at one long bench where a row of women in
blue overalls were doing some sort of assembly work
he was received with affectionate waves, giggles, and
cries of, "Ten-shun!"

"Sorry you can't meet my cousin George," the General said, his voice rising easily above the noise of the
plant. "He's really the brains of this outfit. In London
all this week. It's his plant—I only put in a bit of cap-
ital—couldn't bear sitting about doing nothing when I
left the army. I ring up a few chaps, act impressively
when potential business appears, and try to follow
what's being said at planning meetings. I like the

136

place, you know. It's lively, keeps me fit and on my toes."

He guided me between two files of massive, greasy machines which were thudding up and down, producing shapes out of sheet metal. He talked learnedly about things called the Mark VII, Swedish gauge, and numbers of pressings per minute, and I gathered he knew a great deal about what was happening, and probably did a lot more work for the plant than he let on. He seemed to be a happy man, and I made no effort to understand what he was talking about but floated along on his contentment.

We ended up, about an hour later, at his club, a simple and even drab set of rooms in a quiet street near the Cathedral. The dining room was high-ceilinged and painted a repulsive green, but the food was good solid beef or chops, three kinds of potatoes, and the usual soggy brussels sprouts and cabbage.

"This was once the home of a prosperous merchant," General Nicholson said, tucking in briskly. "It's a businessmen's club now, which I suppose would make the old boy happy if he knew. Somewhat better than the fate that's befallen some of the old houses in Gloucester." He pointed with his fork. "Aha! There's one of our jobs, you see, Model SX98."

It was a large electric heater, the lower part made to resemble a coal fire in an iron grate, with a light bulb inside that made it glow. There was a minuscule two-wire heating unit set into the top among fancy curlicues. If it gave out any warmth I couldn't feel it from where I was sitting.

"You remember, we saw some of those being turned out on the Mark VII," he went on. "We only make the metal case, of course. We subcontract for United Electric; they put the thing together. Very popular, those are."

137

"There doesn't seem to be much actual heat, though," I said, cautiously.

"No, you're right there, Mr. Cannon," the General chuckled. "It's three-quarters appearance. It's what people seem to want, you see. They want to feel they've still got a nice old-fashioned coal fire going, and they're willing to pay for the looks of the thing rather than for efficiency. Progress, that's called. However, more and more people are going in for central heating, now. I've warned George that we shall soon find our orders for those units dropping off. Fortunately, we make a great many other things as well."

"Your shop certainly looked busy enough."

"It did, didn't it? It's fashionable to say that England has changed, you know, but that's all nonsense. Ever since Henry Tudor, perhaps even before, we've been devoted to business. Our merchant guilds were the most active in the world, and our working people the best paid and most thriving. When industry came in, we got cracking long before anyone else. We like to make money, and we jolly well like to spend it, too. But we've always loved to pretend that we're quite different, that we despise trade and that we're really a rustic paradise full of agricultural workers in smocks standing about chewing straws in the most picturesque fashion, and country squires riding to hounds. Not that we haven't got 'em. We have! The Hill People, we call them in Glocestershire. But the Valley People are quite different—just go down to the Stroud Valley, for instance. Where the cloth mills were humming away in the sixteenth century, you'll find modern plants buzzing like beehives today, most of them in the same spots.

"Lots of people say that England's got to catch up to the modern world." He laughed heartily. "Rubbish! We've always been one step ahead of the modern world, still are. We fit it better in many ways than you Americans do, if you'll forgive me for saying so, because you're so frightened of being called Socialists. But we've three major political parties, not fifty like the French or one like the Russians, a balanced and sensible way of governing ourselves, protection and care for the whole population, very little unemployment, and plenty of free time for a sociable pint of bitter. And we can still all go out on a Bank Holiday like the Whitsun weekend and enjoy ourselves. We don't mind what people call us. Never have."

"That's because you've always had the absolute certainty that being English is the ultimate in evolution."

The General regarded me benevolently. "Well, isn't it? But all the same, you know, we've never failed to laugh at ourselves for taking ourselves so seriously. That's our secret, you see. It's what makes us adaptable. And that's why, whatever the modern world has been, we've always been 'with it,' as they say now."

"And yet you just said that people are willing to pay for appearances rather than efficiency. We Americans believe in efficiency rather than appearance. Isn't that a more modern point of view?"

He laid down his knife and fork and his little eyes twinkled.

"Surely you're not serious, Mr. Cannon?" he said, with the relish of a man who enjoyed argument as much as food. "The giant American automobile is no different from our Model SX98 Electric Fire, except that it's five thousand times as expensive. Those immense glass and aluminium buildings I saw in New York last year are anything but efficient—the glass walls look out at nothing but other glass walls, and have to be covered with blinds or drapes so that they won't affect the air conditioning. They are for appearance, aren't they? They *look* so wonderfully modern even if they give the people who work in them the blind staggers. And what about your wars to contain China? I should have said they were a fine example of paying for appearances rather than efficiency. The most efficient way of dealing with that situation would be compromise, I should think. A method we English long ago discovered to be much less extravagant and far more effective. And yet you call yourselves modern businessmen!"

I said, flushing, "We've got ideals, General."

He nodded. "Of course you have. Splendid, old-fashioned things to have, too, provided you don't let 'em interfere with your well being. One might as well boast of having an appendix. No, with all our faults, we English tend to keep clear of ideals. We reserve idealism for whichever political party happens to be out of power at the moment."

"Well," I said, "all this stuff about business sounds to me like mighty peculiar talk from a military man."

"Not at all, not a bit of it. It's precisely because I'm a military man—or was—that I can talk this way. There isn't such a gap as you seem to suppose between sound business practice and good military sense. A military commander tries to secure as much profit as he can with a minimum of waste. Isn't that so? But profit's not much good unless you can enjoy it. One wants to win, after all, without becoming so enfeebled that one can't take advantage of victory. Now an idealist is perfectly willing to throw everything into the balance without regard for the future, and oddly enough the same thing holds true for a greedy businessman, or a bungling officer. They all end up putting themselves out of action in the end, with nothing to show for it. Or don't you agree?"

He said all this with such bland good humor and overwhelming assurance that I found nothing to say in reply.

"I do chatter, I'm afraid," he went on, without any sign of remorse. "Can't help it. It's a reaction against television. Humanity is turning into a silent race which sits passively being talked at by machines. Might as well listen to me, then, eh? What about some cheese? Or the apple tart is quite good here."

When we had settled down in the lounge with our coffee, looking out at a snooty garden enclosed by the walls of buildings, he said, "Now, then, what's been happening? Anything new?"

"Not much." I told him about finding the hammer.

"Proffer or Propter," he mused. "Doesn't mean a thing to me. But depend on it, it was Willie Brock you saw in the woods. Probably his hammer. The name couldn't have been Brock, E.P., for instance? Willie's father was named Edward Percival."

"It's hard to say. The letters were smudged. I don't know, and I won't get another chance to look because the police have the hammer now. Tell me, sir, who's Mr. Lionel?"

"Mr. Lionel? Never heard of him. Why?"

"Mrs. Herne's housekeeper, Sarah, said she thought Neville's murder had something to do with Mr. Lionel and Mr. Richter, and she mentioned some 'stuff' that Mr. Lionel had been in trouble with once before."

"Ah, I see. *That* Lionel. Elizabeth Herne's son. And Richter is the local chemist. But I don't see what they could have had to do with Neville's death. I don't think they've seen much of each other in the past four or five years except for a week or so at Christmas. Lionel's in Manchester now, so far as I know."

"What's he like?"

The General stared thoughtfully out at the dingy garden. "Something of a weed," he replied. "Tall and thin, walks as if he were hung on strings, mouth always dropping open—terrible case of adenoids, I suppose. He wasn't a bad sort when he was a youngster, he acquitted himself very creditably during the war, was wounded early in 1944 and sent home. But after the war, like so many men, he changed. I wasn't here, then, of course, but one hears these things. He was looking for thrills, it seems. Spent a whacking great sum on a dashing Aston Martin and used to go careering around the countryside. He drank heavily, too, and cracked up once or twice so that Elizabeth had to bail him out of trouble. He lost his license in the end. Then he moved to Birmingham and got some girl into trouble, and had to marry her. Now he's in Manchester, and I have heard he's been mixed up with a rather shady crowd there. But I can't say. It seems a pity. I knew his father, Reginald, well. A most delightful man, good company, one of the best raconteurs I've ever met."

"He was Mrs. Herne's cousin, wasn't he?"

"Yes, that is so. He died of pneumonia in the late 'twenties, I forget just when. He had our wretched English habit of taking cold baths and one of them did for him. But he was weak-willed, as well as weak-chested, that was his difficulty. He let Elizabeth dominate him, as she did everyone—Lionel, too. Bad for a boy's character, that sort of thing. I don't go in for this psychology stuff, but I imagine that must have had something to do with it, eh? She alternated between tyranny and coddling, and undermined Reginald's authority. Can't have been a good thing."

"And how about Richter? Were they friends?"

"Ah, well, Richter's another kettle of fish. First of all, he's a foreigner. I don't know whether you could say he and Lionel were friends, exactly. I suppose they were, but not the Damon and Pythias kind. I don't imagine Lionel could ever be really close friends with anyone. But they used to go out together a good deal, riding about in that sports car and hitting the high spots. I saw them together once when I was at home. It didn't appear to me that Richter was enjoying himself, he trailed behind Lionel looking rather like an unhappy hound and got into the car as if he were obeying orders to attack the Russian front. Well, of course, he owed Lionel quite a lot."

"Of money?"

"Oh, no. No, I hardly think so. You see, Richter was a prisoner of war."

"You mean he's a German?"

"Yes, didn't I say that? He was in a camp not far from here, and like many prisoners was assigned to farm labor. He worked for the Brocks, as a matter of fact, among others, and at that time Elizabeth still owned the Brock farm; Willie didn't buy it from her until ten or twelve years after the war. Well, now, I can't tell you this from my own knowledge—in the autumn of 'forty-four I was in the Far East—but apparently that's when Lionel and Richter met. Lionel had served in Europe, and I gather his regiment had once actually faced Richter's so that there was a common bond, you might say. Whether it was that, or the fact that Lionel was bored and was looking for someone to push around in reaction to his mother—I suppose these psychiatric johnnies might put it that way, eh?—well, whatever it was, that was how they got to know one another.

"After the war, Richter applied for British citizenship. He had been a chemist in Germany before being drafted, and the old boy here in Heronwick was persuaded to take him on. I don't know the ins and outs of apprenticeship, but he served for some years with old Mr. Collicke (I've always thought that an appropriate name for a chemist) and then went to Bristol for a two-year course so that he could get his English license. I think, although mind you I'm not certain, that Elizabeth paid for that. And she and Lionel served as Richter's character references, and so did Edward Brock, Willie's father, and Bartram Spendwell."

"Related to the Vicar?"

"His father. A splendid chap, a surveyor and estate agent, and incidentally a great collector of old silver. He'd have sponsored anyone, being a broad-minded man, but Brock was Elizabeth's doing. I imagine she brought all her artillery to bear, for Lionel's sake. Brock was rather down on Germans because he had lost a younger son in the war. However, Elizabeth talked him round; she was even more overpowering twenty years ago than she is today."

"I can imagine."

"Yes, I suppose you can. You're doing business with her, after all, aren't you? I hope you won't find her too sharp for you."

"I know I don't look it," I said, "but I've had lots of experience dealing with sharp people."

"I should say you'd need it. Well, I don't know what else I can tell you about him. He took the chemist's place here more than ten years ago, and he's a British subject now. But I can't say he's been altogether accepted. Keeps to himself, doesn't mix much, a quiet unobtrusive chap.

"You know what it is," the General added, with a sigh. "We're a rum lot, we English. I've been in America, and when someone takes up citizenship over there he becomes an American without question, even if he can't speak the language. But here, this poor devil will be a foreigner all his life. There will always be something faintly comic to us in the way he speaks and waves his hands. Intriguing, perhaps, and even attractive, but amusing like a household pet. It's not

144

exactly snobbery. It goes deeper than that. Perhaps it's our insularity. Might even be a sort of compensation for the filthy climate we have, eh? On the other hand, we've always adored being ruled by foreigners. The Plantagenets from France, James I from Scotland and then his Frenchified descendants, William brought over from Holland, the Hanoverians who at first only spoke German. . . . Odd, isn't it? Almost the only out-and-out Englishman I can think of was Cromwell, and he was also the only dictator England ever had. Damn funny. It's rather as if our sense of independence could only be maintained under a foreign monarch so that we can oppose his power, or even chop his head off without feeling guilty about it."

"I'd never thought of it that way. But about Richter and Lionel, you don't know what the 'stuff' could be? Or what the trouble was that Lionel got into some years ago?"

"Not a clue. The trouble might have been his automobile accidents. Or that girl of his. It could be that, you know. But it happened in Birmingham, not here. Her father was a butcher, something of a bruiser, and he wouldn't let Lionel wriggle out of marriage. So perhaps Lionel tried to get some chemicals, some sort of drug from Richter would would bring on an abortion."

"That's possible. How could he get into trouble, though, if there wasn't any abortion? And I take it there wasn't."

"Quite right. They've got a son, a kid of about thirteen. They all come down for the Christmas holidays and stay with Elizabeth. I'm sure it must give her exquisite torment to be civil to the daughter of a Birmingham butcher. Still, a grandchild's a grandchild. Settles the question of inheritance and keeps the property in the family. As for how that could have made trouble, I've no idea. It was just a thought."

"Hm. Well, could there have been any connection between them and Charlie Neville?"

The General thought for a moment. "Neville used to tag after Lionel, but I never heard the attention was reciprocated. As for Richter, Neville once worked for him for a short time, but that ended in a fight."

"You mean a literal fight?"

"I don't know what it was about, but Neville said he had been insulted somehow. He tore the shop to pieces and gave Richter quite a drubbing. Richter, however, refused to charge him so the matter was dropped."

Before we parted, the General insisted on taking me over to the Cathedral to see its cloisters and its glorious east window. Then we stopped for a moment to chat with a man named John Walter, a bookseller in College Street with whom I'd done some business by mail. I told him cagily that I was on holiday, and would look him up for a longer talk, if I could.

We walked back to the factory and my car. "I've had a great time, General," I said, as we shook hands. "Lucy had me a little scared, but I've enjoyed myself."

"Scared? Why?"

"Oh, she said you'd give me a hard time about American competition. And I don't know anything about business. I've enjoyed talking to you, though."

"American competition? What the devil's she talking about?" said the General. "We haven't any in our field, not to speak of." Then his face changed, and he laughed. "Wretched girl!" he exclaimed. "I know what she means."

"What?"

"No, no, I'll not say a word. She'll have to tell you herself. You make sure to ask her. Serve her right.

146

Goodbye, Mr. Cannon. Don't hesitate to call on me if I can help you."

I drove back thinking he'd make some lucky fellow a good father-in-law.

9

There really *is* something to the English insistence on tea every afternoon. Even if it's no more than a cup and a slice of bread and butter, it gives you a few minutes to unwind, it forces you to break the tempo of the day. I had my tea at the Goat, and I could hear the snick-snick of muscles letting go. This time when I made my phone calls, both Mrs. Herne and the Vicar were in, and I arranged to see the former next morning, while Spendwell asked me to drop over then and there. I strolled up to Church Lane, taking the *Brief Account* along.

"Thanks for the book, Jack," I said.

"Was it useful?"

"It sure was. It gave me all sorts of interesting ideas. For instance, I want to know more about the death of Sir Francis Herne."

He looked puzzled. "I don't think I'm with you. What do you want to know?"

"Call it the working of a naturally evil mind, but I

find something very peculiar about the fact that less than a year after his brother, Alastair, came home, Sir Francis was killed and Alastair got the title."

"And that seems suspicious to you? Why?"

"I don't know why. Maybe I read too many books. How come Sir Francis wheels himself around the house in a wheelchair for fifteen years without breaking a fingernail, and then after his brother comes home he breaks his neck?"

The Vicar shook his head. "As I remember it, a wheel came off his chair. Isn't that what the book says?"

"Yep. And it happened at the top of the main staircase. Lucky, wasn't it? For Alastair, I mean."

"Dave, I think you're going a bit too far," said the Vicar. "You ought to know from your own experience in the past couple of days how dangerous it is to jump to conclusions. From what I've read, I understand Alastair was very devoted, and looked after his brother in the kindest way. Why should he have waited a year? Why not arrange an accident after a month or so, if he wanted to put him out of the way?"

"I don't know. It just has a funny smell to me."

"But what could this possibly have to do with Neville's death?"

"I don't know that either. Anyway, I thought it might be instructive to dig up some background on Mrs. Herne's family."

"What would you like me to do? I'm afraid I haven't any other records of the period. You might try the Reference Department of the County Library in Gloucester. Maybe they have an old newspaper with a fuller report on the accident."

"I was wondering," I said, "whether you knew anybody who might have heard something from a father or mother—you know, if there had been any talk in the village about it, or anything. . . ."

Spendwell took a turn around the room with his hands in his pockets, frowning at the floor. Then he said, "I think I know the very person for you. Someone who was certainly alive at the time—1895, wasn't it?—and may even remember the whole thing. Mr. Savory. He certainly has a good memory."

"He might remember back to Sir Francis's death? How old is he, for God's sake?"

"Nearly ninety."

"Let's go," I said, jumping up.

"Hold on. Not like that." Spendwell waved me down again. "He lives with a grandson. They've no telephone, and I don't think we ought to just drop in. People here like to have a little warning when a visitor from another country comes to call."

"I get it."

"You leave everything to me. I'll stop by there this afternoon before Evensong and see how the old man is, and pave the way. Then I'll ring up this evening and tell you what's what."

"Okay. Thanks."

"But I don't think you're going to find out anything very startling."

"Oh, I don't know. I'm always finding things out. I had a very interesting lunch with General Nicholson today, and got an insight into a British businessman that jolted me. It wouldn't surprise me to hear that he votes Labor."

"Not quite." Spendwell grinned. "He's a Tory all right, but an unconventional one. But then, you know, we're always expecting people to fit certain moulds and they are always annoying us by refusing to do so, bulging out here, a little too thin there. The same misconceptions hold for whole countries. I daresay you've found England to be somewhat different from what you expected? And as we know nowadays, even America isn't as white as it has been painted."

I nodded. "Remember what I said when I first met you? You still don't seem vicarish to me. Now go ahead and tell me you're a Communist."

"Oh, gosh no! But I am for Labor, somewhat to the distress of a few members of my parish. A Labor government may have its shortcomings, but it works for the good of the whole country not just a few privileged businessmen. And after all, that's the aim of my Church, too."

"The General seemed to feel that all Englishmen are businessmen, at bottom."

"That's nonsense. What is true, though, is that we've always had a strong sense of community. We've had our share of wicked landlords and cruel, oppressive rulers, of course, but we've also had an enormous number of people in positions of authority who've felt the sense of their responsibility towards the rest of the land. That's why, by and large, the English working man has been more independent than his counterpart elsewhere. It's also why we've had so much respect for the law without being subservient to it, and why we've had comparatively few violent uprisings. I'm not trying to make our history sound bland and peaceful. But we have a high regard for idealism, which has always tempered our stolid practicality."

I couldn't help laughing. "General Nicholson told me that ideals were old-fashioned and that the English have always steered clear of them."

"Really? Did he say that? I think he was pulling your leg, Dave."

"You don't agree with him?"

He leaned against the frame of one of the big windows and looked out at the lane. "I don't really know," he said. "One can't help thinking of that noble speech in *Measure for Measure*: 'They say, best men are moulded out of faults; And for the most, become much more the better for being a little bad.' I think,

151

myself, that sums up our nature as a nation. Do you know what we like best?"

"Beer?"

"Next to beer. Poetry. I don't think there's another country under the sun which has produced so many poets and so many lovers of poetry. Scratch any bloke here, and you'll find a vein of rich affection for nature, a delight in human eccentricity, an appreciation of lovely words. To be a poet is to be an idealist, isn't it? To have a sense that out of a rich tangle of experience one can distill a few drops of a sublime essence."

"Well," I said, clapping him on the arm with a sudden amicable impulse, "whatever you English are, you're surprising."

He glanced at me, with a chuckle. "You *do* mean that as a compliment, don't you?" he said.

The drug store—what they called the chemist's—stood on the corner of Friday Street, just off the market square. The faded gilt sign said, E. A. O. COLLICKE, and I imagined it wouldn't change even after Richter retired. I was interested to note that this was not only a Dispensing but a Photographic Chemist, whatever that meant. Inside, it was like any American drug store except for its gigantic display of candy.

A thin girl in a white coat came up to me and asked if there was anything I wanted. I looked around. I hadn't really planned what I'd do, I just wanted to look at Richter, if possible. At the end of the shop there was a counter set in a partition, and I could see a man on the other side of it doing something with little bottles. To one side of the counter was a penny scales.

"I just want to weigh myself," I said.

I fished out a penny and stood on the scales. They seemed to say that I weighed around twelve pounds, until I remembered that the English used a stone as a unit of weight. I glanced over at the man behind the counter.

"Excuse me," I said. "How do I translate this weight out of stones?"

He looked up, not really seeming to see me at first. His eyes, deep set in a bony face, had a muddy film like that of a stale fish, and, like a fish's, were round and unblinking. His nose was beaky and bony, and the chalky bone pushed out the pale skin of his jaw and cheek. He seemed dried out, all bone and parchment, the soul half out of his body, not quite all there.

He said, with difficulty, "I don't understand. What do you want to translate?"

His accent was not too thick, and his English, in spite of a few slips, was that of a cultured person so that I guessed he had learned it in school, not during his years of living in Heronwick.

I said, slowly, "This scale shows my weight in stones, and I want to figure it out in pounds."

"You are not English," he said.

"That's right. American."

"Fourteen pounds to a stone."

"Thank you." I stepped down. "You're Mr. Richter, aren't you?"

"Yes. Why?"

"Oh, no particular reason," I said, airily. "I've been staying in Heronwick, and I've got some friends. . . . One of them happened to mention you."

He stared at me with sullen suspicion. "Why should anyone mention me?" he said. "Who was it?"

I didn't answer. My eye had fallen on something on the counter, and there were shivers of excitement running up my backbone.

A telephone book lay next to the phone. On it was lettered neatly, in blank ink: PROP OF E.R.

I became aware that he was saying something.

"What?" I said. "I'm sorry, I didn't hear you."

"I asked you who mentioned me." His voice had taken on a shrill tone. He glanced past me at the girl in the shop, and said more softly, "I haven't so many friends. I am curious."

"Oh, I don't know," I said, with my mind still on that marking. "Does it matter? Maybe it was Mrs. Herne. You see a lot of her, don't you?"

"I don't think it's your business," he said, bristling. "Good day to you, sir. I am busy."

"Okay." I leaned my arms on the counter and bent closer to him. "I was just admiring the way you've got your phone book marked with your initials. I've seen a hammer marked just like that."

If it was possible, his dessicated face turned whiter. For a minute, I thought he was going to fall into splinters.

He said, hoarsely, "I don't know . . . what hammer."

I became a little frightened in my turn. After all, I hadn't any right to question this man. Whether he was guilty of anything or not, I was going too far. It wasn't for me to bully him. On the other hand, though, I had already put him on his guard. I pressed on.

"All I want to know is how it came to be up there in the woods, where I found it," I said, very quietly, so the girl couldn't hear me. "Did you drop it when you went to see Mrs. Herne on Sunday night?"

He was silent for such a long time that I thought he had died standing up. Then he said, "Are you police?"

I toyed with the idea of saying yes. But I didn't have the nerve. I shook my head.

"In that case, get out," he said.

"You won't tell me, eh?"

"Out, please. Get out of the shop." His voice was high and edged again. The shop girl was staring at us.

I shrugged. "Okay, Mr. Richter. Goodbye. I suspect we'll see each other again."

I found, when I got outside, that my face was burning. Under any circumstances, it isn't plesant to be ordered out of a place. Still, the hell with him, I thought, he's just wrapping up his own guilt. If he had done nothing, if he had nothing to hide, he'd have been quite open. The very fact that he asked if I were from the police showed that he had something on his mind.

The clock on the Market Hall said five-thirty. I decided to try the police station again, to see if I could find Inspector Codd.

Constable Baker seemed a bit flustered when he saw me. He said hello, and told me to wait for a moment while he went to find out if Codd could see me. I suspected that he might be feeling the strain of having a Dectective Inspector on his neck.

Codd was at the desk in the office poring over a litter of papers and photographs. He looked up abstractedly.

"Nothing wrong, I hope, Mr. Cannon," he said.

"Not so's you'd notice. On the contrary, I think I've got a piece of information for you."

"Yes?"

"I know who that hammer belongs to."

"Do you?" he said. He pushed his chair back and eyed me keenly. "Do you indeed?"

I sat down, feeling smug. "It belongs to the village druggist—chemist, I mean."

"Is that so?"

"The marking on it stands for Property of E. Richter."

He frowned. "Richter?"

"He's a German, a former prisoner of war who became a British citizen. I'll tell you something else. He

155

went to Herne House on Sunday night, and dropped the hammer on his way home."

"I see."

"He told Sarah, the maid, that he had come to bring Mrs. Herne some medicine."

"That doesn't sound so improbable, does it?"

"No? He came to the front door with his medicine, and part of it was this hammer. Doesn't that sound odd? And then he didn't leave by the front door, which is even odder."

"How do you know?"

"Well, for God's sake—he dropped the hammer in the stream, so he must have gone home down the back way, through the woods."

"Ah, yes. Very logical. And you are certain he was actually carrying the hammer with him that night?"

I hesitated. "Well, no. Not certain. But he must have been."

"Why must he?"

I floundered. "Inspector, when I asked him about it, he looked guilty. He was hiding something. And why was he searching for the hammer Tuesday morning if he didn't drop it Sunday night?"

Codd pinched his lip. "You're being over-zealous, Mr. Cannon. Why didn't he search for it Monday morning, in that case?" He shook his head. "Let me ask you something. Do you think he might have committed the murder with that hammer?"

"I guess something like that was in my mind."

"The murder was done on Monday. If he brought the hammer with him Sunday night, and lost it on the way home, and was still looking for it *Tuesday* morning . . ."

"Okay," I said, sheepishly. "So I'm over-zealous."

"Besides," he went on, "the hammer was not the murder weapon."

156

"Oh? How do you know?"

"I've had a report from the Forensic Lab. In the first place, there is no trace of blood, or skin, or anything like that on the thing—well, of course we didn't expect to find much after it had been in the water. There *are* some fingerprints on it. Yours."

"Mine? Oh, well, sure, I picked it up."

"Exactly," he said, grimly. "That's one of the reasons I warned you not to play at being a detective."

I suddenly had difficulty swallowing.

"In any case, the blow that killed Neville was not delivered by a hammer. The head of a hammer would have made a quite different sort of wound. Neville's wound was produced by a blunt, round object, like the head of a walking stick, for instance, or a club of some sort."

"I had an idea about—" I began.

He held up a hand to stop me. "I know. Constable Baker told me. I gave him permission to look around the house, and he found a—what d'you call it?—a morning star, hanging with some other antique weapons on the upstairs landing. A round iron ball on a short chain, attached to a staff. Very ingenious of you both. We sent it to Forensic, and there are traces of human blood on it."

"Aha!" I cried.

"Aha? You're not thinking. Don't you remember that Neville's wound didn't bleed—at least, not until after he'd fallen? Anyway, they tell me this blood has been on the morning star for a long, long time. The relic of some ancient battle, I suppose. But there are no recent fingerprints, only dust. Sarah's not a particularly good housekeeper, I should think."

"Oh." I felt like a fool. "Well, it seemed like a good idea at the time."

"Yes. But," he continued, sternly, "what is not a good idea is your interviewing witnesses."

"I don't get you. What do you mean?"

He tapped a piece of paper on the desk. I had thought he was doodling, but obviously he'd been making notes, for he replied, "A moment ago you said, 'When I asked him about it, he looked guilty.' That was Mr. Richter, eh?"

Oh-oh, I thought, here's where I get the works.

But instead of scolding me, Codd sat back in his chair and passed his hand over his eyes. In a despairing sort of way, he began to laugh.

"Do you know," he said, "that you're driving me up the wall? As if I didn't have enough on my mind—! You're leaving me with only two alternatives, Mr. Cannon, either to lock you up or—or to encourage you to join the police force. I don't want to do either."

He folded his hands. "Look here, I like you. And you can be very useful to the police. But not this way. You've got no right whatsoever to walk into a man's shop and question him."

"I know. I'm sorry about that. But I did find out that it was his hammer. I found that out without questioning him, anyway, because I saw the words written on his phone book. But then I just couldn't keep my big mouth shut."

"You've got to learn to keep your big mouth shut. If you had any suspicions, you should have come to me at once."

"It wasn't as concrete as a suspicion. I didn't begin to think he owned that hammer. I just found out from something Sarah said—"

"And you were questioning Sarah as well? Really—!"

"Now wait a minute," I interrupted. "Are you telling me I'm not allowed to talk to anybody? For Christ's sake, am I supposed to go around like a Trappist monk? Anyway, I didn't question Sarah. I overheard her."

"I see. Where and when?"

I told him about the conversation in the Falcon. When I had finished, he looked considerably mollified.

"Now that's very interesting," he said. "She said nothing further—no hint about what Lionel Herne's difficulty might have been?"

"No. I asked General Nicholson about it, but all he could suggest was that maybe Richter had supplied something to produce an abortion when Lionel got a girl pregnant."

"Hm. On the other hand, it may not have been anything illegal at all. I shall have to have a word with Sarah. And you say Richter was a prisoner of war who elected to stay on in England?"

"That's right."

"It will be easy to check up on him. It wouldn't be very bright of him to get mixed up in anything illegal. It may be nothing important. Women like Sarah sometimes like to pretend to an awful and mysterious knowledge to impress their friends. In any case, for the love of heaven, Mr. Cannon, don't talk to Richter again. Stay away from him. If he is somehow involved in this affair, I don't want to make him nervous."

"Okay. But I'll tell you something else. There was a connection between Neville and Richter, one that might have some bearing."

"Yes?"

"Some years ago, Richter gave Neville a job. Something happened—I don't know what—but Neville gave Richter a beating."

"Revenge? Dear me, if so, Richter waited a frightfully long time, didn't he?"

"People can do, Inspector," I said.

"Don't misunderstand me," he said, gravely. "I know it very well indeed. It's only that I feel your imagination needs a rein."

"Oh, hell!" I said, getting up. "I can't do anything right, as far as you're concerned."

"Not true. You've been a help, perhaps more than you realize. Just stick to the proper channels, will you?"

He stood up, too, and shook hands warmly. "I haven't said it before, perhaps. Many thanks."

He could be most disarming.

I was reading a science-fiction paperback in my room, about nine that night, with only half my mind on it, when Mrs. Davies called up the stairwell, "Someone to see you, Mr. Cannon."

I went lazily down, only mildly curious. It couldn't be the Vicar because he had phoned up not fifteen minutes before to say that we would go together to visit old Mr. Savory tomorrow afternoon. It might be Jeffrey Parr, I thought, and I had just about settled that that was who it was, when I got to the bottom of the steps and found Richter waiting for me.

"Oh," I said, stupidly. "It's you."

"I want to talk to you, Mr. Cannon," he said. "Please excuse me if I came here."

"Nothing doing," I said, remembering Inspector Codd's warning. But I couldn't help adding, "What did you want to talk to me about?"

"Can we go upstairs?" He glanced around, even though we were alone. The stairs ended in a passage near the back door, quite remote from the bars.

I thought to myself, This will be just dandy if Codd comes back and decides to drop in and talk to me. "Come on," I said.

In my room, I locked the door to be on the safe side. Richter sat on the edge of the straight chair, lacing and unlacing his fingers, the hollows of his bony face dark with shadow.

"Well?" I said. "What can I do for you?"

"I came to apologize." He tried to smile. "It was not very polite of me to speak to you as I did. Particularly as you're an American. I have great admiration for the Americans."

"That's news that will cheer Washington," I said. I didn't mean to be nasty, but I couldn't help remembering how I'd felt being thrown out of his store. And besides, I kept listening for Codd's footsteps in the hall.

He said, with sudden desperation, "You asked me a question. I would like to answer it. I understand that you are very friendly with the detective who is here making some investigations, and I thought, I don't want to get into any trouble. So, just between ourselves, I thought I will tell you what you want to know."

I was puzzled, but I tried not to show it. "All right," I said. "But why? Why not tell whatever it is to Inspector Codd himself?"

"Why did you come to my shop, instead of the Inspector?" he asked.

"It just happened that way."

"We don't have to beat around the bush," he said. "I have heard about everything. Some people think you killed Charlie. Or if not, that you are in some difficulties about his death and that you are trying to put the blame on some other people in Heronwick. Isn't that true?"

I nodded.

"All right. So you go around and ask a few questions, maybe to find out the guilty one, and establish your innocence. In a village like this, Mr. Cannon, there is all sorts of talk and gossip. It doesn't take long to find out what is going on. That's how I know. You see?"

"Okay. But I still don't understand why you don't

go to the Inspector. Unless you have a guilty conscience, maybe."

He bit his lip. "I have no guilty conscience. I don't want any trouble. I don't want to have anything to do with the police."

He raised his eyes, suddenly. "You don't understand? I'm a foreigner here. I became a British subject years ago, but that makes no difference, I am still a bloody foreigner. I will be a bloody foreigner until the day I die. Maybe after that, they will remember me as an English citizen, not a German. To them, this is funny. To me it isn't funny. All my life, the police will know about me and keep one eye on me."

"Why don't you get out of here, then?" I said.

"And go back to Germany? If only I could. I dream about it. I think about it, often. But—"

He had been speaking feverishly, and he stopped suddenly. "I can't," he said. "There is nothing for me there. Here, at least, I have a good job and a house of my own. I have been twenty years in this country, most of the time in this village. It's too long. Anyway, I can't."

This all seemed very evasive to me, but I nodded again. "Go on."

"You are an American, Mr. Cannon," he said. "I can talk to you, because of that. I can tell you all this. In your country you don't know about such things. And I thought—"

"What?"

"Maybe then you can tell the detective to let me alone."

"I? What makes you think I carry any weight with him?"

"I don't know if that's so or not. I only suggest. You can explain to him how it is, that you made a mistake—"

"Wait just a minute. Are you saying that it wasn't your hammer?"

"No, no. It was. But there was nothing complicated —what is it?—no complicity with the murder. Nothing like that."

"Why'd you go to see Mrs. Herne Sunday night?"

"She telephoned me to bring her some sleeping pills. She has arthritis very badly and sometimes cannot get to sleep. That was the only reason I went."

"What about the hammer?"

"But that was a different time," he said, shrilly.

"Sh! For heaven's sake, keep your voice down," I snapped.

"It was another time," he repeated, more quietly. "Charlie had some repairs to make on a bridge over the stream, in the park. He borrowed my hammer and then he told me later that he had lost it."

"That's interesting. You were on such good terms that he'd borrow a hammer from you? I heard that he once beat the hell out of you."

"That was long ago, Mr. Cannon. Five years. We were not on good terms, no, not friendly but not unfriendly either. But sometimes he would seem to be friendly and then he would do something wicked, something vicious, you know? That's how he was."

"I can believe that."

"Ah," he said, with evident relief, "you see? That was why he told me he lost the hammer. I suppose he threw it away. He told me it fell in the water. I once looked for it, but couldn't find it."

"So then you suddenly decided to go back on Tuesday and look again? Or wasn't it you I saw in the mist that morning?"

"It was you, that morning? Of course, you said so, didn't you, in my shop? But why are you surprised that I went back? Charlie was killed on Monday. They said he was hit on the head with a blunt instrument. It was in the newspapers. I was afraid. . . ."

His voice trailed off and he shrugged, but I understood what he meant.

"Well, I can't say I blame you," I admitted.

"It is true. You believe me?"

"I guess so, yes."

He sighed and seemed to relax a trifle. "I am glad," he said. "And you will speak to the detective?"

I lit a cigarette to cover my embarrassment. How was I going to explain to Richter that I wasn't supposed to be talking to him in the first place?

"Mr. Richter," I said, "you've got an exaggerated idea of my influence. Inspector Codd won't listen to me. Your story's perfectly straightforward and puts you in the clear. All you have to do is go to him and openly and honestly tell him the whole thing. It's the best thing you can do."

He sprang up. "You said you would talk to him."

"No, I didn't. What the hell do you mean?"

"But you did. I heard you. You promised you would say you had made a mistake," he cried.

"You're out of your head."

"I? I am out of my head? You—boy scout! You think everything is easy if you go to the police. They'll twist whatever I say. They'll make me guilty whatever I've done or said. They'll beat it out of me. You Americans, you think the world is made of sugar candy and—and money. For you it is. For you everything is easy."

His eyes bulged. His skin was like paper. A line of moisture, like a glued seam, ran down his cheek. All I could think of was Codd, arriving suddenly and hearing the commotion. I strode over and unlocked the door and threw it wide.

"You'd better get out of here," I said, sharply. "That detective you're so afraid of has a room down the hall. He'll be home any minute, and he's going to find you here."

164

That silenced him. He wiped his face with his sleeve.

I said, "I'll do what I can. If I can manage it, I'll talk to Inspector Codd. But I don't think it'll do much good."

He walked past me, and turned in the dim hall with his face so close to mine that I could smell his fetid, frightened breath.

"If something happens," he said. "If something happens to me, it will be your fault. Remember that."

He went down the stairs.

I could have kicked myself. Why, when I had the chance, hadn't I asked him about Lionel? Why hadn't I asked about their curious friendship—about lots of things? But I hung there, hesitating, afraid of meeting Codd. At last, I ran down the stairs, but the lower passage was empty. I threw open the back door and looked out. There was no sign of him, or of anybody.

I stood there in the doorway with the light from the passage behind me, smelling the fresh cool air and listening to the babble of noise from the other side of the house. That poor bastard, I thought, I wonder what kind of a life he has here? According to General Nicholson, he kept pretty much to himself. Who would be his friends, aside from Lionel? What had he done, in twenty years, except grow older? But I was probably making this all up: maybe he had plenty of friends, and didn't want to jeopardize his relationship with them by getting tangled up in a murder case. I knew nothing about him, nothing about any of them here. And as I thought that, a wave of loneliness rolled over me. "A bloody foreigner," Richter had said. I stood looking out at the darkness like an exile, wishing I were home again.

Something rushed past my face. There was a loud bang, and a ringing clatter. I ducked back without thinking.

After a moment of lurking behind the door, I felt brave enough to come out. There was a horseshoe lying on the stone step. It had hit the door frame and splintered a chunk out of the wood. I picked it up. On it, in chalk, was crudely printed GOODBYE YANK.

Somebody else wished I were home again.

10

I said nothing about the horseshoe, just tossed it over my shoulder for luck. But somebody must have talked about it, because shortly before I left for Herne House next morning, Brock appeared at the Goat. He came out of the public bar as I was debating whether to take the car because of the rain. He was wearing a heavy raincoat and a cloth cap which gave him a sinister appearance.

"I've got something to say to you," he began.

I edged away slightly. But I reminded myself that he must have been talking to Mr. Davies in the bar, and if he meant to start trouble Davies would have gotten wind of it and called the cops.

"What's on your mind?" I said. "I've got to go out. I have an appointment in ten minutes."

"Won't take long. I hear somebody tried to cosh you with a horseshoe last night."

I looked levelly at him. "Is that so? I wonder who told you. A little bird?"

"Maybe. And maybe the chap as done it."

"So?"

"I come to tell you that it wasn't me. I don't throw things at chaps in the dark. And I've told some others that whatever they may think, I won't have it. They shan't give you any more trouble."

I said, in astonishment, "I'm not sure I understand, but thanks."

He gave a nod. "You're a good sport, you are," he said. "You hit a six for us, didn't you? Leave it at that."

He jammed his hands into his raincoat pockets and left without another word.

I thought about him as I drove over to Herne House, and wished he didn't seem to be so deeply involved with the murder. With his stony quality, he reminded me of New England farmers I knew, old-timers like Ike Bell and Will Paley whom you could know all your life without being sure they liked you, but who suddenly turned open-handed and warm when there was an emergency and you needed help. I was struck by the idea that just because a man was a murderer he needn't necessarily be unlikeable. It seems obvious, but until now, when I was mixed up in this affair myself, it had just never occurred to me. I didn't know what reasons Brock might have—assuming that he actually *was* the murderer—but maybe they had been good ones, even "good" in a moral sense. How could I tell?

Mrs. Herne was waiting for me in the library. Everything was back to normal. The police were gone, and the house was as chilly and hollowly empty as before, even more so with the rain dripping from the eaves and gurgling in the gutters. She had a fire going in the fireplace, though, and in spite of the greyness the room was almost cheerful. The manuscript lay on the desk, for I had told her on the phone that I was prepared to make an offer for it.

As usual, she didn't bother to shake hands, so I didn't. She seemed colder and more distant today, as if borrowing from the chill of the house, and she wore an iron-grey tweed suit with a hard, unrelenting look to it.

"Sit down, please, won't you?" she said. She herself took the chair behind the desk, upright, with her hands in her lap, and waited.

"I've had a cablegram from my partner," I began, rapidly reviewing in my mind my strategy: an offer, some objections, counter-offer maybe, then I'd up it to the next figure, and so on, bearing in mind that my absolute top was about £2,700. "I must explain that while we are very interested in the manuscript indeed, there are some things about it, as I've already told you, which reduce its value for us. It has no illustrations and no initial letters, even the calligraphy isn't terribly distinguished."

I was watching her closely, naturally, but what I said didn't seem to have any effect on her. Her face remained calm and closed. Something queer happened to me. My first impulse was of irritation, and I decided that I'd start at the lowest possible figure, say a thousand pounds. And I heard myself saying, "Naturally, I'd like to be fair. The manuscript has great historical value for me, and I'd like very much to have it, so I'm going to make the best offer I can to avoid bargaining. I'll give you twenty-seven hundred and fifty pounds."

Inside my head began screaming and rocketing around: What the hell's the matter with you, have you gone nuts? I cried. And I also thought, damn her, this proud, stubborn old bitch expects to be treated like an aristocrat and she deserves it.

She didn't twitch an eyelid. She said, coolly, "I

never haggle, Mr. Cannon, so it's as well we under-stand each other. Your offer seems quite generous. Frankly, it is more than I expected. I accept."

She said this as if she were conferring a knighthood on me. I had been holding my breath, and I let it out in a puff of relief.

"Good! It's a deal. Now, about payment. What's your bank?"

"I have an account at the West Country Bank in Newent."

"Newent? Okay, I'll cable my partner to have the money transferred to me by cablegram at once, in care of your bank. As soon as the draft arrives, which shouldn't take more than twenty-four hours, I'll en-dorse it over to you and you can then give me the manuscript. I'll prepare a proper receipt, for you to sign. Is that all right?"

"Yes, that seems quite all right."

I stood up. "Fine. I'd better be off, so that I can get to the post office and send my cable. I'll have to see your bank manager, as well, and set the thing up. Per-haps you wouldn't mind phoning him to tell him I'm coming?"

"I will do that." She rose, and stood silent for a mo-ment, as if hesitating, and then she said, "There is one other matter."

I waited.

"It may be difficult for you to understand this, Mr. Cannon," she went on, "but in a village like ours we resent interference in our affairs from outsiders. I have not quite the position I once had, but I still feel a certain responsibility for the people. This is particu-larly the case when they complain to me."

"Who's been complaining? And about what?"

"About you, I'm sorry to say. As for who it was, I don't think that's of the slightest consequence. But I have been told by a certain person that you have been persecuting him, making threats, saying that you will set the police after him. I have been very reluctant to raise this question with you, but I see no alternative. The person who spoke to me may, possibly, have been exaggerating—he is sometimes prone to nervous behavior. You will, of course, know best whether there is any truth to the matter. But I must ask you to be extremely careful not to meddle, especially where so grave a situation as this is concerned."

I had been growing progressively angrier as she talked. I even thought, for a minute, of calling the manuscript deal off. But the very notion, coming into my head, calmed me. The thing was mine now, and I was going to pay a hell of a lot of money for it. I counted ten and simmered down. I didn't want to say anything rash that might make her call the whole thing off, either.

"I suspect you're talking about Mr. Richter," I said, trying to match her icy manner with a chill of my own. "I don't know what he's told you, but he came to my room last night and tried to persuade me to keep the police away from him. Naturally, I can't do that. He got hysterical and ran off. If he's done anything wrong, that's his problem—the police will catch up with him sooner or later.

"You seem to think this affair is none of my business. Unfortunately, the police have made it my business by keeping me under suspicion. Richter knows best why he thought it necessary to come to see me. I don't intend to meddle, as you call it. In this case, the meddling was thrust on me. I hope that makes things clearer."

"Yes, it does," she replied, with surprising temperateness. "He did not make it plain that he went to see you. However, you must make allowances for Mr. Richter. He feels strongly that he is an alien and lets it prey on his mind. I am, perhaps, overly concerned since I acted as his reference when he wanted to become a citizen. I therefore have a more than casual sense of being answerable for him."

"I can see that," I said. "And it's certainly very good of you."

"I regret that you should have been disturbed," she said, stiffly, which was a pretty handsome apology, for her. "I shall speak to Mr. Richter. However, I should be grateful if you would keep away from him. He is, as I said, nervous and easily upset."

I could do nothing but agree.

Newent was five or six miles away, a rather drab market town. I found the bank and went up to one of the tellers to ask if I could see the manager. The teller was a young man with thick glasses, and he nodded at me in a friendly fashion.

"I know you, don't I?" I said. "Of course—you're Lucy's brother."

"That's right."

"Your name's Alan, isn't it? I'm sorry, after all we only met for a short time and the light wasn't so good in that pub. Anyway, I'm afraid I was looking at your sister most of the time."

He grinned. "Most people do."

"And you work here, do you?"

"I'm working my way up to be a manager. Father doesn't altogether approve—"

"Why? He wanted you to go into the army, eh?"

"Oh, no. But I think he rather hoped I'd go into industry, perhaps into his factory. He says he'd rather have me handling my own money than other people's."

"Yeah, that sounds like the General. I had a great lunch with him yesterday. He's a terrific guy."

"He is rather terrific," Alan said, with an inflection that gave it a slightly different meaning. "Well, what

172

can I do for you? Did you want to cash a traveller's cheque?"

I told him I wanted to see the manager, and Alan went and fetched him from the office in the rear, a gaunt, stooped, defeated-looking man with an accent so fearfully genteel that you wondered how he had ever sunk so low as to manage a bank.

When I had explained what I wanted, he mumbled, "Ah, yes, definiteleah. Mrs. Herne rang up. . . . . Two thousand, seven hundred, fifty pounds. Quayte a lot of moneh. Howevah, Ay think we can handle the matter for you, Mr. Er."

"Cannon."

"Exactleah. If you will ring us up tomorrow afternoon, Ay shall inform you whethah we have received the cable transfer. And if you would be good enough to bring your passport or some similar identification, Mr. Ah . . ."

"It shouldn't take more than a day. If the money hasn't arrived by tomorrow, are you open Saturday?"

"Oh, quayte, quayte. But in view of the circumstances . . . such a lot of moneh, Mrs. Herne an old and valued customer, your wishing to conclude your business. . . . You may ring me at any time Saturday up to one o'clock. Ay shall do my best to—ah—grease the wheels, ha, ha," he concluded, with the saddest laugh I had ever heard.

"Great. Many thanks."

"Goodbye, Mr. Um," he moaned.

I shook his soggy hand. "Goodbye, Mr. Er," I said.

I drove down to Ross and sent off the cablegram, and had bread and cheese and beer in a pub overlooking the River Wye, now leaden-colored and spotted with rain. When at last I got back to Heronwick, it was time for my appointment with the Vicar. I left the car at his house and we walked to a row of tiny cottages, primly Gothic in the Victorian manner, each with its bit of garden in front neatly marked off with stones or shells. A short, red-faced old man was working on his knees in one of the gardens without regard to the drizzle, and as we came up the path he got painfully to his feet and squinted at us out of pale eyes, the color of well-washed bluejeans.

"Good afternoon, Mr. Savory," Spendwell said. "Isn't it rather wet to be working out of doors?"

"Not a bit of it," retorted the old man. "The plants flourish in it, and so shall I."

I stared at him, for he didn't look to be nearly ninety by a long shot.

"I've brought Mr. Cannon along to see you," said Spendwell.

"Oh, the gentleman from America. Pleased to meet you, sir," Mr. Savory said, and then he did something I had read about but never thought I'd see—he touched a finger to his forehead, and made a little bob at me. The gesture put him suddenly back at the beginning of the century.

"Come inside, sir," he said, "and you, Vicar. I'll just mend the fire and we'll sit down, for it's plain to see you two young gentlemen can't abide to stand talking in the rain."

His cottage, with its scrap of a living room and its kitchen tacked on at the back, seemed too small for the three people who lived there: the old man, his grandson, and his grandson's wife. The two young ones, Spendwell had told me, had jobs and the old man was left to fend for himself all day, which was worrisome because, although he seemed very hale to me, he was apt suddenly to get very shaky and had had two heart attacks. "But if they didn't both work, they'd never manage to make ends meet, you see. They go off every morning never knowing whether they're going to find him at home or in hospital, in the evening. Thank heaven for the National Health.

174

When Mr. Savory was a young man, working people didn't dare fall ill unless they planned to die," Spendwell had said.

Mr. Savory poked the fire and put a lump or two of coal carefully on top. "Have you ever tasted rhubarb wine?" he asked me.

"No, I can't say I have."

"You must have a drop of mine. I make it myself," he said, and got a South African sherry bottle and three very small glasses from the kitchen. The stuff looked like South African sherry which had been out in the sun too long, and had a sticky taste that discouraged tippling. "Tastes like cough linctus, hey? Ah, but you'd be surprised how sloshed you can get on a few glasses," Mr. Savory grinned.

When we were all comfortable, so close together that our knees almost touched, and Mr. Savory's damp clothes were giving off a ripe fume from the heat, he said, "Now, then, sir, the Vicar tells me you're interested in the old days. History, like, would it be?"

"Not exactly, Mr. Savory," I said. "I'm curious about the Herne family, and especially about Sir Francis Herne."

The old man gave a knowing wink. "Yes, family trees and that. I've met many Americans and they have all gone wandering up and down the land looking for their ancestors. One of my sons is in America. In the county of Wisconsin, would that be right?"

"Oh, yes. We'd call it a state."

"He is in a city called Madison, a good long way off. Well, how can I help you?"

"Can you tell me about Sir Francis Herne and his brother, Alastair?"

"That I can. I remember them both. There's not much I've forgot in spite of my age. How old would you take I to be?"

"You look like a man of sixty to me."

"He beamed. "I'm eighty-seven year old, that's what I am. And most of my life I've lived here in Heronwick." He pronounced it *Hernick*. "Not that I 'aven't seen a bit of the world, as well. I were in France in 1916, what do you think of that, hey? Wounded on the Somme I was, and then when they sent I back to action I drove a lorry for two years more without a scratch until it was all over. And what do you think was in the lorry? Why, ammunition!"

I laughed dutifully, and said, "Now, about Sir Alastair. What sort of man was he?"

"A good sort," Mr. Savory said, clicking his false teeth meditatively. "A fine man he was, if a bit short-tempered. Oh, he had been a bit wild, but he sobered later. I ought to know, for I worked at the 'ouse. Kitchen boy, I was then. They was fifteen in service, though you mightn't believe it today. Two cooks, myself, two chambermaids, a butler, footman, coachman and groom, four gardeners—"

"And you liked Sir Alastair, did you?"

"—game keeper, and gate keeper. Is that right? Fifteen, that is. Like him? Dear me, sir, it weren't for me to like or dislike the gentry. Things was different then, from what they are today. But he were a proper gentleman, kind and open-handed. I weren't a scullion by that time, of course."

"What do you mean?" I asked, slightly confused.

"Why, I had become footman, after Fisher was let go. That would be in 1895 when Sir Francis was killed falling down the stairs, and although I were only sixteen I were promoted because I were a good-looking boy, if short. I was taller then; I have shrunk down."

He chuckled, and poured himself another little glass of rhubarb wine. He offered some to me, but I only shuddered. Spendwell said, gently, "I think Mr.

Cannon would like to hear about Sir Francis, Mr. Savory. How he died, for instance. Do you remember?"

"Do I not? I remember everything, Vicar. They say when you get old you forget, but not me. I can remember the old queen, God bless her, when she came to Gloucester, and I went there up behind Sir Alastair. No, don't get into a flap, sir, I 'aven't forgotten what you asked. How Sir Francis died.

"He was forced to sit in a wheelchair, you know, couldn't move about much except by main effort when he heaved himself from the chair to his bed, look. He was strong in the arms. I didn't see much of him, in the scullery where I was, only now and then when Fisher might wheel him in the garden. He had been a fine gentleman in his time, a proper man for hounds and horses, until one day he took a toss and that put an end to his hounding and his horsing. By the time I come to work in the house, he spent most of his days in his study reading his books. And many hundreds of those he had, all sorts, more than the county library. While below stairs, maybe things got a bit slack.

"Let me see, now, Sir Alastair came down from London—of course he wasn't Sir Alastair then but plain Mr. Herne—and didn't things change! He were a proper gentleman, as I've told you, but strict and wanted things just so, and he made us all jump. Said the house had been going to rack and ruin, since Sir Francis could not keep after the servants and there wasn't no Lady Herne then. He soon made things hum, that he did.

"He looked after his brother, too, wheeled him about the garden or took him driving in the dog-cart, and saw to his needs. One thing, he had a frightful temper, just like his father, old Sir Timothy, and if anything wasn't to his liking he would fly out in a rage so that everyone ran for shelter. Worse than the German field guns. That's how it was on the day of the accident, I can tell you."

"Yes, well, what exactly happened that day?" I asked.

"Well, sir, I were scouring some pot or other, and Mrs. Pocket, that was the second cook, was telling I to get on with it, when suddenly there come a tremendous crash and clatter that shook the whole place. *'Lord a mercy!'* Mrs. Pocket shrieked out, and, as for me, I couldn't think what it was but it seemed to come from the hall. I ran out through the passage and there what did I see, right at my feet almost? Why, the first thing I thought was that there had been a smash-up of a carraige. That's how it looked. Then I made out it was the wheelchair with Sir Francis underneath of it and not far off one of the wheels still rattling on the floor."

He paused, his lips squeezed together, frowning. "I was struck all of a heap. I couldn't move at all, for a minute. And then from up above-stairs, on the landing, Mr. Herne shouted out, *'What has happened? My God, he has fallen down the stair! Who's that?'* he cried. *'Savory?'* He come running down to me. *'Did you see it?'* he asks me. I could do nothing but gape at him like a fish out of water. *'A horrible accident,'* he says. *'Run, boy, to the village and fetch the doctor.'* Off I went like a shot. All I wanted was to get away from there. I couldn't bear to look at Sir Francis lying there, his face all a welter of blood, and blood on the stairs and floor."

He shook his head, with a sigh. "Not so very long after, sir, I were to see worse sights, enough to sicken a butcher. But I were young, then, and I'd never seen a man dead except my old grandfather what died peaceful in his bed."

"What happened then?" I asked. "Did the police come?"

"Police?" He opened his pale eyes wide at me. "Whatever for? Why, it was clear enough what happened. The wheel had come off Sir Francis's chair and pitched him over. Sir Alastair was ready to burst. I told you what a temper he had. It was Fisher's job—he was the footman—to keep the chair in good order, and once a week he used to take the wheels off and grease the hubs. Sir Alastair said it was clear he had botched putting one of them back, and sacked him on the spot. Said he should be grateful he wasn't being tried for murder as well. It was a mercy that's all he done, for the kind of man he was I shouldn't have been surprised if he'd horsewhipped Fisher as well."

He yawned, all at once, and leaned back in his chair.

"Perhaps we'd better be going," the Vicar said, softly. "We don't want to tire you, Mr. Savory."

"Tire me?" The old man's eyes snapped open. "It would take more than a little talking to tire me, Vicar. These young kids nowadays 'aven't got no staying power, but not I, sir."

I put in quickly, "I'm sure of that, Mr. Savory. But we have to go anyway. I—er—I have an appointment. I'd just like to ask you one more question. Was Sir Francis in the habit of wheeling himself around alone? I thought you said Alastair always pushed him."

"Oh, no, sir. Only when they went out. Why, for years before Sir Alastair come down from London, Sir Francis wheeled himself about. To go up or down stairs he was carried, but he did not like to be treated as if he was helpless."

"I see." Spendwell was waggling his eyebrows at me to signal that the old man had had enough.

"Thank you very much, Mr. Savory. This has been very interesting."

"Happy to oblige you, sir, I'm sure," he replied, faintly. His eyes had closed again. We softly let ourselves out of the house and left him dozing.

We had to run, for the drizzle had turned into a patter of rain. At the vicarage, Spendwell put the kettle on and we sat at the kitchen table and had some tea.

"He's quite a lad," Spendwell said. "These old people have a way of surprising one with their toughness. Fancy his gardening in this weather. Well, what do you think? Was it of any use to you?"

"I'm not sure. Mostly, I'm not sure because I don't know exactly what I'm trying to find out."

"You said you wanted some background on the Hernes."

"What I think I'm looking for is a motive. Some reason why someone would want to have killed Neville. Right?"

"I don't see what that has to do with the death of Sir Francis. That happened three-quarters of a century ago. . . ."

"And in another country, and besides the wench is dead. Okay, but listen. Suppose Alastair murdered his brother. Suppose he fixed the wheel so it would come off, and that's why the footman was fired so fast—to throw up a cloud of dust, to cover Alastair. Maybe that's why Mr. Savory was promoted, even though he was only sixteen, and short."

"I don't understand. How would that follow?"

"Alastair may have thought the kid had some suspicions, and this would distract his attention. The excitement of becoming a footman might make him forget anything odd or unusual he might have seen. It looks funny to me that Alastair should have been right up there on the landing and should have rushed

180

out yelling that it was a horrible accident practically the minute it happened."

"Not at all, Dave." Spendwell shook his head vigorously. "I don't agree. If he had loosened the wheel, I should think he'd want to be in a different part of the house. What's more, supposing he had loosened the wheel, what guarantee would he have that it would come off just when Sir Frances was conveniently at the head of the stair? It might have fallen off in the library, for instance, where no particular harm would have been done."

"Mm. True. But—oh, what the hell, let's just leave it that there might have been something fishy to that wheel business, and that somehow Alastair did knock his brother off. He had a violent temper. Maybe he needed money and got tired of waiting for Francis to die. He wanted the estate, and hated and resented his crippled brother. That would be his motive."

"I don't know that I go along with you, but all right, let's assume so. What of it?"

"What I'm getting at is this: what if this was a family secret? Suppose only Mrs. Herne knew it? And somehow Neville found out about it and blackmailed her, so she picked up something heavy and let him have it, right in the head."

Spendwell stared at me. Then he sputtered, "You're not serious, Dave? But that's absurd!"

I was a little hurt. "Why? Far-fetched, maybe, but why absurd?"

"But my dear old Sherlock, just *think*. What earthly use would Neville's blackmailing Mrs. Herne over such a matter do him? Suppose he somehow found out this dark secret, that Sir Alastair had murdered his brother to secure the inheritance? It wouldn't make *her* guilty. I don't see how it could affect her, except perhaps by causing some embarrassment."

"But since she's so proud, maybe that would be enough."

"I hardly think so. Her pride rests on her lineage, and that would be unchanged."

"Even if her father were a murderer?"

"I think there's really very little chance of that part of it being true, Dave. Even though the police may not have come into it, a doctor would have seen what the case was and if he certified death by misadventure I think there'd be no reason to doubt it. Even Mr. Savory, who was on the spot, was certain it was an accident. There may have been rumors, but a rumor in a village is like another egg in a chicken house. I don't see how Alastair could possibly have arranged it so that the wheel would come off at just the right moment to spill his brother down the stairs, and I'm sure everyone else there would have thought the same. Or even if he had so arranged it, how could he have been certain that the fall would kill Francis? I mean, people do fall downstairs without killing themselves, don't they?

"Besides, there's another reason Mrs. Herne couldn't possibly have killed Neville as you suggested, by picking up something heavy and hitting him with it."

"What's that?"

"Haven't you noticed that she never shakes hands?"

I thought back. "That's right."

"She can't grip anything with her right hand. Only the thumb and forefinger move. The other three fingers—she was in Bristol, once, during one of the bad raids of the war, and the tendons were severed by broken glass. We were talking of her pride, remember? She won't hold out a hand with nerveless fingers to anyone."

I sighed. "I see what you mean. She'd rather be

182

thought rude, eh? You've got to give her credit. She's got spirit, all right."

"The human skull's an awful hard nut to crack, Dave. No, I'm afraid even if she were strong enough, she'd need all her fingers. That idea won't do. But then the whole story's rather flimsy, isn't it? Alastair must have been able to establish his claim to the title, so the accidental death of his brother must have been fairly plain."

"I guess so. But I still remember Mrs. Herne going on about how things would have been different in her father's day, and how he'd have made short work of any policeman in the house. I can't help thinking there's something phoney about Francis's death. I'll bet a competent, hard-boiled character like Alastair would have known how to handle local cops and doctors. . . . All right. I won't press it. Maybe you're right. I'm just not cut out to be a detective. And it was always one of my youthful ambitions, too."

"Really? Is that what you wanted to be? Not a driver on an express train?"

"Oh, sure, that too. Everybody wanted to be either an engine driver, a cowboy, or a detective. We had a gang called the ICE—stands for Inner Circle of Eyes. We used to prowl around at night looking for clues."

"What sort of clues?"

"Anything. Footprints, mysterious notes, daggers covered with blood. The idea was, first you found the clues and then you discovered the crime. It hasn't changed with kids, either. The Davies' boy, Ted, loaned me a comic book with a big article in it about the secrets of famous criminals, and suggested that I use him as a helper. But I can't think of anything he could do for me."

Spendwell laughed. "My own ambition was different. Oh, naturally, at first I wanted to drive a steam locomotive, and I toyed for a while with the idea of becoming a Field Marshal. But then I dreamed of being an organist in a cinema theater."

"An organist? Was that so beautiful?"

"I wanted to come rising slowly out of the pit, seated at the console of an immense organ with the spotlight shining on me, and I'd turn and smile at the audience and run my fingers lightly and deftly over all those thousands of keys, while everyone listened spellbound. It seemed like the most magnificent thing one could do."

"You were power-mad. You wanted to control a giant machine and a big audience."

"No doubt about it." He glanced at his watch. "I'm sorry, Dave. I've got to leave you. As a poor, downtrodden parson, I'm now controlled by my audience and the machinery of the church. Too bad you didn't get what you hoped for."

"Oh, I enjoyed meeting Savory. I'm grateful to you for taking so much time over it."

"Not at all. Everything else going all right? Your business with Mrs. Herne?"

"All settled. I'm buying the manuscript. If Inspector Codd could just dig up the murderer, I'd be off. As it is, I can't say I'm having a rotten time. I'm going to a dance with Lucy tomorrow night."

His face clouded momentarily. "Oh?" he said. "Where?"

"At the Market Hall."

He smiled again, rather sadly. "I hope you'll enjoy yourselves," he said. "I don't expect you'll find it as gay an affair as an American dance, but it may be fun."

I faced him squarely. "Listen, Jack, maybe I've got no business saying this—I've been told I say things no Englishman would ever mention—but I feel like a heel. I didn't intend to crowd you out with Lucy. If she's your girl—"

"She's not my girl," he interrupted.

"I'm sorry. I'll be leaving Heronwick pretty soon, anyway. Unless they lock me up."

"It's nothing to do with me. I've no sort of claim on Lucy. And certainly none at all on you."

"I just wanted to have it out."

"There's nothing to have out. Let's not talk about it, shall we?" he said, coldly. Then he added, "I didn't mean that to sound rude. But I really don't want to discuss it any longer."

"Okay," I said, and irrationally I felt thoroughly angry at him, but even more at myself.

I went to bed early and out of sorts, that night. I had a couple of whiskies, and tossed around for a while before falling asleep. I awoke suddenly, in the dark, and lay wondering what had disturbed me. There were steps in the hall outside, and I guessed that Codd had just come in; it must have been that. I began to drift off again, and abruptly I was wide awake. I knew how Sir Francis had been killed.

I had come into my head with the thought of Codd. I remembered him saying that a wound like the one Neville had received didn't begin to bleed until later. I visualized Sir Francis in his wheelchair at the top of the stairs, the wheel coming off, and him going over. And I heard Mr. Savory saying, "all a welter of blood, and blood on the stairs and on the floor."

So much blood from bumping down the stairs? No, sir! I said, sitting up in bed. But if Sir Francis had been hit with the iron ball of a morning star . . . that old dried blood from a long-ago battle could have been his.

Alastair loosens the wheel. He does it sometime during the morning, maybe, when nobody's watching.

He waits until his brother is out on the landing next to the head of the stairs. He gives him a good smash with the morning star and over he goes. Naturally, the loose wheel goes flying off. And didn't Codd say that Constable Baker had found the morning star in a trophy of arms on the *upstairs* landing?

It figured. At least to me, at that hour, it seemed plausible and possible.

I got up and turned on the lamp, and fished out the bottle and had a drink. I lit a cigarette and looked at the time. It was just after midnight. I didn't feel sleepy, and I wondered whether Codd felt like talking. I slipped on my bathrobe and went out into the corridor.

There were voices in his room, and I stopped and almost turned back. One of the voices was that of the Superintendent, and I heard ". . . that chemist chap, Richter."

I was consumed by curiosity. I couldn't just walk in and ask them what they were talking about, and I knew that it was wrong, and wicked, and naughty of me to want to eavesdrop but it didn't take much effort to overcome my scruples. Then I had a sneaky idea, worthy of one of the founding members of ICE.

Next to Codd's room was the bathroom. In England this generally means a room with a bathtub in it and nothing else. This one, built in after the tourist trade got started, had been made by throwing up a partition wall which, unlike the earlier parts of the building, was pretty flimsy. I stepped into the bathroom, sat on the end of the tub, and pressed my ear to the wall.

Codd was saying, "But I only got the report at ten-thirty."

"You should have knocked him up then," said the Superintendent. Now that he wasn't playing the wicked uncle, his voice was pleasant enough. I remembered that the head of the bed was against this wall. He was probably lying on it again, and the wall was so thin I could hear him strike a match. When he spoke again, it was between puffs at his pipe. "Must consider—if he scares easily he might do something—regrettable."

"Skip out? Where would he go? No, I hardly think so. He let us look at his boots this afternoon without making a fuss."

"And naturally, they checked on Richter?"

"And no luck there?"

"None. I told him I'd talk to him again tomorrow, and he just nodded. Well, after all, there was no positive link with Herne." I heard the rustle of papers. "Let's see. Nineteen-fifty-seven, Lionel Herne picked up on a tip to the Vice Squad that he was peddling dexadrine to teenagers. Nothing proved, although a quantity of the stuff was found in his flat. Claimed he used it himself, just to keep going, as he said. Wouldn't say where he got it: 'Here and there,' he said. Nineteen-sixty-two: this time it's purple hearts. Again, no proof that he was selling the stuff, and since it was before the 1964 Act we couldn't bring him to court just for possessing it.'"

"And naturally, they checked on Richter?"

"Naturally, since they'd been friends, and Herne and his mother had sponsored the fellow. Couldn't find a thing wrong, there. Richter's Poison Register showed nothing out of the way—but of course, it's not difficult to cook the records for this sort of stuff. Still, the suspicion remains, doesn't it?"

"And since that time?"

"Nothing that we can bring home to him. Manchester have kept an eye on him, but he's been careful."

There was silence for a time. Then the Superintendent said, reflectively, "I suppose there just might be a connection, but it's hard to see what it could be."

"Exactly. He went to Herne House Sunday night, all right, just as Cannon said. He insisted that it was because he had to take a sleeping potion to Mrs. Herne. He showed me the entry in his book."

"One of the ordinary proprietaries?"

"Yes."

"Mrs. Herne confirmed it?"

"That's right. Doesn't mean a thing, of course. And the hammer in the stream. . . . Only Neville could tell us whether there's any truth to that, and he's not talking, poor lad. Still, I see no great reason to doubt it. But the whole thing feels wrong to me. I can't say why. If Lionel Herne and Richter were up to something, and Neville found out, it might have come to murder. Who knows? They might have forced Brock to do it for them. And Mrs. Herne might have played along to keep her son out of trouble. Not that there's much love lost between them. She doesn't say so, but it's clear she detests him."

"Mhm. About Cannon. Are you going to keep him hanging about?"

"I don't see why not. It won't do him any harm. You know what Americans are like: cocky, self-confident. He bounces up each time brighter than ever."

After a pause, the Superintendent said, "You're not enjoying it, by any chance, are you, Len?"

When Codd answered, he sounded uncomfortable. "No, not really. But you know how it is, Superintendent. It's hard to forget the war—that chap with all his dollars, and Gladys, and that time at Brighton and so on. No, honestly, I've got nothing against Cannon. He's a nice lad, and God knows he's done us a bit of good in his own peculiar way. The thing is, he makes a good red-herring. It may be a trifle hard on him, having people think he's suspected of murder, but after all he'll be going back to the States where it won't make any difference. Meantime, it may make someone else relax his guard, bring him out into the open."

"I see. All right, but don't carry it too far. We don't want any unnecessary complications."

"I'll be careful."

"You'll see Richter tomorrow, will you?"

"First thing. Unless I oversleep."

"Take damn good care not to."

I heard them stirring around, and wondered whether there was any chance of them coming in to take a bath. I'll see you out," Codd said, "and lock up after you." When I heard them go creaking down the stairs, I ducked out and went back to my own room.

I was cold with fury. The son of a bitch, I thought. That mealy-mouthed, flat-footed son of a bitch. This was the guy I had thought was so straight, and—wholesome. The word turned my stomach. So I was a nice lad, was I, and useful enough in my own peculiar way? And cocky like all Americans? And I was being kept dangling around, under suspicion of killing a man, just to provide Codd with a cover. Or worse, to satisfy his sadistic impulses because he had had trouble with some soldier during the war? Great! I said to myself. That does it. Screw them all. I will jolly well get the hell out of here, old chappie, and you can take your murder and shove it up your polite English ass. It was obvious Codd no longer thought of me as a possible suspect. There wasn't a thing he could hold me on. I would take the *Raimond* manuscript and kiss Mrs. Herne goodbye, and I would tell Codd what I had heard him say, and then I would blow.

No, I wouldn't. I had to wait until the money arrived. And I had a date with Lucy, and that was one appointment I was going to keep. At the moment, I didn't care if I stepped on anybody's toes. I didn't like

English voices, or inflections, or the way they smiled, or drank tea, or looked at me. That didn't go for Lucy, though. I was going to meet her, and dance with her, and have some fun. And then I would take off, and Codd could find himself a more pliant red-herring for his stinking business.

11

The funny thing was, when I woke up next morning I didn't remember to be angry, at first. My curtains were moving in a warm breeze, a rod of sunlight speared through the crack, and birds were calling and chirruping outside. I lay looking at the shaft of sun and thinking, A nice day . . . what's today? Friday? The dance tonight. And I must check with the bank this afternoon. Then I recalled the conversation between the two detectives, but without much rancor, and I had to flog myself into a sluggish kind of resentment. Damn them both, I thought, but half-heartedly, and got up yawning.

Codd was just finishing breakfast when I came down, and he greeted me amiably, so amiably that I had to remind myself he didn't know I had overheard him. The thought gave me so much satisfaction that I was able to recover most of my irritation of the night before.

Mrs. Davies brought me the usual giant breakfast.

"Did you sleep well, love?" she asked, as she always did, and added, without waiting for an answer, "That's nice."

I told myself crossly that the English never listened properly.

"As a matter of fact, I was restless last night," I growled.

Codd said, "I hope it wasn't my fault. I came in rather late."

I glanced at him. "You didn't bother me at all," I replied. But of course, the double meaning was lost on him.

He drank his coffee while I began scaling the mountain of eggs, bacon, and fried bread. Finally since I made no conversation, he folded his napkin and got up. "Well, I must be off," he said.

"Got lots of arrests to make?" I asked.

He checked, looking at me quizzically. Then he decided that it was a joke.

"No, no. Just routine work."

"Yeah. One man's routine is another man's poison."

He blinked. Then, rather stiffly, he said, "I'm sorry you didn't sleep well last night, Mr. Cannon." And off he went. I was glad I had soured the top of his morning.

At the same time, as I pensively stirred my coffee, I changed my plans. Instead of leaving as soon as possible, I would stay, even if my money should arrive this afternoon. It was obvious that Codd had his own theories about the murder. But I now knew something he didn't. My best revenge on him would be to stay and follow up my lead in the hope of proving him wrong.

From what I'd overheard, it was clear there was some sort of traffic in drugs between Richter and Lionel. If Neville had found out about this, it might provide a motive for Richter's killing him. But thinking about Richter as he had appeared in my room, I wondered whether he were capable of killing anyone. I supposed it was possible; after all, I didn't know much about what made a man a murderer. Maybe Codd, with all his experience, knew better.

Furthermore, the theory—if it could be called a theory, since I was only guessing in the dark—that Richter and Lionel might have fixed Neville's wagon, because he wanted to crash into their game, didn't take Brock into account. How did he come into it? But, I reminded myself, maybe he didn't. Maybe Brock had really only been poaching in spite of what General Nicholson felt.

What I did know was that someone else might have had a motive for wanting Neville dead, for I knew—I felt utterly certain—how Sir Francis Herne had died. I was willing to bet that he had been murdered by his brother, and that although this had taken place nearly three-quarters of a century before, it had something to do with Neville's demise. There were lots of holes in my theory and I hadn't any proof of anything, but I told myself with gloomy satisfaction that it made at least as much sense as Codd's.

I hoped the money would arrive from Bob without delay. Because if I should be right, and Mrs. Herne were somehow involved in the murder, I wanted to have the *Raimond* manuscript in my possession before she was wafted off to jail. Selfish and narrow of me, no doubt, but anyone with passionate interests in some field of collecting will have no trouble understanding.

And thinking of the bank, and the money, an idea occurred to me. An idea so interesting that I went right to the phone and called the Nicholsons' number.

"Hullo, Dave," Lucy said. "You'll want to know about tonight. Why don't you come here for tea, and then we can go on to the dance. It begins about seven-thirty."

"Great!" I said. "I'd love it. But I'm also calling about something else."

"Yes?"

"I'd rather not talk about it on the phone. Can I drive by in about ten minutes and pick you up?"

"It sounds deliciously mysterious. Have you found a clue?"

"I don't know. Maybe. It depends on you."

"On me? How exciting! Yes, come on."

She was waiting in front of the gate when I drove up, her hair bound round with a blue scarf, her hands thrust deep in the pockets of a tweed jacket. A blue turtle-neck cashmere pullover came to her chin, so that her porcelain skin and dark gold hair were set off like a jewel in a velvet case. I found myself gaping, and shut my mouth and tried to look intelligent as she got into the car.

"Where are we going?" she said. "What have you found?"

"Nothing, yet," I replied. "Gosh, you look lovely today."

She arched her eyebrows. "I thought we were going to talk about clues and things."

"Okay," I sighed. "It's a hell of a note when a pretty girl won't let herself be complimented."

"I'm not stopping you. Fit it in along with the other."

"Too complicated. What do you know about Mrs. Herne's father?"

"Sir Alastair? Not much, I'm afraid. What's he got to do with it?"

I told her about the *Brief Account*, and about my visit to old Mr. Savory, and the morning star and my conclusions about Sir Francis's death.

"I see," she said, thoughtfully. "And you think that

Charlie found out about it somehow and threatened to blackmail Mrs. Herne? Whew! How on earth could he discover such a thing? You're only guessing at it."

"I haven't any idea."

"And do you really believe she'd feel so strongly about having it known that her father murdered his brother that she'd have Neville silenced?"

"I admit that part of it seems wobbly."

"I'd say it seemed positively dilapidated. It might be a rotten thing to have known, but I doubt she'd want someone killed for it. I don't see how the information could harm her. I shouldn't imagine they'd take Herne House away from her."

"That's what Jack Spendwell said. But look, leave out that side of it for a minute. Her bank is the West Country, in Newent. Your brother works there. Do you suppose we could find out from him whether Mrs. Herne drew any sizeable amount of money out of her account recently?"

She pursed up her lips in a soundless whistle. I wanted to kiss her. Before I could make a move, however, she said, "I'm sure there must be rules against that sort of thing, Dave."

I was taken aback. What kind of rules could there be against kissing? Then I pulled myself together. "You mean the bank wouldn't let him tell you?"

"I'm almost certain of it. Oh, dear. Don't look so disappointed. I suppose it wouldn't hurt to *ask* Alan."

"Could we? I thought we might drive up there. It isn't far."

"Alan goes to lunch at twelve-thirty," she said. "We can drive slowly. We've plenty of time for any nice things you care to say."

I took a long route, going round-about into Herefordshire to a pretty town called Ledbury where there were some fine old black-and-white buildings, and out again through the winding country lanes. We talked nonsense, and laughed a great deal, and I began to feel as if I were on a vaction for the first time in days. I told her about my business, and about Bob, my closest friend as well as partner, and about Dad, and about my first love affair which had ended when Alice got drunk and socked me in the eye, and about Connecticut and how you could love some things about it and hate others all at the same time. I told her about the first peepers and the redwing blackbirds perched on the willow wands in spring, and about the maples waiting for the first touch of frost, and about the neat villages with their white clapboard churches and their volunteer fire departments and their town meetings, all astonishing and new to her. I told her about the hurricanes that came roaring up from the south, and the ice storms that locked us in exasperatingly in February, and the breathless, steamy summer nights when all you could do was search out someone with a swimming pool and lie dead in the water. And the more I talked, looking out the car windows at the neat patchwork of English fields, and the occasional timbered cottage with its cap of slate or thatch, the more homesick I got.

She said, "It must be lovely there. It's so difficult to picture what it's like as you know it. I'd adore to go there some day. I don't suppose I ever shall, though, unless Daddy makes a frightful lot of money. He's been, but he always says he can't afford to take me."

"You'll come someday," I said. "You've got to come."

I pulled over to the side of the road and stopped the car. "Come back with me this fall," I said, smiling, turning so that I could look at her.

Her cheeks grew very pink. "Is that a proposal?" she laughed.

Our eyes clung, and suddenly we both became very grave. My throat closed up. I couldn't think of anything else to say, so I put my arms around her and kissed her.

"Well! I didn't expect that," she said, when we had at length moved a little apart. She sounded as breathless as I felt.

"Lucy," I said, "come to Connecticut with me."

"You're mad," she said, in that same queer, choked voice. "We don't even know each other."

"You want a formal introduction? My name is David Cannon. How well do you have to know somebody to know that you don't want to let go of them?"

"How can you know that?"

"It's your English accent that hooks me. That, and your funny mouth. You have a funny mouth, you know?"

"You're an idiot. One of your eyes is higher than the other. I noticed it the first time we met."

"When you laughed at me in the church. I always carry one eye higher than the other. It helps to see over things."

Suddenly, we were kissing each other again.

A car went by, slowed as it passed us, and tooted its horn merrily. We drew apart.

"Nosey," I said. "Now it'll be all over the whole neighborhood. Dave loves Lucy."

"Do you?"

"I don't know. I guess so. Could you ever fall in love with a man under a cloud? Maybe I did knock Neville off, after all."

A shadow crossed her face. "That's one thing that's serious, Dave."

"One thing? Don't you think *this* is serious?"

"I don't know," she said. "Are you serious?"

I took both her hands. "I'm very mixed up," I said. "But I do think I'm serious. I think maybe I love you. I want you. I want to spend time with you. I want to take you home with me. Whatever it is, it's serious."

She gave a long sigh. "It's too quick. I don't know what I feel. It's all—it's very strange."

"But a little serious with you, too?"

She looked away from me, out of the window. She said, as if to herself, "To go away, maybe forever." She turned back to me, and added, softly, "I think, perhaps, it is a little serious."

I started to take her in my arms again, but she put up a hand to hold me off. "No," she said. "Not now, not for a while."

"Whatever you say," I said.

I started the car and we drove for a time without talk. It wasn't a tense or a disagreeable silence, but a contented one, a shared quiet in which I was just happy to have her beside me and to remember her lips and everything we had said.

After a bit, I broke it. "Do you think your father would object?"

"No," she said. "Why should he?"

I thought of Codd. "Not all English people like Americans."

"He does. At least, some Americans. I know he likes you."

"Oh, that reminds me. He said something odd to me that day we had lunch together. You remember, you told me not to be upset if he mentioned 'American competition?' Well, he said I should be sure to ask you what that meant, and said it would serve you right."

She chuckled.

"Well?"

"It's a rather sad story. No I don't mind telling you. You see, Daddy had it all fixed up that I was to marry Jack Spendwell."

"Wait a minute," I said, stopping the car again. "All right, now that I'm standing still, go ahead."

"Jack and I had known each other since childhood.

I mean, since I was a child—he's ten years older than I. But what was really the point was the fact that Daddy and Mr. Spendwell, Jack's father, had known each other all their lives. They more or less took it for granted that Jack and I would get married.

"After the war, Jack decided to go into the Church, and about eight years ago he was offered a living here and came home to be vicar of Heronwick. A year or so later, Daddy began hinting to me that the vicarage was a nice, big, empty house and that Jack needed someone to cherish him. You'd have thought he was proposing a corporation merger."

"Couldn't Jack speak for himself?"

"No, it wasn't quite so bad as all that. You see, Jack really did love me and wanted to marry me. He had talked it over with Daddy, and Daddy more or less jumped the gun. The trouble was, I was already in love with someone else."

"Oh?" I began to feel chilly. "Who?"

"An American. Dick Segal. He was an awfully good-looking boy, the son of a friend of Cousin George's. He had come over to study British industries, or business methods, or something like that, and of course Goerge invited him to stay with them in Painswick. He had the sweetest short haircut! The first time I met him I fell madly in love with him. I don't think he felt quite the same about me. But we met often; I had my little car then, before it got smashed up, and I drove him around to see the sights —and the factories. Heavens, we must have looked at a thousand of them. He had all sorts of introductions to people."

"I see," I said, dourly.

She gurgled with mirth. "You're jealous! But Dave, it was six years ago. It's long since over and done with. It didn't last very long. Dick went back to the States and I got one letter from him, the sort of letter

199

that says what fun it was and how much he enjoyed it and how he hoped we'd meet again some day. . . . We never did," she added, wistfully.

"You're sorry?"

"Well, of course I'm sorry. You told me about that awful girl—Alice—the one who used to get drunk in public and start taking off her clothes—well, weren't you sorry when it was all over?"

"No. I was relieved."

"All right. It was different with me. He was such a charming boy. Even though I couldn't help giggling at the way he spoke. You know. Anyway, I got over it. But it took Daddy longer than it took me. He was convinced that Dick had ruined Jack's chances and broken up the marriage plans. For quite a long time afterward he was very stuffy about Americans. His favorite phrase was 'American competition.' He'd go on about Americans thrusting into British markets, British business, British cultural life, and then he'd work his way around to personal relationships and finish up triumphantly by pointing out that we'd have had a splendid king in Edward VIII if it hadn't been for Mrs. Wallis Simpson's interference."

"My God, and you just told me he *likes* Americans."

"Daddy's much too fair-minded a man to carry a grudge forever. He's really a poppet in spite of his bark."

"A poppet? Is that what you call it?"

"He went on a business trip to America three years ago, and saw Mr. Segal in New York, and met Dick again—he's an executive now, with some gigantic firm or other—and they gave Daddy a royal reception. Wouldn't let him go for three days. They live in Long Island—somewhere with an unpronounceable name, and they kept pouring whisky and good food into him, and introducing him to all sorts of marvelous people, until by the time he got out of their clutches he had been thoroughly brainwashed."

I nodded. "And Jack Spendwell got left out in the cold. Now I understand."

"What?"

"Something he said. It doesn't matter. But do you ever wish you'd married Jack after all?"

She shook her head. "I wouldn't have married him. At least, I don't think so. I always liked Jack. I thought of him as a close friend, a dear friend, but I can't imagine him as a lover and never could."

"Can you—?" I began.

"Yes," she said, without letting me finish.

"Telepathy," I grinned. "You see? Our minds are in tune."

I started the car, and now I had to drive for real as it was a quarter past twelve. In Newent, I waited in the car while Lucy went off to track down her brother.

I passed the time in thinking about her and imagining her in New Canaan. I was alternately elated and cast down, as I kept telling myself I must be out of my mind because I hardly knew the girl and she didn't know me and I didn't have any right to make plans, and pushing all that aside with the memory of how she had returned my kisses and how she had said, "Perhaps a little serious." How could this kind of thing happen? You went along from day to day, busy with your affairs, and all of a sudden, *pop!* you jumped through a hoop into a totally different world in which there was someone else, someone more important than anything you knew.

She came walking up the street towards the car, smiling with the sun in her eyes, and everything went out of my head except the thought, *Sweet Christ! I'm crazy for her!*

I opened the door and she got in. "Do you want to talk here? Or drive out of town?" she said.

"Is it good or bad? It must be good. You're grinning like the Cheshire cat."

"It's good."

"Tell me."

"Alan objected, at first. He said the bank had very strict rules against divulging any information about clients, just as I suspected. They wouldn't even tell the police anything like that, he said. I said we weren't the police, and that it was the least he could do to help you, and that we wouldn't breathe a word to anyone—you mustn't, you know. Alan might very well lose his job. Promise?"

"Absolutely. Cross my heart."

"Well, at last he said that it was funny we should want to know what we did because, yes, Mrs. Herne had telephoned the bank manager Saturday morning just before closing time and told him that it was imperative for her to draw out a large sum of money. Naturally, Alan didn't hear the telephone conversation, but the manager grumbled about the matter because he had to drive to Heronwick with the money. A thousand pounds, it was. Alan says it's nearly all she has in cash in the bank."

"I knew it!"

"That's not all. She came in Tuesday afternoon and put it all back into her account again."

"There you are! What does it sound like to you?"

"Somebody wanted all that money and then suddenly didn't need it after all."

"Just so. Didn't need it because he got killed."

"Gosh!" she exclaimed. "It looks that way. What now? Shall we go to the police?"

"Uh-uh. What are we going to tell them? You made me promise to keep my mouth shut about the bank.

Anyway, I've got reasons of my own for not wanting to spring this on them."

"Pride, I'll bet. 'American amateur sleuth out-guesses Scotland Yard.' Right?"

"Shut up," I said, affectionately, "or I'll slug you."

"Oh, how I wish I could speak American," Lucy said. "Will you teach me?"

I slumped behind the wheel and tried to think.

"It's no use," I said, at last. "I can't figure out what ought to come next. I can't cross-examine Brock—I haven't the authority. Or the guts, come to that. If we could get into Neville's house maybe we could find something that would involve Mrs. Herne, some kind of note from her, for instance. Something like that would prove she had a motive, wouldn't it?"

"Dave, that's a wonderful idea!" Lucy said. "It makes sense, too. Charlie hadn't a phone, so she might well have sent him a note."

"Mm. But don't you think the police have already searched his place?"

"It's likely. But they wouldn't have known what they were looking for. Suppose the note said something ambiguous—oh, Lord, I don't know—something like, 'Bring the goods on Monday and I will pay you.' That wouldn't have looked like anything at all to the police. But we know now what it would mean."

"True. Still, I can't back it up with the information about her drawing out the money and putting it back."

"Let's face that when we have to," she replied. "I know where Charlie lived. I'll take you there."

"Oh, yes," I said, as I pulled away from the curb. "His little 'chapel' in the woods. I've heard about it from Jack. A regular two-bit den of iniquity, he said it was."

There was no reply. I glanced at her. She was blushing furiously.

"You've been there," I said. "I remember, now. In the Goat, when Charlie came over to our table, he said something about it to you."

"Let's not talk about it," she broke in. "It's not a happy memory."

I began to feel a little sick. I fumbled for something to say, but she saved me the trouble.

"All right," she said. "I can see it's hurting you. You needn't be dismayed. He took me there one evening, and tried to rape me. I got away from him. That's all."

I said between my teeth, "The son of a bitch. I wish I *had* killed him."

She put a hand on my arm. "I'm glad you didn't."

"But how could you go out with him? I mean, he was such an unsavory-looking mess."

"Not always," she answered. "You didn't see him ten years ago. I don't mean I was in love with him, nothing like that. But he was *dashing*. He was a rebel. He dressed in outrageous clothes, embroidered waistcoats and Edwardian jackets and tight trousers, and he carried himself with an air that made us all think of—of—oh, the Scarlet Pimpernel, or someone like that."

"This *is* Charlie Neville you're talking about?"

"I know. Seeing him when you did, you'd find it hard to believe. But then, when I was sixteen or seventeen, he seemed to defy everything smug and proper and respectable and old-fashioned. He frightened me, but he drew me, too. Do you understand?"

"Sure. Why not? Lots of girls went for Elvis Presley years ago for the same reason."

"Yes, it was something like that. It's curious . . . in a tiny place like Heronwick, Charlie was like a wind from outside."

"An ill wind."

"Poor Charlie," she murmured.

204

I said to myself that women were peculiar creatures. Poor rattlesnake!

We stopped at a pub and had a bite, and then drove back to Heronwick. About a half-mile out of the village she told me to pull up where a wooden stile broke the line of a stone wall.

As we got out of the car, a young man went by on a bicycle. I recognized him: the blond yob with the flattened nose. He gave me a venomous stare.

"I don't know whether I ought to leave the car by the roadside," I said to Lucy. "He's one of the ones I fought with at the Goat. He'd probably love to slash my tires."

"Alfred Fewes? Not he. He wouldn't dare, now we've seen him. Just lock up."

We climbed the stile and took a faint footpath along the edge of a field. Another stile led over another boundary wall, and we were in a wood of dusky, heavy trees, thick with ivy and mistletoe, through which the path twisted.

"All this land, the fields and the wood, once belonged to the Neville family," Lucy explained. "Now there's only the cottage and its right of way. Do you remember passing a large, very handsome eighteenth-century house set back among gardens on the right? That was Neville Hall. It's split up into flats, now."

We came in sight of the cottage soon after. It was of stone, filigreed with vines, its roof sagging like an old horse's back, its windows small and so dirty they looked as if they were curtained. To my chagrin, the door was locked.

"Of course, it would be," I said. "I wonder what the sentence is for breaking in?"

We went around to the rear. There was one small window next to the back door. A board had been nailed over it. I pulled gently, and the nails came away from the rotten wood of the frame. The pane beneath had a large hole in it.

"I don't suppose you could actually call this *breaking* in," I breathed.

I laid the board carefully on the ground, reached through the hole and unlatched the window. I climbed into a small scullery, and Lucy followed although I protested that it was too dirty.

The scullery led us into a narrow kitchen with a small coal stove, a cracked sink with one faucet, and a wooden table with two rickety chairs. Dirty dishes were stacked on a dresser, and on one wall hung a calendar with a picture of Ann Hathaway's cottage on it. I was surprised. I'd have thought Charlie's taste would have run to a different sort of pin-up.

We poked about among the pots and crockery, and looked in the drawer of the table, but found only some stained cutlery there. The sitting room yielded nothing, either. We climbed the stairs and found two bedrooms, one empty. The other was almost filled by a large, carved mahogany bed. The rest of the space was taken up by a tall wardrobe and an armchair. The roof sloped, and a dormer window cut into the thick walls opened to the woods. We searched this room but the wardrobe was empty and there was nothing under the mattress, or in the chair, or anywhere else.

"Well, hell," I said. "Unless he's got a wall safe hidden somewhere, this is a wash-out."

"I imagine the police must have taken all his personal effects," said Lucy. "So if there were a note, it would be in the police station. We never thought of that."

I rested my elbow against the beam that spanned the dormer and looked out at the dark trees. "His great grandfather used to write poetry here," I said. "Have you ever read any of it?"

"No. I never even knew about it."

"It must have been a sweet little place in those days. Now look at it, a pigsty."

I glanced around the room in distaste, at the filthy walls, the grime on the furniture, the grey curls of dust in the corners. There was even a bird's nest under the peak of the dormer.

"Okay," I said. "Let's go."

We started to leave, and then it hit me. I grabbed Lucy's arm and stopped her.

"Wait a minute," I said. "How come a bird built inside this room?"

"That's not so strange," Lucy said. "I'm only surprised there aren't rats' nests as well."

"Did you ever see a bird's nest without the marks of droppings under it?"

She stared at me.

"And Charlie wouldn't have been the man to clean them up," I added.

I reached up. As I had suspected, the nest came easily away: I could see, now, that it was held in place by two nails driven into the wall. Inside it were a thin, old, gold watch, three gold coins, a pair of massive cuff-links, and two pieces of stiff, thick paper folded up and held by a rubber band.

I opened them out. They were photostat positives. On one appeared a single line; the other page was covered with writing, cramped together, crossed out here and there, spattered in places as if the writer's pen had hurried, and almost indecipherable. It all looked very familiar. I had seen it before, and I knew just where and when: it was a photocopy of the letter that had been folded inside the leather case of the *Raimond* manuscript. And I could see now that the superscription I had originally read as "Chas. Nowlle" was, in fact, "Chas. Neville."

"So that's what he meant," I said.

"Who meant? What is it?" asked Lucy, eagerly.

"Charlie. He said, 'I only take what's mine,' He meant this letter. It's addressed to him."

She took the pages from me. "Surely not," she said. "It's got a date at the top. 5 May 1895. This Charles Neville must have been his grandfather."

"His great grandfather," I said. "The poet. The friend of Sir Francis Herne. That's who it was."

Quickly, I told her how I had first seen it. "Afterwards, I forgot all about it," I finished. "I'd just had a brush with Charlie and then I had to deal with Mrs. Herne. I had put the letter aside, and Charlie saw it on the desk and read the name on the outside. Of course, he thought he had a right to it. And he wasn't going to say anything about taking it, because his mind probably jumped at once to ancient documents which could be sold profitably."

"But this isn't the letter itself, it's only a photostat," Lucy said.

"I think I can guess why," I replied. "But let's read it first. Or anyway, let's try—the handwriting is fierce."

After much stumbling and guessing, we were able to puzzle it out:

I am writing to you, my dear Charles [it said], *in some haste and distress. Must tell you this unbelievable as it sounds so that someone else will know. For God's sake, come to me here at once. Or if it should be too late, act on this information.*

Alastair is not my brother. He is a nameless guttersnipe.

I learned this from my father before he died. I do not know how to begin. You remember my father. In spite of his severity, you remember how he doted on my mother almost to distraction. You will have seen it even more than I, for when I was a child you were al-

ready a youth. After I was born, it seems she was left ill and nervous and Doctor Shrubb warned them to have no more children. My father, with customary independence of spirit, ignored this and nine years later she was again expecting. However, the baby was born dead. Knowing Mother's frailty, my father feared to tell her. With the connivance of the midwife and Dr. Shrubb they explained that babe taken away to be nursed for a short time because of its weakness. You must recall how Father dominated everyone in those days. Dr. Shrubb was as terrified of him as anyone else, and fell in with the whole scheme. Through a baby-farmer, the midwife procured another child, almost of the same age, which they gave to my mother. My father gave the midwife a pension and packed her off to London. As for the doctor, my father easily crushed his opposition. Told him, among other things, that if he ever spoke and my mother should be harmed by the news, Shrubb would be responsible. A weak man. To the day of her death, my mother never learned truth. Her own child was buried secretly—I fear by my father's own hand, in some unknown spot.

In Father's last illness, when at his request I was putting his papers in order, I found a letter from a Mrs. Harkness—the midwife as it turned out—complaining she could no longer live on what he sent her and asking in what I thought over-familiar, even rude terms for an increase in pension. I taxed Father. I will not tell you what I thought at first. By degrees, the story came out. He seemed relieved, asked my forgiveness, but I think he needed to confess to someone. A horrible crime, Charles, but some extenuation?..

I must hurry. I have made a mistake. The day before yesterday, Alastair and I had words—I have been learning much about him which is ugly—there are certain debts, and now I find a shameful relationship which must be bought off. I lost my temper, like a fool. I told him all, saying that in spite of his pretensions I would find means to cut him off should he prove unworthy of the name he now bears.

Since that time, I feel certain he means to do away with me. He has threatened me. Watches me day and night to prevent my sending for help. He has intimidated or bribed the servants, so I scarce know whom to trust. However, there is a good young man here, young Savory whom you know, and I believe I can find means of giving him this letter. Come to me at once, for the love of God. But if I am already dead, use this letter, let Alastair see that he cannot escape judgment.

Francis

When we had done wading through it, we looked at each other for a long moment over it, without finding words. At last, Lucy exclaimed, "Crikey!"

"Crikey, indeed," I said. "What a shock that must have been for Alastair. Enough to unhinge anybody. And he doesn't sound, from the few hints here, like a model citizen. He must have reformed later. Remorse, probably."

"But this is ghastly!"

"Yes. Francis must have hidden the letter in the slipcase of the *Raimond* manuscript. Alastair probably wasn't much of a reader and wouldn't think of looking among the books. That explains, too, why it was never found later. Mrs. Herne told me she didn't do much reading, either. The slipcase had only been opened twice since Francis's death, once by me and once by the appraiser from Saxby's who, if he could read it at all, must have ignored it as I did, once he saw it had nothing to do with the manuscript."

"But if he glanced through it, surely he'd have called it to Mrs. Herne's attention?"

"Would you?" I asked. "He was English. Skeletons in the cupboard—? Surely, it would be a family affair he would consider none of his business. So Francis wrote the letter on May fifth—I suppose he had just tucked it safely away, when his brother came in fully determined to finish him off without waiting any longer."

She shivered. "It's enough to give one the creeps."

"Yeah. And it gives you a motive, too. No wonder Charlie knew he was on to a good thing when he read this. Mrs. Herne, with her family pride, wouldn't have cared two cents about her father murdering Sir Francis, but she couldn't bear to have it known that she was descended from a—what does he say?—a nameless guttersnipe. And if the news got out, I'll bet she'd lose the property and the title. I don't know the law, but I'll bet there's something governing illegitimate descent, and Alastair wasn't even adopted into the family, just accepted. Mrs. Herne not only has a son, for whatever he's worth, but a grandson. It would be the end of all of them."

"I can't believe she'd have had Charlie murdered."

"I know. Murder's a difficult thing to swallow. But just think how staggered she must have been when Charlie showed her this letter. Knowing him, I'll bet he read it out loud to her and had a good time doing it. Her lineage was chopped off right then and there. Not a Herne, not a descendant of baronets and lady of the manor, but Mrs. Nobody, the daughter of Nobody. A nameless guttersnipe! It makes you feel for her, all right. My God, she only had two choices: either to kill herself for shame, or to sponge out Neville. And I don't think she hesitated long."

"Yes, I can see that. And Charlie wouldn't only have taken her money, he'd have treated her like dirt in the bargain, afterward. He'd have jeered at her every day, made her life unbearable. She certainly

211

saw that, and she never would have borne it. But who could she have got to do the murder for her? And how?"

I shrugged. "She is a very resourceful woman. Anyway, now we know why this is a photostat. It's what I suspected right away. Rule one for blackmailers—don't hand over everything because next year you might need money again. I'll bet you anything that Charlie went right off to Gloucester Friday afternoon, after he read this, and had it photocopied so that he could hand her the original with a light heart."

I made for the door. "Come on. We've got to show this to Inspector Codd. I'm going to enjoy watching his face when he reads it, the bastard."

She looked at me in surprise, but I didn't go into details. We climbed out through the scullery window and I put the board back. We hurried to the car and drove to Heronwick. As we came into the High Street I had to slow down: the street and the market square were crowded, and there were cars parked all over the place.

"Oh, dear," Lucy said, "I forgot. It's market day."

I could see the booths, piled with cheap clothing, fruits and vegetables, and hardware, lining the open arcades of the Market Hall. I could also see something else. The crowd was thickest over to our right, across from the Market Hall where Friday Street began, and in front of the shop marked E. A. O. COL-LICKE Dispensing and Photographic Chemist stood a uniformed policeman, not my friend Baker but a stranger. People were staring and pointing and jostling in front of the shop, and there was a large, official-looking van parked nearby.

Lucy leaned out of the window and hailed a red-faced woman with a market basket who was heading out of the crowd.

"Mrs. Dunk! What's happened?" she called.

"Ooh, haven't you heard, love?" Mrs. Dunk replied, coming purposefully towards us. "Wherever have you been? It's Mr. Richter. Killed himself this morning and sent poor Ann Wilson into a fit."

12

We both said, "What?" as if we had been rehearsed.

Mrs. Dunk looked pleased at finding somebody who hadn't heard the news. When it came right down to it, however, she hadn't an awful lot to tell. Most of that was what the unfortunate Ann Wilson had seen —she was the girl who worked in the chemist's shop.

Soon after the shop opened that morning, Constable Baker had come in. Mr. Richter was in the back of the shop making up a prescription, and Ann was at the counter. The constable had said to Richter, in a low voice, but she had overheard him, "The Detective Inspector would like a word with you, sir, if you please." Richter had replied, "Very well. In a moment. Excuse me, I must just finish this." The policeman had turned away for a moment, and the next thing they knew Richter had crumpled to the floor. The policeman had darted through the curtain and tried to pick him up, and Ann had seen Richter writhing for a moment in the constable's arms with an awful look on his

214

face. Then the policeman had laid him down again, told her to stand still and keep cool, and picked up the telephone. From then on, it was all chaos and confusion, but when the Detective Inspector and the doctor and some other policemen had come, she had made out from their conversation that Mr. Richter had poisoned himself with a few crystals of cyanide. She had had hysterics, and had been slapped by Constable Baker—"such a nice young man"—and had been sent home to become the object of more attention and admiration than, said Mrs. Dunk with satisfied disapproval, "as if she was a film star."

We got away from Mrs. Dunk at last, when we found there was nothing more to be learned from her. I drove through the market square with some difficulty and out to Kingsmill. The policeman's cottage had four or five cars parked around it, with people coming and going, and I went up to the door with some misgivings. Constable Baker met me, looking careworn and pale and considerably older. No wonder! I thought, with the house full of his superiors and the man he had been supposed to bring in lying dead.

Inspector Codd, he told me, was in the chemist's shop with some other officials. No, he didn't know when he'd be returning. Yes, he'd say that I was looking for him, but he couldn't promise that the Inspector would have a moment to spare until quite late that night if not tomorrow morning. No, he regretted he couldn't give me any information about Mr. Richter's death.

I went back to the car. "No dice," I said. "I couldn't find out a thing."

"But I imagine Mr. Richter's suicide—and I suppose it couldn't have been anything else—means that he was guilty, doesn't it?" said Lucy.

"Maybe."

"Did you leave the letter for Inspector Codd?"

"No, I didn't. I want to hand it to him myself," I said, grimly.

"Dave, what's going on?" she demanded. "You said a few things earlier on that made me think you're very annoyed with the Inspector. Now this. Has something else happened?"

"I don't see why I shouldn't tell you," I said. "I eavesdropped on a conversation between Codd and his Superintendent last night. They say that eavesdroppers never hear anything good about themselves. It's true. I found out that Codd has been keeping up the pretense that I'm a legitimate suspect in the case partly to make whoever's guilty relax his guard, but partly because he has some sort of grudge against Americans. From the war, I think. How do you like that?"

"I think it's disgraceful! Can't you complain to his superiors?"

"Ha! You forget his superior was right there in the room with him. But it's more than that. Call it pride—that's what you said before, you know. 'Amateur sleuth outguesses Scotland Yard.' But he's kept on telling me not to play detective games, and I'd just like to see his face when I show him this letter and tell him how Sir Francis was murdered."

"I think you're absolutely right," she said, firmly.

"Anyway, there's no rush. They're going to be busy with poor old Richter's suicide for a while. They may even find something which will go this document one better."

She said, hesitantly, "Do you still want to go to the dance tonight?"

"Sure, why not? There's nothing more we can do now. Codd will probably get in touch with me when he's free. Meanwhile, there are still lots of things I want to tell you. Didn't you say something about our having tea together?"

"As it happens," she said, "Daddy won't be home to

216

tea, and Alan doesn't get home until about six. So whatever you have to tell me ... I don't think we'll be disturbed for a while."

By seven-thirty, all traces of the market had been cleared away except for a few vagrant bits of wrapping paper and a cabbage leaf or two. The policeman had gone, and Richter's shop was locked up and dark. There were a few people loitering about staring at it, and a few others in knots in the market square. The Market Hall was lighted, and from outside we could hear the thumping of music.

We made our way up a broad staircase to the room in the upper story. It was large and long, with a stage at one end on which the band was playing, and a balcony opposite, on the front of which was painted, in much faded letters, JACOBUS REX—A.D. 1620. Folding chairs were set out underneath the balcony, and others lined the walls on either side. The band was about what I had expected: a group of earnest-looking young men with extravagant coiffures, wearing blazers without lapels and elastic-sided shoes, and armed with electric guitars, a saxophone, a clarinet, and drums. They weren't bad either, except that each piece they played sounded pretty much like every other piece.

The hall rapidly filled with dancers. There seemed to be two different groups, in a general sort of way. One consisted of a kind of beat crowd, in denim, leather, or plastic, the girls with long lank hair and thin faces and tight little buttocks like apples, the boys shaggy, with large hands, awkward in their cheap versions of mod styles. The other group were well if casually dressed, clean, loud-voiced, tending towards arrogance, the girls fattish and thick-ankled in expensive frocks, the boys in bright waistcoats and unmatching slacks and jackets, and all looking as though they could do with an operation for adenoids.

You could tell them apart by their speech: the culti-vated neighing on one hand, the rustic grunting on the other. But we all danced pretty much the same dances, and in the intervals the young men of both sorts went amicably, side by side, to the bar where the woman from the Falcon presided, to forage for themselves and their girl friends.

Lucy knew quite a few of them from both sides of the fence and many in between. I did a lot of parry-ing of joking thrusts, and buying my share of drunks, and most of the people I met were polite and pleas-ant. But there was a small crowd who watched me with a hostility which grew more open as the evening wore on.

They were led by my old friends and fellow-batt-lers, Alfred Fewes, the bony-faced blond fellow, and Henry Dawlish, the runt with the permanent wave. At first, they were content to stare at me and whisper to each other and to their friends. I returned their looks as distantly as I could. Then, after a while, they began saying things more loudly, taking pains to be near enough to me so that I could hear them.

"Hey, Alf, notice a funny smell in 'ere?"

"Coo! Sort of dead rat?"

"Oo, no. More like something from Connect-i-cut."

And so on. Heavy-handed, but effective. It got under my skin in spite of all I could do to ignore it.

I had a feeling we were going to tangle before the evening was over. I decided that it might be best if Lucy and I left before that could happen. When I mentioned it to her, in an intermission between dances, she said, "They won't try on anything here, Dave. But we'll go if you like."

"One more dance?"

"All right."

"How about another drink?"

I got her a gin and lime, and a whisky for myself. I

was just turning away from the bar when someone jostled me roughly. The whisky slopped out of my glass and over my slacks.

I looked round angrily, into the face of Alfred Fewes.

"Wet your drawers, have you?" he said, blandly.

We were close together. I gave the other glass a jerk and splashed gin and lime over the front of his pants. He jumped back, but too late.

"I'm so sorry," I said. "Somebody pushed me."

It was childish, but it gave me considerable pleasure.

He said, shrilly, "You bloody bastard!"

People turned, at that, and a hush began to spread out around us.

I put the empty glasses on the bar behind me. I felt exceedingly detached, as if I were watching from a slight distance.

I said, "I don't like what you've been saying all evening. And I don't like being called a bastard."

I was bigger than he was, and heavier. He backed away a step or two, glaring at me with real spite.

"You touch me—" he snarled.

His friends were gathering behind him. I saw glittering eyes and sideburns of various shapes and sizes through the grey coils of cigarette smoke. I kept my attention on Fewes.

One of them said, loudly, "Why don't you get out of it, Yank? Nobody arst you to come here."

"Now look," I said. "I didn't start this."

They surged a little closer, and it seemed to me that there were suddenly a lot of them. I didn't want to move. I was conscious of the bar table at my back and I thought fleetingly of grabbing a bottle and charging into them. But only fleetingly.

Fewes said, hoarsely, "You can bet he done for Charlie. And now he comes dancing here like he was a bloody big shot. Thinks he can push anybody around."

Lucy was beside me, although I hadn't seen her come. She stood close, her shoulder touching mine, and I could feel her trembling. I glanced at her; her face was set and angry.

"You ought to be ashamed of yourselves," she burst out.

"Don't you talk about shame," cried one of the girls. "We know about you and your Yank boy friends. And what did *he* do? Set the police on my Aunt Sarah, that's what. Heard her talking private in the Falcon, and ran straight off and told the coppers."

"Yes, and poor Mr. Richter, too," said another girl with her hair piled unbelievably high. I recognized her: Ann, the thin one from the chemist's shop. "He come in there and started the whole thing. I saw him. It was him sent the police and made Mr. Richter take that poison."

"Run him out," said Henry Dawlish, licking his lips.

They pressed in on me. Some of them were grinning. I had never felt so naked before, or so helpless. There may have been plenty of people in that room who were on my side, but I couldn't see any of them. They were all too law-abiding. I couldn't fight this whole mob. I didn't know what to do, and I was scared clean through, not only for myself but even more for Lucy.

And at that point, a sharp voice said, "Let me through, please."

There was a kind of boiling among the crowd, and Fewes was abruptly shoved aside. I never thought I'd be so glad to see Inspector Codd.

"That'll do, then," he said, in the same business-like tone. That mild and innocent air of his was gone, and he looked perfectly competent to clean out the place single-handed.

Many of them must have recognized him. They fell back in silence.

He said, "Mr. Cannon, will you come with me, please?"

I caught Lucy's hand and followed him out of the hall.

Down in the street, he turned to Lucy and touched his hat. "Miss—Nicholson, isn't it? Have you a car? No? Then perhaps I can give you a lift home."

"My car's parked just down the High Street," I said.

"I want you with me, Mr. Cannon," he replied. "I shall want to have a talk with you, if you've no objection."

We got into his Vauxhall, and Lucy told him how to get to her house. He drove us without speaking, and we sat in the back seat holding hands, because there wasn't room for three in his front seat. When we arrived, I got out with her and she clung to me in a goodnight kiss.

"Phone me tomorrow morning," she said. "And don't worry."

"Not me," I said. "Don't worry. Goodnight."

"Goodnight, darling."

I got in front with Codd, a little tipsy from that "darling."

"I sure am glad you showed up when you did," I said. "How'd you know I was there?"

"From Mr. Davies," he replied.

"I thought it was going to turn into a real brawl."

"I'm happy it didn't."

His tone didn't encourage conversation, so I shut up. To my surprise, he drove not to the Goat but to the police station. We didn't see Constable Baker. Codd let himself in and took me into the office. The Superintendent was there, in a straight chair tipped back against the wall, and he nodded at me over his pipe. Codd pitched his hat on the desk and ran his fingers through his scanty hair in that automatic gesture he had.

"Take a seat, Mr. Cannon," he said.

"Okay. I suppose you got my message."

"I got a message," he said, "but it wasn't from you. I think," he went on crisply, "you have some explaining to do."

"About what?"

He passed me a sheet of paper. On it was scrawled: "Ask American why him and Lucy Nicholson broke into Charley Nevilles house."

"Who sent you this?" I said. "Never mind. I can guess. It was probably delivered by a guy named Alfred Fewes. He passed us on the road this afternoon. I suppose he sneaked back and watched us."

"I didn't know that," Codd said. "It was pushed under the door, in an envelope addressed to me. It's true, then?"

"Sure."

"Mr. Cannon, we cannot put up with this any longer," he said. His voice shook on the last couple of words.

I looked up at him, seeing him clearly for the first time that evening. His cheeks were sunken, his mouth drawn down tightly, and his eyes had a feverish brightness. I suddenly realized how much of a strain he must be under. At the same time, I grew tense. I'd had a nasty experience, and I didn't intend to be bullied. Certainly not by him.

"I've warned you again and again," he was saying. "Your meddling has become intolerable. That incident at the dance tonight—I heard some of what was being said. It was lucky, indeed, for you that I got there when I did. We can't have this sort of thing! We've had another death today. No doubt you know about it. You must ask yourself whether your interference there might not have helped push Richter into

222

such an act. You've got a large section of the village up in arms against you, and now you've added house-breaking to the rest."

I clasped my hands together over my chest to keep myself calm, and sat back in my chair.

"I wouldn't have been in that spot tonight if it weren't for you, Inspector," I said.

That brought him up short. "What do you mean?"

"I think you and the Superintendent here know what I mean. I heard you talking about me last night."

My control broke and I jumped to my feet. "You've been having a ball with me, haven't you? You needed a decoy and I was convenient, and you don't like Americans any more than Alfred Fewes and his gang do. And how come you don't want me playing detective, as you put it? Afraid I might find out something you don't know? You wouldn't have known about Richter in the first place, if I hadn't put you on to him."

The Superintendent took his pipe out of his mouth, and said calmly, "Take it easy, Mr. Cannon, Sit down, sit down. I see we owe you an apology."

Codd's face was flushed with embarrassment and he had that rather helpless look I had seen when he had first shown up at Herne House on the day of Charlie's death.

He said, "So you heard . . . I'm sorry, Mr. Cannon. Truly sorry. But you must believe that my feelings about Americans—whatever they are—had nothing to do with my decision. It may have been wrong, proba-bly was. I didn't think you'd be harmed."

"I know," I said, drily. "Americans are bouncy, like tennis balls."

"I apologize for that. The fact is, I—I had a rather unfortunate experience during the war."

"In Brighton, with Gladys and a rich American?"

"You really did overhear everything, didn't you?" he said, with such a rueful expression that I couldn't help smiling. Once I did that, of course, my anger was broken although I tried not to show it.

He smiled, too. "Not exactly a rich American. In those days, your chaps had an awful lot of money compared to us. Just soldiers' pay, I suppose, but ours was about a tenth what yours was. It made for rather bitter feeling. Do you know, he used to pay for everything with pound notes, and just cram the change into one of his pockets saying that he couldn't be bothered to figure out the funny British system? And things were short . . . there were lots of things he could afford that I couldn't. And we were all tired, you know. . . . It wouldn't have mattered if I hadn't cared for Gladys. I never quite got over it, I'm afraid. She's living in America, now. I haven't seen her or heard from her in nearly twenty years."

He gave a slight shrug. "You certainly do manage to draw things out of one. I've mentioned that before, I think. Well, never mind."

He went around to the other side of the desk and dropped heavily into the chair. "I'm sorry, too, if I sounded harsh a moment ago. I've had quite a day of it, and we've only just come back from Bristol."

The Superintendent put in, "Now, Mr. Cannon, I hope you're satisfied."

"Yes, I'm satisfied. More or less. But I still don't like your saying that my interference might have pushed Richter to suicide. Unless it's true. Is it? Can you prove it?"

"No, no. I think Inspector Codd was simply speaking out of fatigue," said the Superintendent. "I'm afraid he—ah—we were both exceedingly disturbed by Mr. Richter's death."

"Richter was guilty, then?"

"I don't think we'll discuss it."

"No?" I said. "I wish you would. I'm awfully curious. And I am kind of snarled up in this thing now. You still haven't heard why Lucy and I broke into Neville's cottage. We found something very interesting. I suppose you've got a law against withholding evidence from the police, eh? But before I tell you what we found I want to know why Richter killed himself."

The Superintendent sat up straight, snatching his pipe an instant before it flew out of his mouth. Codd slammed his hand flat on the desk. Then he put his head back and laughed wearily.

"You see?" he cried. "I told you, Superintendent! He's incorrigible. What's one to do with a chap like this?"

"I'm also helpful in my own peculiar way, as you said last night," I pointed out. "Come on. We're safe here. I won't tell a soul."

"You're a scoundrel, Mr. Cannon," the Superintendent said, but then he snorted. "Go ahead, Len. I don't think it'll do any harm to tell him what little we know."

Codd said, "Richter was a morphine addict. Even if we hadn't established it from going through his records, which we did, it was apparent in the post-mortem. All our pressure on him made him realize that it was going to come to light. And the drug made him unstable, anyway. He's been taking it for years. When PC Baker came for him, it must have been the final nudge."

I thought about that. "And he didn't leave a note, or say anything? Then it was guilt about taking drugs, not necessarily guilt for having committed a murder, that made him kill himself."

"We don't know," Codd said.

"I gathered from what I heard you two saying last night that Lionel Herne is probably a drug addict, too, and a pusher as well. It makes a couple of things clear, doesn't it?"

"Such as?"

"Why, that Lionel must have gotten his supplies from Richter."

"We don't know that either. We expect Mr. Herne to be here tomorrow morning, and perhaps then we'll learn something from him."

"Hm. When Richter came to see me at the Goat, I asked him why he didn't go back to Germany if he was so unhappy here. He said that he just couldn't, and refused to discuss it. Well, if Lionel was using him as a source of supply, he wouldn't have let Richter get away, would he? He could have threatened him with exposure, to keep him right here in Heronwick with access to all sorts of tasty drugs. Maybe even poisons as well."

Codd glanced at the Superintendent, who said, "That's a very interesting point. Certainly worth considering."

"Yes," said Codd. "And we have wondered why Mrs. Herne was willing to employ someone like Neville. It occurred to us that perhaps she did so at her son's insistence. I remembered, too, that Neville had once worked for Richter and that they had had a quarrel. Well, perhaps Neville found out what they were up to, and wanted to be a partner. Richter refused; Neville beat him up. And perhaps then Richter and Lionel kept him quiet with the bribe of an easy job. But if he learned still more about their dealings—"

"Then Richter would have told Lionel, and Lionel would have forced Richter to shut Neville up by killing him," I finished.

"Quite so." The Superintendent nodded. "Very neat."

"Well," I said, "there's only one monkey-wrench in the works."

They raised their eyebrows at me. "Monkey-wrench?" Codd said.

"A kind of spanner," said the Superintendent. "Go on."

"Here's what we found today." I took the photostats out of my pocket and tossed them on the desk.

The Superintendent joined Codd, and together they read the letter—with a little help from me. When they were done with it, I told them how I had found it and where I had first seen it. I also described my researches into the Herne family's history and ended with my conjecture about Sir Francis's death.

Codd put his hands behind his head, stretched, and blew out a long breath. "Good God!" he groaned. "We should have run you out of the village long ago. My sins have recoiled on me with a vengeance. You've certainly complicated this affair for us."

The Superintendent thoughtfully filled his pipe. "I don't know," he murmured. "True, all this seems to give Mrs. Herne a jolly good motive for wanting Neville out of the picture. But I don't see that it affects the other side of the case. If Neville blackmailed her, she may have paid him off on Saturday or Sunday. I don't suppose we shall be able to find out easily; banks are notably reticent about their clients' business."

I opened my mouth and quickly closed it again. I didn't want to get Lucy's brother into trouble.

"If she paid him off," the Superintendent continued, "we may still be able to find the money. We shall have to have another look at Neville's cottage, Len. Obviously, we didn't do as thorough a job as Mr. Cannon has done. Perhaps a bit of digging's in order. But the two things—this letter, and the drug taking, or peddling—may not necessarily have anything to do with each other."

Codd yawned. "Well, I propose to leave it for the

morning," he said. "I'm absolutely dead beat. At the moment, Mrs. Herne should be quite easy in her mind. If she had anything to do with it, and Richter was her tool, she will assume that she's safe with him dead. She doesn't know that her son will be here to-morrow, so that won't make her nervous. And Master Lionel may be able to tell us a good deal we don't already know. Come along, Mr. Cannon. I'll drive you home."

"Fine," I said. "And, by the way, Mr. Davies is allowed to serve liquor to residents after hours. If you can keep your eyes open a little longer, I'd like to buy you a drink. I feel I owe you one."

"I think I can manage," he grinned.

The Superintendent shook his head. "Remember his highly personal questions, Len," he said. "If you feel chatty, remember what we used to say—everything you say may be used in evidence against you."

13

I had an early breakfast, but early as I was, Codd
had already left. I felt better disposed towards him
this morning. We had had a couple of whiskies the
night before, and in the mellowness compounded out
of those and his weariness he had loosened up and
shown himself the pleasant sort of guy I had taken
him for in our first meetings. He had told me a little
about his career and the sense of high purpose which
had driven him into the police force, but all this with
a kind of deprecatory modesty which told me more
than any words. I was surprised to find out how poor-
ly he was paid and how tough, actually, a detective's
life could be; for all that, he seemed to be one of
those rare and lucky people who honestly like their
jobs.

And at one point, I'd said to him, "You know, the
Vicar told me he thought the English were poets and
idealists. But General Nicholson told me you were all
businessmen geared to the modern world. What's
your feeling? Which are you?"

He said, "Why do you want to know?"

"There's a detective for you," I said. "Let's put it that I'm curious because I want to understand you people."

"Oh," he said, "if you go about asking questions like that, you'll never get a serious answer. We know what we're like, but we're jolly well never going to let on that we do."

Considering that, this morning, I remembered a mailbox I had seen in London, which in a funny sort of way summed up the exclusivity of the English for me. It had two slots. One said, LONDON. The other said, haughtily, ALL OTHER PLACES.

Mr. Davies came in as I was finishing my breakfast.

"I hope you will not think I am prying into things that do not concern me, Mr. Cannon," he said, portentously, "but I heard that you had a nasty experience at the dance last night."

We had said nothing about it the night before; in fact, we had said little more than hello and goodnight to him.

"It did get a little tense there for a minute," I said. "But it wasn't too bad. How'd you find out about it?"

"Oh, word gets around," he said, vaguely. "Please do not imagine that we are all like that in Heronwick. Those were a few rowdies. It is not the way we normally conduct ourselves here. We have a great respect for law and order. I do not mean that we pull off our hats and perform minuets of respectful admiration when we see a blue uniform, but we are peaceable citizens and we do not like to see crimes go unpunished. What is more, many of us have a great liking for—ah—visitors who come to us from distant lands." For the first and only time, he seemed a little embarrassed, perhaps by the excessive emotion this betrayed.

"I understand," I said.

"Particularly," he said, "when they are good enough to come to our aid, in need. As Jeff Parr was saying only last night. He was having a last pint just before closing time, and he said, 'That Mr. Cannon,' he said, 'stepped in without knowing any more about cricket than I do about the controls of an interplanetary spaceship,' he said, 'and broke the clock with a six. It will take a lot of forgetting, that will,' he said."

"Well, that was very good of him," I said. "It wasn't really anything."

He raised a finger to show me he hadn't finished, and continued. " 'Why,' he said, 'I never would have thought to find a cricketer among baseball players, any more than to find an oak tree in a desert. If I wanted to find an oak,' he said, 'I would look in a forest. Be sure to tell Mr. Cannon that for me,' he said."

I felt a little confused by all this adulation. "He said that? That was very nice of him."

Mr. Davies eyed me in a peculiar, meaningful way. "I hope you understand the message, Mr. Cannon. If anyone wanted to hide an oak tree, they'd hide it in a forest, surely?"

I puzzled over it as I strolled out to the bridge behind the pub for a smoke and a look at the stream. It was certainly friendly of Parr to have gone out of his way to say something like that. I decided, at first, that he must have said it to counteract that disagreeable episode at the dance. But he hadn't been there, and how could he have heard of it so quickly? And why should he make such a point of hiding oak trees in forests?

Wait a minute, I said to myself. It had been Mr. Davies who had said that. Parr had talked of *finding* oaks in forests.

I hit myself on the forehead. I was an idiot! Davies had clearly been anxious that I should get the message, and get it straight. But neither of them, for all their friendliness with me, wanted to draw attention to himself or violate the unwritten village code by coming right out and saying anything plainly.

I got to the police station in record time, and found Codd fuming because the police car that was bringing Lionel Herne down from Manchester had not yet arrived.

"Yes, what is it?" he said. "I'm rather rushed this morning."

"I'll come right to the point. I just found out where the best place is to hide a pair of boots. In a shoe repair shop."

"A pair—?" he began, and then he got the message, too.

"Who told you?" he said.

"I can't tell you that. Take it that a friend tipped me off."

"I see. Whose boots are they?"

"I don't know for sure, but I can guess."

"Never mind."

He pawed through a heap of papers on the desk and came up with a batch of large, glossy photographs of footprints. He jumped up and left the room, and I heard him saying in the hall, "Tom, you come along with me. Baker, if the car arrives keep Herne in your sitting room. I shall probably want the office." Then I heard the door slam. Since nobody had told me to go, I took one of the straight chairs and moved it softly into the furthest corner where I sat down and tried to look like a design on the wallpaper.

My disguise didn't work. Codd came crashing back, shortly, burst into the office and jerked his head at me.

"Sorry, Mr. Cannon. I shall be questioning someone in here."

"That's fine," I growled, resentfully. "And I can't listen, eh? Some gratitude."

I began to go, and then remembered something important. "Well, look, can I at least use the phone? I have to call a bank in Newent."

He fingered his chin. "It's not really permitted. . . . Do you need some money? I'm sure I can arrange things for you."

"I have to find out whether my partner has cabled the payment for this manuscript we're buying from Mrs. Herne."

"Ah," he said. "I see." He thought for a bit, and then nodded. "All right. Go ahead."

I sat at the desk and called Mr. Er at the Bank. The cablegram had arrived, and I could come in any time up to noon, or after ten Monday morning. Since it was now only a couple of minutes past nine, I thanked him and told him I'd come as soon as I could make it. When I hung up, Codd was looking at me in a contemplative way.

"It's there, is it?" he said.

"Yep."

"Had you planned to get it this morning and conclude your business with Mrs. Herne?"

"That's right."

"You'd really like to know what we found out about those boots, wouldn't you?"

"Oh, yes. I would."

"Mm. It may be rather a squeeze for Mrs. Baker, but perhaps you can sit in the kitchen until I'm finished in here. Then I'll—um—talk to you for a moment."

So I went to the kitchen like Cinderella, and talked to Mrs. Baker, a thin, pretty woman, who told me her troubles as a policeman's wife, but laughingly, until PC Baker, who was looking older and older, came in and summoned me to the office again.

Codd was alone. He sat with his hands shoved into his pockets, lounging back in his chair, a rather smug look on his face. I half expected him to lick his lips and couldn't help glancing around to see if there were any canary feathers on the floor.

"Well?" I said.

"Well, that was a good lead you gave me."

"They were Brock's boots, weren't they?"

"That's right.'

"Have you questioned him?"

"Oh, yes."

"My, you're a real blabbermouth this morning," I said.

"I'm sorry. I have several things on my mind. No, he admitted they were his boots. We had to go through every pair in the shop; the cobbler wasn't very cooperative. But we found 'em. Brock says he took them there after he met you, that morning, because he was afraid he'd be accused of the murder."

"But he claims he didn't do it?"

"That's it. He dropped the story about snaring rabbits. Now he says he had to go to Herne House on private business. No one answered the kitchen door, so he went in and when he got to the end of the passage he saw Neville lying on the floor in the hall. He didn't go any further, just turned and fled."

I shook my head. "I gather you don't accept that yarn either."

"I think we've got our man dead to rights," Codd said, exultantly. "First, when he met you on the way back, he had no reason to tell you he'd been fishing. He could have said, quite easily, that he'd been at Herne House on business. He had been palpably worried during the cricket match the day before, enough to put him off his game. All this makes it quite clear he had a good deal on his mind both Sunday and Monday. Another point: I asked him how he could be so sure, standing at the end of the passage, that Neville was dead. Surely, one's first impulse would be to go and see? He answered that he was just sure, that's all."

He rubbed his hands. "I'll soon break him down. Because, you see, I'm pretty certain I've got the weapon."

"You have? What is it?"

"I've sent a man to Brock's house to fetch me his cricket bats."

I sat, thunderstruck. At last I said, weakly, "How about that!"

"Just so!" he chuckled. "You remember your experience with a cricket bat, of course. The back is rounded, isn't it? I've spoken to Forensic on the phone and I'm told the wound on Neville's head might very possibly have been produced by the back of such a bat. And Brock's certainly powerful enough to have killed him. It seems clear to me that he entered the house, took off his boots, and crept up behind Neville. Neville may have heard a slight sound and turned. At that point, Brock hit him."

"I see. It certainly figures."

"I have no doubt we shall find that bat. Even if we find nothing but its splinters. And when we do, I shouldn't be surprised if Brock confesses."

"Where is he now?"

Codd motioned with his head. "In the sitting room, thinking things over."

I said, "That lets Richter out, doesn't it?"

"Not yet." He began drumming lightly with his fingers on the desk. "No, not quite yet. I'm still waiting for Lionel Herne. It is possible that Herne and Richter somehow forced Brock to do the murder for them. He may even have been involved with them in the drug game. On the other hand, Mrs. Herne may have been the moving spirit. We are carefully searching Neville's house inside and out for some trace of the money, or some indication that she paid him. It's very possible that we may be dealing with two separate, unconnected crimes. I shall be having another session with Brock, in a moment. But meanwhile—"

He stopped drumming abruptly, and fixed his eyes on me.

"Now, I've been very fair with you, haven't I? I really had no business telling you as much as I have. After all, it's still highly confidential, and I hope you'll repay me by keeping absolutely quiet about it. And in another way, as well."

"Of course, I'll keep—" I began. Then I paused. "What do you mean, 'in another way?'" I said.

He clasped his hands together on the desk and bent forward.

"Now look here. Richter slipped through my fingers, because he was aware we were closing in on him. I don't know how Mrs. Herne comes into all this, but I don't want to lose her in *any* way. I don't mean to imply that she'd commit suicide. But someone will certainly carry word to her that Will Brock has suddenly been detained by us, that his boots have been found, that something new is in the air. I don't want to alarm her. I don't want her to feel threatened, so that she'll do anything rash, try to get away, or—well —destroy any evidence. And I don't want to pick her up until I've got a bit more to go on. You see? The obvious thing to do is to make her feel that we're on a completely different track. Let her think we've been led in another direction, that someone else has come under surveillance."

I narrowed my eyes. "I think I can guess what's coming."

"I know this is a great deal to ask, but it would be extremely helpful to me," he continued. "I'd like you to be a red-herring again. Voluntarily, this time.

Phone Mrs. Herne and tell her you can't come with the money for your manuscript this morning because the police are holding *you* for interrogation. Then go back to the Goat and stay there, in your room. Don't take any telephone calls. Don't talk to anyone. Just sit tight and wait until I let you know all's clear. Will you?"

My first instinct was to yell, "Nothing doing!" I couldn't wait to get my hands on the *Raimond*, and it was mine now, except for a few formalities. At the same time, I knew that I couldn't just turn my back on him. I was too deeply involved in the case. It sounds sententious but being an American in this situation had something to do with it. I wasn't going to give Codd another chance for complaint.

I couldn't help saying, "You don't do things by halves, do you? And you *are* a cold-blooded character. That's why you let me phone the bank. And that's why you took me into your confidence about Brock. Something for something."

He answered, gently, "I really haven't any right to ask such a favor. I know you want to complete your business and wash your hands of this place where you've had nothing but unhappy experiences—"

"Oh, come on! You'll have me in tears in a minute. Let me see the phone book, I don't know her number offhand."

I trudged back to the Goat, wondering if I was behaving like a shnook. I thought, resentfully, that my mother should have warned me against becoming friendly with cops.

The Davies boy, Ted, was sitting on a bench in front of the pub, whittling a pistol out of a piece of wood.

I said, "No school today, huh?"

"No, sir."

237

"That's a nice-looking six-shooter. Know how to fit it with a rubber band so you can shoot spitballs?"

"What's a spitball?" he asked, eagerly.

"It just so happens," I answered, "that I am one of America's leading spitball experts. Got a piece of paper?"

I showed him the proper method of chewing and folding so as to get maximum trajectory and zing. We got a thick rubber band and I showed him how to fasten it to the front of his pistol. We fired a couple of rounds for effect.

"Hoy! That's all right, that is," he said.

He looked up at me. "Did you see him?" he said, suddenly.

"Him? Who's him? What are you talking about?"

"*Him.* Mr. Richter. When he was dead."

"Oh. No, I didn't, Ted. I heard all about it, but they whisked him away for the post-mortem in a hurry. Anyway, I wasn't even in Heronwick when he killed himself."

The boy made a derisive noise. "Killed himself? Not half, he didn't. He was done up."

"Is that so?" For a second, I wondered whether the kid really knew something nobody else knew.

"'Course! Didn't you read that story in the comic I loaned you? The one about famous crooks and how they work? It says there that murderers always have to do another murder because they got to shut up a witness or somebody what helped them."

"And you think whoever murdered Charlie Neville killed Mr. Richter?"

"Well, don't you? Somebody sneaked in and done Mr. Richter up by maybe putting poison in his tea that morning."

"Gee, I don't think so, Ted. That isn't the way it happened."

"Why, everybody says he was poisoned. How *did* it happen? Did the coppers tell you?"

"He ate a mouthful of a stuff called cyanide, when the police constable came to pick him up. It works very fast, so he couldn't have had it in his tea earlier."

Ted sighed. With wide, innocent, cherubic eyes, he said, "I bet he looked awful. All twisted and gha-a-astly. Wish I'd seen 'im."

"I'm glad I didn't," I said, getting up.

"I still think there was some way it could have been done," he insisted.

"Maybe."

"Are you going back to America soon?"

"I'm not sure yet, Ted. Pretty soon, I guess."

He closed one eye and moodily aimed his pistol at a passing sparrow.

"I wish we had a place like Disneyland in Gloucester," he said.

I shivered, and went quickly upstairs.

I smoked a cigarette, leaning out of the open window and watching some small, black-capped birds who were very busy in the garden. I had only been shut up in my room for fifteen minutes or so, and already I was fretting with boredom. Heaven knew how long I'd have to stay here because of my stupid promise to Codd. I had finished my science-fiction novel, and hadn't anything else to read. I dug out the comic book Ted had loaned me and studied some of the Methods of Master Criminals, but the page kept blanking out in front of my eyes: the Great Train Robbery wasn't half so perplexing as the Heronwick troubles, in spite of Codd's cheerful air of having everything under control.

I had one vital piece of information which he didn't, and which made everything at once simpler and more complicated. I knew that Mrs. Herne had drawn a lot of money out of her bank and had put it back again after Neville's death. It meant that some sort of blackmail attempt had been made and dealt with. Or at any rate, I couldn't think of anything better it might mean. But it got me no closer to understanding what had happened, or how.

Brock had been uneasy on Sunday and he had been equally disturbed on Monday—at a time when the murder had already been committed—disturbed enough to have told me a senseless lie. So even without the proof of his boots, I could assume that he really had been at Herne House that morning. But Richter had been at Herne House, too. That had been on Sunday night. And he had been worried and upset, far more than could be accounted for by the story of his hammer.

And what about that hammer? I thought. It bothered me, now that I thought of it along with everything else. I tried to remember exactly what Richter had told me about the incident, but I couldn't recall anything but the general sense of what he had said. Charlie had once borrowed it from him to make some repairs to the bridge in the woods, and had claimed he lost it. Then Richter, worried because Charlie had been killed by a blunt instrument, went searching for it. But if Charlie was such a liar, if he was given to doing unpredictably vicious things, why should Richter have assumed he had really dropped the hammer in the stream? It would have been more like Neville to have sold it for a few shillings and then to say he lost it. Surely Richter, who must have known him well, could have seen that? Why trouble to search the stream—one of the most unlikely places for the police to start looking, some way from the house, deep in the woods?

Richter and Brock, both worried, both concealing something. Both with at least a shadow of a reason in the background for hating Neville. And Mrs. Herne with a damn good reason for wanting him put out of the way.

I picked up the comic book with a groan, and looked at cartoons in which there were characters named Lord Soapy and Twiddlewinks and the Whizzo Twins, all drawn as if by a blindfolded amateur. A large balloon formed over my head labeled THINKS.

And I thought: Could it have been Mrs. Herne herself? I didn't see how. An old lady with a bum hand against a tough yob who wouldn't have scrupled to knock the bejesus out of her if he had been threatened? Not likely. And why should she have done so, when she could have found someone else to do the job for her? The someone else might well have been Richter. His entanglement with Lionel in a drug operation would have been enough of a hold over him. Assuming, of course, that she knew of it. But very little escaped that lady, I felt certain.

Still, was Richter the murderous type? Come to that, what *was* the murderous type? I had nothing to go by. For all his feverish excitability, he had never made the slightest violent move towards me. On the contrary, he had struck me as being a man easily intimidated rather than prone to action. But he was a former German soldier, maybe an ex-Nazi, perhaps used to violence and to concealing it. And he had been a morphine addict as well. *Unstable,* Codd had called him. Unstable enough to kill?

Then, Brock. There was no evidence that Richter had been anywhere near Herne House on Monday, but Brock had been there—he had been inside. And he was hard and strong; once moved to do something, I felt, he wouldn't have turned aside.

And yet . . . I didn't want it to be Brock because I rather liked him. Gloomily, I read a page of jokes: "How does Batman swim? He does the bat-stroke." I didn't feel like laughing. The bat-stroke. Maybe that

241

had been the stroke with which Brock had crushed in Neville's skull.

Then I knew what was wrong: I honestly didn't think Brock was the kind of man who would sneak up behind someone to kill him. He had gone out of his way to apologize to me for the horseshoe incident. He needn't have done it, he needn't have said anything. But he had said to me, "I don't throw things at chaps in the dark." I believed him. I couldn't see him creeping up behind Neville—Neville, of all people! He'd have gone straight up to that no-longer-juvenile delinquent and smashed him. Why, then, should he have taken off his boots first? And on the other hand, if he were telling the truth, how could he have known Neville was dead, from a distance?

The whole thing was crazy. Maybe Jack Spendwell had done it. They always said, in mystery stories, that you had to look for the most unlikely person. I began to have the eerie feeling that maybe I had done it myself, while suffering from a temporary loss of memory. Or maybe Mrs. Herne had called in some Master Criminal from outside, someone whose name she had gotten from reading *Whizzo!*

I decided to put it all out of my head. I lit another cigarette and read a page of creaky old conundrums: "What has four wheels and flies? . . . What's black and white and read all over? . . . What goes up a chimney down but won't go down a chimney up? . . . Who jarred Charlie Neville's teeth loose and made such a mess of him? . . ."

And suddenly, I had it. An idea so preposterous, so far-fetched and unlikely, that I began to laugh, sitting there all by myself with *Whizzo!* comics and a sluggish September wasp who came cruising in at the open window.

I stopped laughing. I got up restlessly, shooed away the wasp, and pitched *Whizzo!* into a corner. The more I thought about the idea, the less improbable it seemed. The more I considered it, the more it made other things fall into place. It had to be checked on. That would be—well, not exactly easy to do, but not too difficult. It would be tricky, and even dangerous, if I were wrong. There were problems, not least of which was the fact that I'd promised Codd to stay put. But the desire to put the idea to the test was so compelling that I couldn't resist it.

I looked at my watch. It was a quarter past ten. If I was going to act at all, I had to act right now. The prospect brought a cold nervous sweat out on my ribs. But my curiosity was too strong. I ran down the stairs two at a time and grabbed the phone.

"Dave, darling! I've been waiting to hear from you," Lucy said. "Is everything all right?"

"Everything's fine," I said. "I'm about to stick my neck under a guillotine. No, no, I'm just kidding. Lucy, you're going to have to help me with something."

"You know I will."

"Good. I'll come by for you in the car in about five minutes. I'll explain everything then."

She was my girl, all right. When I told her what I wanted her to do, and what I was after, she barely blinked. All she said was, "Do try to live more quietly after this is over, won't you?"

I let her drive while I tried to be invisible, just in case Codd or one of the policemen should be in circulation. We drove up between the sooty herons of the gateposts and into Herne Park, and before we got to the house Lucy slowed behind a thick mass of overgrown rhododendrons and dropped me off.

Using the bushes as a screen, I made my way around to the rear of the house. The grey stone wall hung over me threateningly. The back door was unlocked. I slipped through, into the flagged kitchen which smelled of cabbage. Sarah was by now, I trusted, in the lounge of the Falcon savoring a shandy, one of those gruesome English concoctions of warm beer and lemonade. And if everything had gone according to plan, Lucy should be at the front door proposing to discuss with Mrs. Herne a marvellous new suggestion for a last-minute change in the Harvest Festival decorations. I fervently hoped everything had, indeed, gone according to plan.

I climbed the back stairs, torn between the need for haste and the need for silence. Oh man, I thought in anguish, England has certainly led me into some peculiar byways: fist-fights, trouble with the cops, breaking into Neville's cottage, and now this. How was I going to explain away my creeping around the house if, for instance, Sarah *wasn't* at the Falcon but upstairs making beds? The old floor of the landing complained underfoot. I wished I weighed less. I wished I had taken my shoes off. I wished I was in Zanzibar.

I got to the library and paused to listen. I could hear muffled voices down below: Lucy must be with Mrs. Herne in the sitting room. Five minutes was all I needed.

Well, I found what I had been looking for. I had just turned away, with triumphant pleasure submerging my trepidation, when I heard footsteps on the stairs. And I heard Lucy's voice, high and strained, saying, "But I'm sure I heard nothing, Mrs. Herne!" She was warning me.

That's when I made my mistake. I should have taken off, full tilt, along the landing and down the back stair. I'd have been seen but I'd have made a getaway. Instead, like a fool, I backed into the library again with some sort of panicky idea of climbing out the window, or hiding behind the door. So I was standing in the middle of the room with my mouth open when Mrs. Herne walked in holding a shotgun.

"Mr. Cannon!" she said.

Her eyes flicked to the writing table. So did mine. The *Raimond* manuscript lay there. She must have had it out, ready for me, and when I phoned she had neglected to put it back.

"I see," she said. "You never intended to pay for it after all. Very clever."

"Now, wait," I said. "You don't understand—"

"I think I do. A very skillfully designed plan, I should say. That telephone call this morning saying that the police were holding you. Then Miss Nicholson keeps me busy in the sitting room while you nip up here and take the manuscript. It's a lucky thing I heard you moving about."

The muzzle of the shotgun was pointed at my stomach, and there wasn't a tremor in her. Lucy's face, white and drawn, was behind her shoulder.

"I think we'd better have the police," Mrs. Herne said.

"Okay," I said, in desperation. "Let's call them. We'll have to have them in any case now. And since your hearing is so good—maybe you can explain to them why you didn't hear Neville fall down the stairs. Because that's what he did, isn't it?"

A change came over her face, like a sudden alteration in the light on a field when the clouds shift.

She said, in a softer voice. "Oh? Perhaps it wasn't the manuscript after all?"

She raised the shotgun a trifle. "I think," she said, "I'd be perfectly within my rights to shoot a thief caught in the act."

I could barely keep my voice level. I didn't doubt for one instant that she meant what she said. "Are you going to shoot Miss Nicholson, too?" I said. "You'll have one hell of a time explaining."

She hesitated. I went on, "Will Brock is sitting in the police station right now, under suspicion of murder. You were the one who kept talking to me about responsibility and honor and all that stuff an American couldn't understand. Is that your sense of honor—to let him take the rap for you? Some honor! If that's honor, I'm glad I don't have any."

She lowered the gun. "So you do know," she said.

"That's right. And the funny thing is," I said, "that I got it out of a comic book. I was reading some of those silly old riddles, you know? There was one: 'When is a door not a door?' I suddenly thought of the answer. When it's a weapon.

"Of course, the minute I saw that, I saw everything. All I had to do was come over her and look at the door. Well, generally, on a door the stop—that long strip of wood it closes against—is nailed in place. This one has been screwed in with two screws. And the hinges are two-way hinges. That's why Richter was here Sunday night, isn't it? You had him under your thumb because he had the morphine habit. I suppose your son had to tell you about that whole business after he got into trouble with the police. You forced Richter to come over and change the hinges, and pull the nails out of the door stop and replace them with screws. That's why he had his tools with him. I suppose he went home through the woods in blind terror of being seen, and lost his hammer in the stream on the way.

"You had told Neville to be here Monday morning with the letter, and you said you'd give him the money then. It wasn't hard for me to imagine how you could set the thing up. The landing is narrow and the stairs are steep—the first time I came up them I almost lost my balance and fell, myself. I guess you stood in the doorway of the library and took the letter from him. Then you started to hand him the money and dropped it. He bent to pick it up, and at the right moment you only had to give the massive door a good hard swing. I looked at the knob. It's a solid, round, iron one. It caught him square on the forehead and over he went, down the stairs, as if he had been hit by a club."

Something else occurred to me. "You had to rehearse the whole thing so that you would know just where to drop the money and when to swing the door. You used Richter for that, too. No wonder he was nearly out of his mind when he left here. And no wonder he killed himself. Quite apart from his pilfering morphine, and his involvement with your son in peddling drugs, he was an accessory to the murder. My God! I'll bet you reminded him of that, in the hope of sending him over the edge. His death made it look as though he were guilty."

From her expression, I could guess that I was right.

"Sarah was out of the house," I continued, "and I wasn't due until eleven. So you had plenty of time. You went downstairs to make sure Neville was dead. You had some whisky ready and you poured it over him. Then all you had to do was screw the door stop back into place and wipe off the doorknob. That done, there was nothing to show that the door would swing outward. If there had been any big splashes of blood you'd have been in trouble, but maybe you didn't think of that. Or maybe you had a story ready for that eventuality, too."

She still said nothing, just stood there, but now the gun was shaking slightly.

I was struck by another thought. "And Brock! Tied to you by loyalty, or some kind of feudal feeling—one of those virtues you were telling me about, once. I'll bet you asked him to do the job for you and he turned you down. That's why he was so shaken on Sunday—who wouldn't be? Then you decided to do it on your own. He must have known you were going to try something on Monday. He came here to stop you, to warn Neville. Or maybe he came to try to get you to change your mind. When he got to the hall, he saw he was too late."

She drew a long breath. Her back was as straight as ever, her eyes never left mine, and when she spoke at last, her voice carried the same old commanding note. Whatever the truth about her father, she had lost nothing of her accustomed authority.

"I knew that you were a clever young man," she said. "And you've just worked this all out, have you—just now?"

"I can't think of any other reason why somebody'd have a door rigged like this. Can you?"

She gave me an acid smile. In a few strides she was beside the writing table.

"In that case, no one else knows of it, Mr. Cannon," she said. "It's very ingenious. Far too ingenious. Perhaps you would do better to keep it to yourself."

She rested the muzzle of the shotgun on the *Raimond* manuscript.

"Hey!" I cried. "Watch it!"

"It's for you to say," she rapped out.

All I could do was stare at her, and then at the blue steel of the gun barrel and the beautifully seasoned leather case that housed the chronicle of Raimond de Poitiers.

In my fog, I became conscious of a loud knocking downstairs. Mrs. Herne's head jerked, and she swung round, bringing up the gun. In a flash, I realized that Lucy still stood in the doorway and that the gun was pointing at her. I didn't stop to think, but launched myself forward. I covered the ten feet or so between us without feeling myself touch the ground. I grabbed the barrel of the gun and twisted it upward. It went off at the same time, with a crash that showered plaster on us both.

I kept hearing the echoes of that crash, but it was

only feet pounding up the stairs. Inspector Codd burst into the room.

"You again!" he grated. "I might have guessed!"

Still, I knew I'd be able to soothe him.

He had finally broken Brock's defenses down. The farmer had admitted that Mrs. Herne had asked him to kill Neville for her. He had refused. She had taunted him with being a coward and had told him that in that case she'd manage by herself. He had come on Monday, as I'd guessed, hoping to find Neville and warn him. With this information, Codd had not waited any longer for Lionel's arrival but had come at once to arrest Mrs. Herne.

"Will you get the *Raimond* manuscript after all?" Lucy asked me.

We were waiting in PC Baker's beweaponed sitting room for Codd to take my statement.

"I don't know. I don't see why not. And she'll need the money, now."

Her fingers tightened around mine.

"Dave," she said, "there's one thing I want to ask you."

I smiled at her. "About us?"

"Not exactly. Well—yes. But that can wait. This is something else."

"What is it?"

"When Mrs. Herne threatened to destroy the manuscript unless you kept quiet about how she'd done the murder. . . . Would you have agreed?"

"Ugh!" I said. "Don't talk about it. The memory makes me feel sick."

"But I can't help wondering. I mean, you're wild about your old books and manuscripts and things. On the other hand, the law's the law."

"That's true," I said.

"But which?"

I put my arm around her. We were alone in the room.

"I don't mind telling you," I said, "because I can always stop your mouth."

And I did.

In the great tradition of **THE GODFATHER** and **THE UNTOUCHABLES**

B95-1082 THE CONTRACT by Ovid Demaris...95¢
Carl Vincent was a veteran. He knew once a contract was made, it was filled. He had filled over forty of them himself. Then, he decided it was time to move up in the organization. It was a mistake. Now there was another contract out, but he would not be the one to fill it. His name was on it.

B95-1094 THE MAFIA by Noel Clad...........95¢
John Running Tree was a full-blooded Indian who learned his trade in the war. Now, he was the best hit man in the syndicate. Why would he suddenly refuse an assignment at the risk of his own life? Why did he go soft?

B95-2029 MAFIOSO by Peter McCurtin........95¢
Nick Lanzetta was a Mafia soldier, young, handsome and ambitious. One by one, he eliminated the "old blood." Then the Don's daughter was kidnapped and Nick saw a way to go right to the top. If he played his cards right, a seat on the council was waiting for him. If he made one mistake, he was a dead man.

TWO BIG NOVELS

BY DAVID MARKSON

The author of THE BALLAD OF DINGUS MAGEE
has done it again with these two tough, powerful,
moving novels of murder, suspense, sex and love.

Belmont Productions, Inc. 185 Madison Avenue
New York, N.Y. 10016

Please send me the books listed below.

ORDER BY BOOK NUMBER ONLY

Quantity	Book No.	Price
....	....	....
....	....	....
....	....	....
....	....	....
....	....	....
....	....	....
....	....	....
....	....	....
....	....	....
....	....	....

I enclose $............

Name ....
(please print)

Address ....

City................. State........ Zip Code........

Send check, cash or money order

Add 15¢ for every Canadian dollar order.

Please allow 2 to 3 weeks for filling orders.

Please add 15¢ per copy for mailing.